WHITE NIGHT

JJ MARSH

PREWETT
BIELMANN

White Night

Cover design: JD Smith

Published by Prewett Bielmann Ltd.

All enquiries to admin@jjmarshauthor.com

First printing, 2020

ISBN 978-3-9525191-7-2

For The Woolf Pack, who do so much more than howling at the moon

Chapter 1

Demonstrations were not unusual at this time of year. For one thing, the weather was more conducive to getting out onto the streets. No matter how passionately people supported or opposed a cause, temperatures of -15° plus wind chill off the Baltic Sea tended to keep them indoors in winter, voicing their discontent in bars or on the Internet.

Today, however, the summer had blessed Helsinki with a warm breeze, weak sunshine and long hours of daylight. People were on the march, placards held aloft: 'OUR COUNTRY, OUR FUTURE', 'No More Nuclear', 'LokiEn = GREED!', 'Protect Our Environment!', 'NO WAY, BOOMERS!', 'There Is No Planet B', 'Say No to Neljä' and multi-coloured flags fluttered in the breeze. Chanting slogans, banging drums and blowing whistles, the protestors dressed in bright clothes filled the streets with noise and colour. It was a good-natured affair, with pushchairs, dogs, children on their fathers' shoulders and several heavily pregnant women in the centre of the throng. A large number of those at the front of the march were teenagers and children of school age. The occasional police officer stood inside the line of barricades, observing the slow-moving procession or directing people towards the public toilets. Photographers crouched beside the pavement or scrambled up lampposts to get a meaningful shot, and a TV news crew kept pace with the leaders.

Similar marches had taken place in Turku, Tampere and here in Helsinki two weeks earlier. No one expected any trouble. As the marchers closed on the object of their ire, the atmosphere changed. Smiles morphed into frowns and sing-song slogans became angry demands. The police presence was still very much in the background, but outside the headquarters of LokiEn, a barricade encircled the forecourt of their huge glass building at the top of the broad steps. Around fifty members of a private security firm formed a human wall right behind the physical barrier. All wore sunglasses.

The sight of such heavy-handed protection appeared to enrage the crowd. The leaders stopped marching and a furious debate took place. Police officers spoke into their radios and expressions of concern emerged. Eventually, two people stepped away from the crowd and approached the cordon. A young man and woman strode up the steps towards the centre of the barrier and addressed the man in the centre. Whatever request they made was instantly denied. He shook his head and waved a dismissive hand. The young woman tried again, holding up a document of some kind. The security guard shrugged and leaned away to look over her shoulder. Voices from the crowd grew louder, shouting, 'Let them through!' 'We have a right to speak!' Earnest gestures from the young man seemed to indicate a plea for reason, but the security guard merely folded his arms.

The girl whirled around to the crowd and lifted a megaphone. "They refuse to let us deliver our report. This petition, signed by hundreds of thousands against the modular nuclear reactor, represents our legal right to protest, to defend our future. Why won't LokiEn listen? They cannot ignore us. Our politicians cannot ignore us. We will not be silenced! We DEMAND to deliver our report! We DEMAND to be heard!"

A huge roar went up from the crowd and a swell of movement rippled to the front. People surged forward in support of their representatives and the police mobilised fast to try to come between them and their antagonists. A big man with dreadlocks stormed forward and took the papers from the teenager, heading right for the middle of the cordon. He was followed by around ten assorted activists who loosely assembled into a V shape to counter the U formation of the security team. A scream rang out and a uniformed guard shoved the big man to the ground. Police officers tried to force their way through the crowds but a sense of outrage galvanised a disparate collective into a furious mob. Fists flew at the barriers and one guard lifted a cosh to smack against someone's head.

Sirens blared and officers came running from all directions, trying to push back the mass of bodies. A woman with a bloody nose fell and her partner helped her up. Placards soared over the heads of those at the front line, aimed at the heads of security guards. Riot shields appeared and a line of police penetrated the battle, putting themselves and the physical cordon between the warring groups. The security firm retreated inside the building. Officers formed a uniformed barricade outside. Ambulances drove into the square to tend to the wounded.

As the first crew ran towards the injured lying at the base of the steps, an elderly woman diverted them. "There's a man over here! He's hurt ... not breathing! Please come. He hit his head. He's not breathing."

Two crew members followed her to the edge of the steps where a middle-aged man lay awkwardly on the steps, his head facing the bottom and a long-lens camera under his chest. The medics knelt to attend to him as the woman continued her repetition of what had occurred. "They pushed him, you see, and he was off balance. He fell and hit his head."

The female paramedic stood up. "Can you come with me? We'll need to take a few details."

"Yes, of course. Is he going to be all right?" The woman clutched her arm. "He's not ...?" Her eyes filled with tears.

"Come with me. You did the right thing in letting us know.

There, now, don't upset yourself. There's nothing you could have done."

She guided the woman in the direction of the ambulance. Her colleague covered the man with a tarpaulin and radioed to base. When he finished the call, he became aware of a sudden silence. The sobs and shouts of the crowd had subsided to a shocked hush, all eyes staring at the tarpaulin.

A police officer materialised by his side. "I'll get this area cleared and put up a cordon. Is that one of the protestors?"

"Don't think so. Looks like a journalist to me. Poor sod."

Chapter 2

VALO: The only independent news site to shed light on the truth

Journalist killed at protest march

HELSINKI: The authorities have named the man who died amid Saturday's violence as 43-year-old Juppo Seppä, a freelance photographer from Espoo. His death is being treated as accidental. Seppä suffered a severe head injury and was pronounced dead at the scene. He leaves behind a wife and seven-year-old twin boys.

Shocking scenes

On Saturday 13 June, teenage climate activists charged the headquarters of LokiEn, the energy giant responsible for the newest of Finland's existing nuclear power facilities and the long-awaited Neljä modular reactor plant at Kolkko. Initially peaceful, the protestors gathered at Pohjoisesplanadi at 10.00 and marched towards the LokiEn offices on Senaatintori to deliver a petition. When refused entry, a small group of young people at the head of the march attacked the security guards protecting the building from malicious damage. Fighting broke out around 11.00 and over twenty people were seriously injured, several of whom are still in hospital. Police struggled to control the violent disorder, during which many of the marchers were seen to throw their placards at officers' heads. So far fifteen people have been arrested and there may be more to come, according to a police spokesman.

'We are examining CCTV footage of the incident to assess why and how a peaceful demonstration turned into a civil disturbance. There may be more people we wish to speak to.'

Marches against the concept of new nuclear modular reactors built close to urban areas have previously taken place in various cities, including Helsinki, but this is the first time the young activists have disturbed the peace and sparked violence. Questions are already being asked about how to contain potential disruptive elements and protect the public next Saturday, when the new plant is due to open. The high-profile ceremony will be attended by senior politicians, the three chief executives of the companies behind the joint venture and most assuredly a small but vocal group of objectors.

There is no doubt these young people feel strongly about their beliefs and have a right to express them. The tragedy is that an innocent bystander had to lose his life in order for them to be heard.

COMMENTS

- HariV: These kids have been brainwashed and don't even understand the facts. Send them back to school until they learn what they are talking about.
- *This comment has been deleted by a moderator because it does not meet our standards*
- TruFinn: Little swine! If my kid tried to join them, I'd lock her up.

- LennonAgain: There's no evidence the young people started it. Why didn't LokiEn let them deliver their petition? It's not like it will make any difference.
- MrMobile: @LennonAgain – they may not have started it, but they certainly participated. Have you seen the TV footage?
- OhLordi: @LennonAgain – if it won't make any difference, why did we bother signing?
- *This comment has been deleted by a moderator because it does not meet our standards*
- UrsiMinor: Why do they object to the new reactor? Don't they learn in school how important nuclear energy is to this country? Or should we still be dependent on Russian gas?
- Ergmann: @UrsiMinor Bitching about energy sources is what got this guy killed. Grow up.
- HansUp: I will be at the opening ceremony and I will not take any crap from a bunch of 'woke' millennials.
- MobileFoam: Someone needs to stand up to the atomic whores! The rest of the population are duped. Go Warriors!

Comments on this article are now closed

"Good evening, ladies and gentlemen and thank you for your patience. My name is Detective Sahlberg of the Helsinki Police Department. As promised, I have a statement for you regarding the unfortunate events of yesterday morning. We have made a total of nineteen arrests, all of which are concerned with public disorder offences. We will not release the names of any of these nineteen unless charges are brought. I would like to stress that no one is being held in connection with the death of Mr Juppo Seppä.

The second reason for calling this press conference this evening is for another very serious matter. Two of the protestors leading yesterday's march are officially missing and we are concerned for their welfare. We would like to locate them as a matter of urgency. Valpuri Peura, aged sixteen, and Samu Pekkanen, seventeen, represented Gaia Warriors, the central organisation behind the protest. These two were given the responsibility of delivering the petition. Neither has been seen since. If you look at the screen behind me, you will see recent photographs of Ms Peura and Mr Pekkanen. If anyone has any information on the whereabouts of these young people, it is essential you contact the police on this number. Now I would like to allow the parents of Ms Peura and the mother of Mr Pekkanen to address you all. Mr Peura."

Journalists rustled and shifted to get a better look at the distressed father. He appeared startled to find himself the centre of attention and turned to the detective, who whispered in his ear. The man scanned the faces and fixed on the camera directly in front of the podium. He cleared his throat.

"Valpuri, please come home. You are not in any trouble, far from it. Your mother and I are so proud of you. You stand by your convictions and we love you for that. We want you to come home because we are worried about you. If you see this, or if anyone watching knows where Valpuri might be, I beg you, please contact us or the police. Please."

The man sat down, clutching at his wife's hand. The commissioner leant forward to address the woman at the end of the row. She got to her feet, white-faced and trembling. But her voice was strong enough to make everyone pay attention.

"My son is seventeen years old. He is caring, generous, sensitive and principled. He is a wonderful person. I ask you, all of you, help us find him. Someone knows where he is. You must tell us what you know. He is all I have. Samu, I love you. Come home."

The woman's presence transfixed all faces so the moment she sat down, comforted by Mrs Peura, the journalists seemed to wake up, transferring their attention to their keyboards, notepads and phones. The police detective thanked them and the press conference was over.

Chapter 3

Heikki aimed the remote at the screen, switching it off just as a talking head came on to analyse the events of the weekend. Karoliina opened her mouth to tell him to leave it on, until she became aware of how peaceful the kitchen was. It was vital to keep abreast of developments, in particular public opinion. And what better bellwether of public opinion than the media? At the same time, the urge to shut out the world, just for a few hours, overcame her. Her husband crossed the kitchen and opened the fridge, taking out the bottle of wine. Without asking, he refilled her glass.

Using her fork, Karoliina scooped up the last few leaves of salad and chewed them without tasting. Her mind bounced and rebounded like a monkey in a cage, desperate to do something although she had no idea what. Heikki replaced the wine and came to sit opposite her at the breakfast bar.

"It's not your fault, you know," he said. "Not the journalist, not the missing kids, none of it. This has nothing to do with you. It's all on the demonstrators."

Karoliina dropped her fork with a clatter. "Don't be so naïve, Heikki. This has everything to do with me and LokiEn. What the hell do you think they were demonstrating about in the first place? We have to present an official response, at the very latest by tomorrow morning. That response will need to be coordinated and agreed upon by the other two CEOs. You can imagine how smoothly that is likely to go. I should call them tonight." Her voice was weary.

Heikki reached across the table and smoothed her forehead with his thumb. "It's Sunday evening. You can't do anything tonight. Contact them first thing in the morning and decide on a plan of action. But I say again, this is not your fault."

"Not all of it, no. Nevertheless, I am responsible for dealing with the fallout. We made some mistakes and we have to acknowledge that." She shook her head impatiently. "This is not the time for recriminations. Now is the time to act. There are three things we need to do and time is of the essence. Top priority is finding those kids. I need to call the police and offer any support I can, while making a public statement of concern. Nothing I can do will bring that photographer back, but I can make a gesture of sympathy and offer some kind of financial assistance to his widow. Then we have to face the fact that next Saturday is going to be a powder keg and we have to do something to mitigate that. It might even mean calling off the opening ceremony if those young activists are still missing."

"Karoliina! You can't do that! For one thing, the consortium wouldn't let you. Next Saturday is a major milestone in the history of Finnish energy production. No more reliance on coal or wood to heat our homes." He drained his wineglass.

"Yes, thank you. I've read my own press releases."

"The point is, the whole country will be celebrating."

She gave him a sardonic look. "The whole country?"

Heikki pulled a face of disgust. "Apart from a handful of raggedy-arse protesters, yes. Most right-thinking people know how important this plant is, not just for Finland's future, but the whole of Europe. You can't let a couple of muddleheaded kids spoil something you've been working towards for almost a decade. Let's face it, they're probably shocked that their violent actions led to someone's death and they've gone underground out of shame. I'd be very surprised if there were anything like the scale of protest we saw today. They've learned a lesson. Pity someone had to die to teach them."

The doorbell rang and Karoliina pushed back her chair, glad of the interruption. She hated it when Heikki started talking like a tabloid.

He looked at the doorway. "Are you expecting someone?"

She shook her head, brushing the crumbs from her shirt. "Yes and no. I've made no appointments but it's only a matter of time before the police turn up asking questions. I'll see who it is. Thanks for making dinner, by the way." She took a last sip of wine and arranged her face into professional mode as she walked down the hall to the front door. The porch light was on but Karoliina could see no figures awaiting admission. She hesitated a moment before opening the door. Outside, there was no one on the porch, on the path or either side of the doorway. She looked at the street which was empty of vehicles. The island was silent apart from the distant buzz of a motorcycle. She was about to retreat inside when something at her feet caught her eye. An envelope bearing her name: Karoliina Nurmi.

It wasn't the first time Karoliina had received anonymous post and she was well versed in how to deal with it. She left the envelope on the mat, returned indoors, walked past the kitchen and into her study. She found the drawer she was looking for instantly and retrieved a pair of rubber gloves and a re-sealable plastic bag. When she emerged, she saw Heikki standing at the front door.

"Don't touch it!" shouted Karoliina.

He jumped and whirled around. "Touch what?"

She didn't answer him, instead donning her rubber gloves, picking up the envelope and taking it back into her study. She slid a gloved finger underneath the flap and looked inside. The content was a folded sheet of paper, no powder or signs of any other toxic substance. Placing the envelope on top of the plastic bag she withdrew the letter and unfolded it.

The message was printed in a large font and across the page there was a splatter of red.

You have blood on your hands. Today, the blood of three people. From Saturday, the blood of millions.

You must be stopped. You must be killed.

For our country. For our planet.

Karoliina rolled her eyes and laid the letter on top of the envelope. She was so very tired of this posturing.

Heikki was at her shoulder, the cat in his arms, reading the message. His eyes widened. "Is that a death threat?"

She quelled a temptation to say 'No, it's a shopping list' and moved towards the telephone. "Certainly looks that way."

He stood there, watching as she called the police and reported the incident. She paced to look out of the window at the sea while talking, keeping her husband in her peripheral vision. It wasn't that she didn't trust him. Her concern was more that her impulsive husband might easily pick up the letter for a closer look. At least while he was petting the cat, his hands were full. She replaced the receiver.

"The police are coming to collect the letter and take it for analysis. Their opinion is that it's simply designed to frighten us. No need to panic, but we should ensure we keep ourselves safe." As she spoke, she refolded the letter, placed it in the envelope and sealed it in the plastic bag.

"Easy for them to say. Someone came here, to our house, to Kulosaari in order to hand deliver a personal threat. This isn't a practical joke! Someone went to a lot of trouble to frighten us. Was that…?"

Karoliina removed the rubber gloves. "Was what what?"

"On the letter. Was that… blood?"

She exhaled something short of a snort. "I doubt it. I'm no expert, but blood tends to dry dark, more brown than scarlet.

That bright red splatter probably came from food colouring or an ink cartridge. Look, Heikki, why don't you go and check our security system? See what the cameras picked up. It's possible whoever sent this delivered it by drone, but if it was delivered by hand, we might get a clue from the footage. Would you check?"

He put down the cat and was already halfway out of the room, muttering. "Yes, you bastards. We've got you on camera. It will not be difficult to find out who is threatening my wife."

Karoliina closed the door behind him and returned to the phone. She had another call to make.

"Björnsson?"

"Hello, Roman, this is Karoliina Nurmi calling, from Helsinki. I'm sorry to disturb you on a Sunday evening."

"Karoliina. I haven't heard from you in months. Are you well?"

His relaxed, unflappable tones drew an involuntary smile from her. "I'm the picture of health, thank you. How about you?"

"Healthy, happy and enjoying the summer sunshine. So what's up? Why are you calling me out of the blue on a Sunday?"

"Well, while my personal life is smooth sailing, I'm having a few difficulties at work. It crossed my mind to hire a private investigator. When we were at that conference in Oslo, I recall you saying you had a connection in the business. I know I could find someone online with some diligent research but this is the kind of situation where I would prefer a personal recommendation."

Roman was quiet for a moment, prompting Karoliina to worry if she had offended him in some way. She should have known better. The Icelandic detective rarely took anything personally, but it was in his nature, like hers, to think before he spoke.

"Yes, I could personally recommend a PI who used to hold a senior position in the London Metropolitan Police. Since retiring, she's established quite a name for herself in the private detective sphere, in more ways than one. She's based in Britain, but I know she's keen on international jobs." He made a noise which sounded like a laugh. "It's funny, you know, you remind me of her. I can't even say why, but you do. I have a feeling you two would get along. Do you want me to email you her address?"

A long sigh of relief escaped Karoliina. "Yes, please, that would be great. And as I'm under time pressure, could have a telephone number? Just to speed things up a bit."

"Sure." Roman dictated the number and Karoliina scribbled the digits onto a notepad.

"Thank you, Roman. I owe you one. Seriously, any time I can do you a favour, just say the word. Oh, by the way, what's this woman's name?"

She could hear the smile in his voice. "I will hold you to that, Karoliina Nurmi. The detective's name is Stubbs, Beatrice Stubbs. Give her my love."

Chapter 4

Beatrice hated being in the back seat. She could not sit still, peering through the rear windscreen at the street behind them. She twisted round in her seat and folded her arms, gazing at the passers-by pottering up and down Hollybridge High Street. Then she checked her phone, leaned forward once again to look past DS Perowne at the coffee shop and above his head at the rear view mirror. If she crouched a little, she could just see the entrance to the church. Her companion, in contrast, sat still as one of the stone angels in the graveyard.

"I don't think he's going to show. He is onto us; he knows it's a trap. He should have been here by now. What if he gets into the churchyard by some other route? We might miss him altogether. I think he's around here somewhere, watching us and deciding to back off. Too risky with the cops around." She leaned forward once again, scanning the population of Hollybridge, but spying nothing more sinister than two women with toddlers in pushchairs, an elderly couple wheeling their shopping home from the Spar and three teenage girls sitting on the churchyard wall, poring over their phones.

DS Perowne met her eyes in the mirror. "Ms Stubbs, with all due respect, if anyone is watching the vehicles on the street, the only one likely to attract attention is this one because of the fidgety female in the back seat. Sit still, keep your eyes peeled, watch the mirrors and wait. If he comes, he comes. If he doesn't, there'll be another time. As for entering the churchyard via another route, it would have to be over the wall and DS Gage has got that covered."

"Has he though? Can you see him from where you're sitting?"

"Yes, he's at the bend in the street, looking at the estate agent's window. He's ready, we're ready and all we need do is sit tight. The one thing we cannot risk is alerting him to our presence."

He was right, Beatrice acknowledged. That a detective sergeant should have to remind her of the importance of stillness on a stakeout was rather embarrassing. She'd spent more nights on surveillance than she cared to remember while she had been a detective inspector, hissing at her own team for scratching, shifting, whispering and shuffling with impatience.

"Sorry, detective sergeant. I really should know better. I will practise some deep breathing," she announced.

She did try. She inhaled, expanding her lungs to the maximum before exhaling a long steady breath. She tried again but her mind whirred into activity, checking each item off the list. Everyone was in position; Wendy in the café, wearing a big hat so as not to be recognised. She and DS Perowne in an unmarked car parked no more than one hundred yards from the entrance to the graveyard. DS Gage in plainclothes at the other end of the street. Her assistant, Theo Wolfe, dressed in costume, ready to spring his surprise. The stage was set and all they needed now was the key player. Beatrice gave up on the breathing and turned back to DS Perowne.

"What if he doesn't turn up? What if he gets away? The Devon and Cornwall police force will never trust me again and henceforth regard me and my assistant as poisoned cellos."

Perowne kept his gaze forward, checking all three mirrors intermittently as he replied. "If he gets away this time, there'll be another occasion. We have a lot more information on him and his organisation thanks to the efforts of you and your assistant.

We will apprehend this man. Most importantly, Mrs Wendy Carys is not about to lose her life savings to some romance fraudster. If nothing else comes out of today, I consider that to be a major ... ah now, let's have a look at this."

Beatrice's spine stiffened and she looked into the wing mirror. A taxi pulled up in front of the church and the driver got out to help his passenger from the back seat, a well-dressed gentleman carrying a red umbrella. Once the cab had pulled away, Beatrice had a clearer view of the suspect.

"Bingo!" she whispered.

Beside her, DS Perowne spoke into his police radio, informing his colleague their operation was about to commence. Beatrice twisted around in her seat, her impatience and anticipation barely controlled. DS Perowne lifted a hand to still her as he signed off.

"Sorry, sorry."

"It's all right. The minute he goes through the gateway, we get out of the car and stroll along this side of the street, looking in shop windows and taking our time. Once opposite the graveyard, we cross the street and wait either side of the hedge until he approaches Mr Wolfe. This fella will be on high alert for anyone watching. Do not scare him off."

Beatrice unclipped her seatbelt and with a glance over a shoulder to see if there was any approaching traffic, got out into the street. She joined DS Perowne on the pavement and they strolled casually past the café, the supermarket and the craft shop. The detective looped his arm around hers and guided her across the street towards the church.

Peering above the yew hedge, Beatrice spotted their quarry, moving with a slight limp towards the church door, leaning on his umbrella for support. He stopped and took out a handkerchief to mop his brow, surveying the churchyard as if looking for something. In that instant, a movement caught Beatrice's eye. From the far end of the church, a figure emerged, its upper half concealed by a bright red parasol. The lower half, dressed in a long summer skirt, tiptoed along the path towards a line of gravestones. The figure's back was to the church, so that neither Beatrice, DS Perowne nor the new arrival could see the person's face.

As if alerted by a signal, the man with the handkerchief focused on the figure with an intense stare. He replaced his handkerchief and his hat, and began walking in the direction of the red parasol. Beatrice and DS Perowne, both keeping low and out of his sight line, entered the churchyard and crouched behind a large family sarcophagus. When Beatrice had got her breathing under control, she raised her head just enough to see above the mossy stone.

The parasol-holder had stopped to kneel on the grass, apparently paying respects to a gravestone. The man approached, his limp less noticeable now. He came to a halt several paces behind the stationary figure and cleared his throat.

"Hello, my dear. I'm sorry I'm late." His voice was smooth as melted chocolate. Even at this distance, it was immediately recognisable from all the recordings Beatrice had heard. "Have you been waiting long?"

The person with the parasol straightened. DS Perowne moved from a kneeling position into a runner's crouch. Beatrice held her breath. The figure turned, revealing a tall black man in a dress.

"Bleeding ages, mate. Where the hell have you been?"

The older man stumbled backwards several paces, then turned and broke into a run. DS Perowne leaped into action to cut him off and the man attempted to duck inside the church in order to escape. But Theo was too quick for him, even in a full-length skirt. He jumped over two rows of gravestones and caught the tail of the man's jacket, dragging him backwards onto his behind. DS Gage skidded to a halt beside them, ready with a pair of handcuffs.

A small crowd gathered to watch the officers guide the arrested man across the road and into the police car. Beatrice and Theo stood at the gates of the graveyard, watching them depart. Beatrice lifted her eyes to the window of the Hollybridge Café and met those of Wendy Carys. The two women exchanged a smile and a cheerful wink.

Beatrice turned to Theo and shook his hand. "Well done! That's one more romance fraudster off the streets. I think we've earned ourselves a slap-up tea with extra custard. Do you want to come back to Upton St Nicholas for a slice of pie with me and Matthew or are you heading straight back to London?"

"I'm coming back for tea. Because if I don't, you'll tell Matthew you were the hero of the hour and I want my moment of glory."

"As if I would cast myself in the starring role! Although I will say, catching someone with their pants down like this is largely down to administrative ground work." Beatrice laughed at his outraged expression. "No, seriously, you did a brilliant job and I just wish I'd been a tiny bit closer. I badly wanted to see his face when you turned around."

"It was priceless!" said Theo. "If I never do another investigative job in my life, that was a career high. 'Hello, my dear. I'm sorry I'm late. Have you been waiting long?' How could I resist a cue like that?" He let out a loud hoot, setting Beatrice off again.

"Oh dear," she said, wiping at her eyes. "Here's my car. Where's yours?"

"I parked the Mini behind the Co-op. Meet you back at the cottage?"

"See you there. Are you going to keep your dress on?"

He grinned. "Do you mind?"

"Not at all," said Beatrice. "It rather suits you."

Chapter 5

Theo accepted another slice of blackberry and apple pie after his third rendition of the afternoon's events. The three of them sat at the garden table, under the shade of the horse chestnut tree, enjoying the afternoon sunshine. Having already heard the story from Beatrice, Matthew seemed no less fascinated by Theo's retelling.

"How marvellous! It must be enormously satisfying to see all your efforts come to fruition. Are the police pleased with the operation?"

Beatrice offered Theo the jug of custard and brushed a fly away from the remaining pie. "They had jolly well better be. They should hand out gold stars after all we've done. Apart from the actual arrest, the fact this man is now in custody is 100% down to Stubbs and Wolfe. And while today was all action and excitement with a few belly laughs, the vast majority of the job has been a tedious paper trail."

"Paid off, though, didn't it? We got our man. Cheers, Beatrice!" Theo raised his teacup.

"Cheers! We most certainly did and earned ourselves a decent bonus to boot. Wendy Carys is a very generous woman."

"I offer you both my heartiest congratulations." Matthew poured himself more tea. "You obviously make quite the team."

Theo's grin spilt his face as he replaced his spoon in his empty bowl and reached down to tickle Huggy Bear behind the ears. The Border Terrier's teeth stuck out as if she was smiling. "Yeah, it looks like I finally found a job I'm good at. Crap translator, useless barman but detective-cum-female impersonator? I'm a natural! What's next on the agenda, boss?"

"Ah, that reminds me," said Matthew. "There's a message on the answering machine for you, Old Thing. You might want to listen to that in the office. Judging by the approaching commotion, it sounds like the girls have arrived."

Beatrice grabbed her chance and ducked into the conservatory just as the garden gate opened, the dog started barking and Luke, Matthew's grandson, came charging up the path like a pint-sized American football player. She trotted into the study and closed the door behind her. For a moment, she sat at the desk, relaxing into the silence before her curiosity prodded her into pressing the flashing red button on the machine.

This is a message for Beatrice Stubbs. My name is Karoliina Nurmi and I am CEO of LokiEn, one of Finland's top energy suppliers. I am seeking a private investigator as a matter of some urgency. Roman Björnsson of the Vikingasveitin recommended you. I would prefer not to leave details on an answering machine for obvious reasons. I am sending you an email with an outline of the situation and I would be most grateful if you would call me back at your earliest convenience. My mobile phone number is as follows ...

Beatrice jotted down the numbers with one hand while opening up her laptop with another. She skim-read the promised email and rested her cheek on her fist.

It was an interesting situation. Two missing youngsters, a CEO receiving death threats and an imminent showdown at the new facility opening on Saturday. Plus it would be well paid and an opportunity to visit Finland, a country she had never seen.

But, and it was a very big but, there was another major event next Saturday – Tanya's wedding. The big day had been seven months in the planning, ever since Matthew's youngest daughter and her ridiculously handsome boyfriend had made the announcement last November. With less than a week to go, anticipation and tension were nearing a peak. It would be unthinkable to take off to a foreign country for a few days at this late stage.

Then again, if she left tomorrow, she could be back on Thursday. Plenty of time to do the wedding rehearsal, get her hair done and lend a hand with last-minute emergencies. And, she thought with a guilty smile, she could get out of the whole splicing hysteria and hide behind work.

She adored Matthew's daughters, she really did. But she was not their mother, so when it came to planning the wedding dress, flower arrangements, favours, table placements, bridesmaids, photographers, the wedding breakfast, a band for the reception and all the thousand and one other things to be fretted over, Beatrice was happy to leave it to Pam. It made perfect sense. As Tanya's mother, as a hotel events manager and as a great enthusiast for weddings generally, Pam was the obvious choice.

Except it wasn't that easy. Tanya wanted Beatrice to have an official role. She was determined that Beatrice and Matthew should be involved in every stage of the planning process. No matter how often Beatrice told her she was far more comfortable in the background, it was not to be. The final week before the shindig was always going to be utter murder. Yet this case had unexpectedly fallen into her lap and she could see a way out.

She printed a copy of the email for Theo and sealed it in an envelope. Then she took a deep breath, opened the door and headed towards the noise and mayhem in the garden.

An hour and twenty minutes later, Beatrice managed to drag Theo away from the attentions of the family and escort him to his Mini.

"Thank you for today. You really handled it beautifully. Drive safely and when you get home, have a look at this." She pressed the envelope into his palm.

"What is it?" he asked. "Bit early for my first bonus."

"You've already had your first bonus. Two slices of blackberry and apple pie. No, this is a potential job. The thing is, if we were to take it, we would need to fly tomorrow. Don't look at it now, but when you get home, think it over and give me a call."

Theo studied her, his hands clasping the envelope. "Fly where? What about the wedding?" He glanced behind her towards the garden. "They can't talk about anything else."

"You let me worry about that. Is Finnish one of your many languages, by any chance?"

His eyebrows shot up. "Finnish? No. But my Swedish isn't too bad and that's an official language in Finland."

"That might come in rather handy." Beatrice placed a hand on his shoulder and guided him into his car. "Safe trip and I look forward to hearing from you later this evening. Take care now!"

She watched as the scarlet Mini whizzed off down the lane, Theo's arm still waving as he rounded the bend. She steeled herself and returned to face the music.

In the garden, Matthew was fighting a losing battle in trying to teach Luke how to play croquet. Four times out of five, the boy's mallet either missed or flew out of his little hands. On the rare occasion he did connect with the ball, Huggy Bear grabbed it before it could reach the edge of the lawn. When Beatrice returned, Matthew gave up and came to sit at the table with her and his two daughters.

Tanya immediately appealed to Beatrice. "Will you talk some sense into this woman?" she pleaded. "She seriously thinks she's in with a chance with Theo! He's out of your league and far too young, you cradle snatcher!"

Marianne lifted her hair off her neck and puffed out a breath from her bottom lip. "Phew! I'm roasting. She's exaggerating, Beatrice. I only asked if he was single. Just out of curiosity, because with a face like that, he shouldn't be. Anyway, no one cares about age gaps any more these days. Look at Keanu Reeves."

Beatrice had no idea who Keanu Reeves might be and who she was dating, but nodded as if she understood. "I don't know if Theo is single or not. In my opinion, he lacks a daisy in his attitude to relationships. Catinca tried it on but nothing happened. Pity, because he is devilishly handsome."

For once, the sisters were in full agreement.

"Who's devilish handsome?" Luke asked, abandoning the mallet to the grass and the ball to Huggy Bear.

Tanya wrapped her arms around her son and planted a kiss on his hot, pink cheek. "You are, me 'andsome. And so is my husband-to-be. How lucky am I, living with the two best-looking men on the planet?"

Luke accepted the kiss and gave his mother a tolerant smile, then pulled away to wipe his sweaty face with the neck of his T-shirt. "I'm hungry. Are we having tea here today?"

"No, not today," Marianne replied. "You're going round to Grandma's tonight."

Luke wrinkled his nose. "Do I have to?"

"Yes, because your mum and I have got stuff to do." She prodded Tanya. "We should get a shift on. Dad, don't forget you're babysitting on Tuesday because it's the hen night. The minibus will pick you up at ten past seven, Beatrice, OK?" The two women got to their feet.

Beatrice bit her lip. "Ah, yes, the hen night. I may not be able to make that. The thing is, a job offer has just come in. I'm not sure exactly what it will entail, but if I have to take off for a couple of days, I hope you will understand."

The silence that followed was filled with the same kind of tension as just before a balloon bursts. Matthew slipped away from the table, cajoling the croquet ball from Huggy Bear and exhorting Luke to collect the mallet.

"You what?" Tanya's hands were on her hips. "It may have escaped your notice but I'm getting married on Saturday. This Saturday, not in two weeks' time. You know how much we have to do in the next week. You can't go rushing off to London five days before my wedding, Beatrice, you just can't!"

Beatrice dipped her gaze to the table and up again at the two outraged faces. "It's not London, actually. It's Finland. But it would only be for a couple of days, as I say. Back on Wednesday, Thursday the latest."

"Thursday?" Marianne's voice had raised in pitch. "What about the hen night? What about the dress fittings? Catinca arrives on Tuesday, Adrian and Will are coming down on Wednesday for the stag do and the dress rehearsal is on Friday afternoon. Beatrice, I know your work is important to you, but surely it will keep till the following week! It's not every day Tanya gets married and we need you here."

Beatrice reached a hand behind her head to massage her shoulders and caught sight of Matthew peering out of the kitchen window. Rotten coward, leaving her to deal with this all alone.

"Girls, listen to me. None of the things that need doing this week depend on me. Tanya, your mother is not only enthusiastic but also has a great deal more knowledge and expertise on the subject than I do. I appreciate the fact that you've included me and made me feel a part of things, but at this stage, I would prefer to take a rain check. Please don't take this personally, but I'm not really the wedding planning sort."

Tanya sat down again and took Beatrice's hand. "I know you're not. That's not the reason I want you involved. You are part of the family and it's important that we all enjoy not just the day but the preparations too. Can you really not postpone this job for one week?"

"If I could, I would do so in an instant. The fact is, two children have gone missing and someone believes I can help. I know the timing is awful, but if there is just a whisper of a chance that I can help find these youngsters, I have to go. Surely you understand that? I swear on all I hold dear I will be back in time for the wedding. I solemnly promise."

Marianne looked at Tanya, her expression defeated. She knew as well as Beatrice how the concept of a missing child would touch a chord with her sister.

"I see." Tanya's expression was grave. "In that case, you must go. I wish you didn't have to, but I understand why. Does Dad know about this?"

Beatrice shook her head. "No one knows because I just found out myself this afternoon. I've given Theo the details but I'm not sure he will want to come with me. I'm sorry about the timing and I'm very grateful for your understanding. Both of you." She reached up for Marianne's hand and the three of them sat for a moment, linked like a daisy chain.

Matthew emerged from the conservatory with exaggerated caution, with Luke and Huggy Bear in his wake. "Is it safe to come out now?"

"It's safe," said Tanya. "Come on, Luke, we have to go. Beatrice has something she needs to tell Granddad." She bent to kiss Beatrice on the cheek, kissed her father and reached for Luke's hand. Marianne said her goodbyes and hugged Beatrice, whispering in her ear, "Thank you for getting another online fake off the streets."

Finally, Beatrice and Matthew took the detritus of afternoon tea indoors and sat in the kitchen. He looked across at her with a stern frown, his hands gripping the edge of the table.

"You may have won those two over with your feminine wiles but I warn you, you'll find me a much tougher customer. Come on then, spit it out." His rugged pose was spoiled somewhat by the cat jumping onto his lap. Dumpling reached up to butt his grey head against Matthew's chin.

"Nothing is certain yet, but there is a strong possibility I will have to fly to Finland tomorrow in order to help locate two missing children. I have given the girls my sincere assurance that I will be back at the very latest on Thursday."

Matthew narrowed his eyes. "That's an awfully elaborate excuse to get out of the hen night," he said. "And I don't mean this to be insulting in any way, but why you? One would think a case of missing persons would fall under the jurisdiction of the Finnish police."

"Good question. Apparently, the person who wants to hire me is one of those who might benefit from the young people's disappearance. I believe her aim in involving me is a case of proving herself innocent. I'd say I'm her insurance policy. Whatever her reasons, I plan to do the very best job I can in the short time I have available. Do you mind terribly?"

The rattle of Dumpling's purr drew his attention downwards. He stroked the cat, a smile playing on his lips. "If the girls are fine with it, so am I. Just as long as you take good care of yourself, Old Thing."

"I always do, you know that. When have I ever given you cause for concern?"

Matthew gave her a sidelong glance but said nothing.

"By the way, what excuse are you going to use to get out of the stag night?"

He looked shocked. "I don't need an excuse. I'm looking forward to it. This is Gabriel, the son-in-law I always wanted, remember. There'll be no kissograms, discotheques or yards of ale at this bachelor party. Just me, him and a few of the chaps having a quiet pint and a steak and kidney pie at The Star. I might even push the boat out and have a plate of chips. Talking of which, what's for dinner?"

On hearing that word, Huggy Bear leaped out of her bed, ran to Matthew's side and jumped up on her hind legs, wagging her tail.

Chapter 6

Valpuri came round to the strangest sensation. It reminded her of school playgrounds, swinging high in the air until the momentum ran out and her stomach dropped, then whistling back in the other direction. She lay, inert, trying to make sense of what was happening. A sharp metallic pain throbbed across her nose and through her sinuses; her arms were stiff and bundled against her body, and she desperately needed something to drink.

The jerking motion continued as if she were in a basket being carried downstairs, and she could make out distant voices shouting, although she could not understand the words. She opened her eyes to blackness, casting around for some kind of clue as to where she was. The voices lifted in both volume and pitch, with an edge of panic, and solid ground rose to support her. The realisation that she had been winched through the air provoked a sudden nausea and she swallowed several times to control the urge to vomit.

Hands fumbled with the fabric swaddling her and the restrictions fell away, releasing her limbs. The hood covering her head eased back and she found her cheek resting on soft sand. A silvery light played across her face and she detected the sounds of the sea. She opened her eyes again to see two figures crouching over her. They too were hooded and on seeing her conscious, they stood up and moved away.

"She's awake!"

"Shit! Let's get out of here!"

"Do him first! We have to do him."

"I'll do it. You watch her. If she moves, you know what to do."

Valpuri blinked, tilting her head from one side to the other, trying to identify what was wrong with their voices. They spoke like computers, strangely distorted electronic sounds although the people making them were clearly human and female. The pain across her nose and face had spread like a metal band around her skull. She made an indistinct noise and the person standing guard took a pace backwards.

"Quick! She's coming round."

Another voice came from high above, this one a more natural man's shout. "What's happening? Why are you taking so long?"

The robot-person nearest to her shouted back. "Coming! We've released her and she's awake. We're just untying him and we'll come up."

The man yelled again. "Leave him! Leave the stuff and get out of there. Now!"

Sounds of rattling tins and a thump of something heavy came from behind her. Unsure she could sit up, she attempted to roll onto her back in order to see what was happening. The two figures were running away from the light into the darkness. Far above, there was a different kind of light, a hole in the roof through which people were shining torches. In the beams, she watched the two robot-people climbing some kind of ladder, one following the other. She lay on the sand, blinking her dry eyes and watching the progress of the steadily shrinking figures. Eventually they clambered out of the hole and pulled the ladder up behind them. The torches went out. Then there was silence apart from the steady wash and rush of the waves.

Until someone groaned.

Chapter 7

The call came as Karoliina was parking in the underground lot beneath the LokiEn headquarters. She rolled her eyes, convinced she knew who it was before even checking the display. She was right. The woman on the end of the line was PA to Ville Ikonen, asking if they could relocate the meeting due to start in ten minutes time to a different site. The secretary cited some bullshit excuse about security concerns, but Karoliina saw it for what it was. Ville Ikonen was playing power games, switching the venue from Karoliina's office to his own at the eleventh hour. That meant she would inevitably be late, ruffled and on the back foot. Whereas Ville would receive her on home turf, relaxed and in control. She would bet every last Euro in her purse that the third member of the party had been informed either earlier that morning or late last night. The boys always looked after each other and that was unlikely to change.

She assured the secretary she would be there, if a little later than expected. Driving in rush-hour from the centre of the capital to Scanski Solutions HQ would take at least half an hour. She was about to reverse and battle the traffic when a roar filled the garage and a leather-clad figure on a BMW motorcycle pulled into the space next to hers. For the first time that morning, Karoliina smiled.

The motorcyclist switched of the engine and pulled off a

matt-black helmet, releasing a cascade of thick blonde hair down her back. "Good morning, Karoliina!"

Her Swedish assistant always brightened Karoliina's spirits but especially so today. "Astrid, you're a sight for sore eyes. How fast could you get me to Töölö, do you think?"

"Around fifteen minutes. Twenty if the traffic is shit. And the traffic is always shit. Why are you in a hurry to get up there? Is Ikonen jerking you around again?"

"Right first time."

Astrid opened the pannier behind her and withdrew a spare helmet. "In that case, you'd better get on. We'll be there in ten."

As predicted, when the secretary accompanied her to management level at Scanski Solutions and showed her into the corner office, Ville Ikonen and Jouko Lahti were already there. The two men sat at the conference table, sipping coffee and laughing at some private joke. The jollity left their faces as they saw her, replaced by businesslike half smiles.

Ville stood. "Karoliina, I cannot apologise enough for the inconvenience. It only occurred to me this morning that meeting at LokiEn's headquarters might be an imprudent move, given the events of Saturday morning. I spoke to Jouko and he agreed to come here instead. I'm so glad you were able to make it. And only a few minutes late."

Karoliina shook his hand with a smile, hoping he could not see her teeth were clenched. Then she briefly clasped Jouko's clammy paw, resisting the temptation to wipe her palm on her skirt. She kept her tone light. "Of course I was able to make it. I could hardly miss a meeting of this significance, could I? Oh, is that coffee?"

The secretary poured her a cup and she sat on Ville's right, directly opposite Jouko. Once the woman had closed the door, the meeting began, five minutes later than planned. Naturally, Ville took the chair.

"I would like to open proceedings by expressing great sorrow at the loss of Juppo Seppä on behalf of myself and the entire organisation. That Saturday's disorder resulted in the death of a Finnish citizen is a matter of profound regret. May I suggest that whatever press statement we release at the end of this meeting begins with those sentiments?"

Jouko's jowly face sagged still further in what he must have fancied was an expression of heartfelt sorrow. Karoliina bowed her head, partly out of respect to the dead man and partly to hide the fact she was crossing her eyes in frustration.

"Personally, I'm shocked by what happened," said Jouko, shaking his head like a bulldog with a flea in its ear. "I do believe the whole country feels the same way. Up to now, we have indulged the younger generation and allowed them to express their opinions; no matter how ill-informed they may be. However, on Saturday morning, these protesters crossed the line and broke the law. That is unacceptable and cannot happen again."

Both men looked down at the blotting pads before them. Karoliina took a sip of her coffee and raised her eyes to the blue sky behind Jouko's head. "It's true that Saturday was a dramatic escalation from any previous protests. I can't help wondering why that might be. Most factors were more or less similar; number of protesters, length of route, level of media interest and number of participating groups. There's only one element that differed on this occasion and that was the presence of a private security agency." She sat back and waited for the theatrics to begin.

Ville did not disappoint. His jaw retracted into his neck and eyes bulged as if he were a turkey that had just seen the stuffing. "The private security agency was something agreed upon by all three of us as partners, I'll thank you to remember. The reason for their presence was to protect and defend your headquarters. Jouko and I agreed to share the bill due to the fact the new plant is a venture supported by all three companies. The fallout from Saturday is tragic and ugly but the one thing we can and should be grateful for is the lack of damage to LokiEn's headquarters."

"That's right," agreed Jouko, now nodding as if he were in a rocking chair.

Karoliina's temper was hanging by a thread. "If either of you gentlemen thinks I give more of a shit about bricks and mortar than the safety of environmental activists and freelance journalists, then you are living under a delusion. Yes, I agreed to the presence of security guards, in principle. My mistake was in allowing you or your henchmen to brief them. My understanding was that a small security presence would be inside the building when the protesters entered to deliver the petition. Instead, they were confronted by what amounted to a private army, who refused them access. Not only that, but if you have studied the media footage in any detail, those heavy-handed goons were the ones to strike the first blow."

Jouko blew out his cheeks. "Hardly!" He reached into his briefcase and withdrew a printed article. Before he even began, Karoliina knew it would come from Valo, the right-wing, trouble-making news site. With insufferable self-importance, he shook the paper and commenced to read.

Shocking scenes. On Saturday 15 June, teenage climate activists charged the headquarters of LokiEn, the energy giant responsible for the newest of Finland's existing nuclear power facilities and the long-awaited Neljä plant at Kolkko. Initially peaceful, the protestors gathered at Pohjoisesplanadi at 10.00 and marched towards the LokiEn offices on Senaatintori to deliver a petition. When refused entry, a small group of young people at the head of the march attacked the security guards protecting the building from malicious damage. Fighting broke out around 11.00 and over twenty people were seriously injured, several of whom are still in hospital. Police struggled to control the violent disorder, during which many of the marchers were seen to throw their placards at officers' heads. So far fifteen people have been arrested ..."

"Oh please, Jouko, give it a rest! Instead of an internal enquiry as to the conduct of the private security company, you prefer to spout hysterical ill-informed bias across this table. Put that mouth-foaming crap away and listen. We have to take partial responsibility for what happened this weekend. But as far as I'm concerned, that is a secondary consideration. Two of the protesters leading the march have now disappeared. Their welfare must take priority. If they have not been found safe and well by Saturday, we cannot possibly go ahead with the plans for the opening ceremony."

The two men raised their voices in protest and Karoliina shouted over both of them. "You can threaten to go ahead without me all you like. How do you think that will look? No, I'm sorry, but we need to handle this with extreme delicacy. This is how we're going to do it."

Ville pressed two fingers either side of his temples. "Karoliina, I must ask you to lower your voice. This is a meeting of chief executive officers, not a fish market. Before you continue with your mission of appeasement, I feel there is something important I need to share with you both. Yesterday evening, whilst entertaining some international guests, I received this through my letterbox." He reached inside his jacket and pulled out an envelope which he placed on the table between them. On the envelope, there was nothing more than his name: Ville Ikonen.

With a face-palm, Karoliina released a growl of infuriation. "Let me guess. It's a threatening letter and you didn't see who delivered it. Because you know best, you decided to pick it up with your bare hands, thereby obliterating any existing fingerprints and exposing yourself to potential toxins. Rather than reporting it to the police, you chose to bring it into the office to share with me and Jouko."

This time, Ville did not attempt to disguise his hostility. "You think you're very smart, don't you? I'd like to see how you would handle such intrusion into your privacy."

"Would you really? Then why don't you ask the police? They are in possession of a death threat delivered to my home and the security camera footage from outside our house last night. Jouko, if Ville and I have had threats, yours will only be a matter of time. Pick it up with gloves, bag it and inform the authorities immediately." She spotted his shifty expression. "Oh, great. You had one too. What did you do with it?"

Jouko thrust out his chins. "I burnt it. They don't scare me."

"Nor do you scare them," Karoliina sighed. "The only sense of unease they feel is the knowledge the police have at least one copy of their work. Mine. If it happens again …"

"We'll involve the police," snapped Ville. "The only reason neither of us saw the need to do so is that unlike you, paranoia is not our constant companion."

Dinosaurs, thought Karoliina. *The pair of them should be in a museum.*

She pressed on, taking advantage of their momentary discomposure. "The threats are another reason I see Saturday as a major problem. We need a plan of action. First, a press statement. I will draft something this morning and share it with you both for approval. The response should come from all three companies as a united front.

"Second, we launch an internal enquiry into the violence on Saturday morning." She held up her hands to forestall their indignation. "We do not have to share the results with anyone, but we must be seen to do the right thing. Third, from our privileged position, we offer the police our unconditional support in finding the young activists, while making a few enquiries of our own."

Jouko snorted. "Those flag-waving, snot-nosed, over-privileged little shits. They've gone into hiding, don't you see?

This is what they want. A huge handwringing media circus, trying to find the poor ickle protestors. Only when they have disrupted our opening ceremony will they crawl out from whatever stone they've been hiding under, smiling all over their smug faces."

Ville cleared his throat. "Yes, well, perhaps you had better leave addressing the press to me."

"No." Karoliina drained her coffee and got to her feet. "As the CEO of LokiEn and the chief stakeholder in the project, I represent the Neljä project. Any enquiries, send them to my team. A unified front, remember. We believe we are doing the right thing for the Finnish people and if takes a little longer to get everyone on board, so be it. Have a good day, gentlemen."

She left the room with a brief nod at the secretary, aware of two pairs of eyes boring into her back. As soon as this project was over, she reassured herself, she need never see Jouko Lahti or Ville Ikonen ever again. That prospect provoked the second smile of the day.

Chapter 8

On arrival at Helsinki airport, the plane taxied in the direction of the terminal and came to a dead stop. After a few moments, the captain's voice sounded over the intercom system, informing passengers there was a problem with the skybridge at their gate and there would be a few minutes delay. Five minutes became ten, then twenty and Beatrice's impatience grew, along with that of the other passengers. People switched on their phones, looked at their watches and craned their necks to stare out of the window.

Beside her, Theo sat perfectly still, his eyes closed. Beatrice peered past him to watch the petrol tankers, baggage vehicles and catering vans waiting to service their aircraft. She sighed again and turned her attention to Theo, vaguely annoyed that he did not share her frustrations. His head rested on the seat, his face completely relaxed, long eyelashes resting on his cheeks. His chest rose and fell steadily, as if he were asleep.

"Are you doing yoga?" she asked, a touch of belligerence in her voice.

His lips curved slightly although he did not open his eyes. "Not exactly. More mindful breathing. Does it bother you?"

"No, it doesn't bother me. It just feels like you're not here."

The plane started to move and Theo opened his eyes. "That's the whole point. I am here, a 100% in the moment. You, on the other hand, are straining towards to the future, itching to be in that terminal, rushing to the next part of the day."

The seatbelt lights went off with a ping. The captain apologised for keeping them waiting and wished them a good stay or onward journey. Passengers unclipped their belts and began the mad scramble of putting on jackets, unpacking overhead bins and queuing to get out of the aircraft. Beatrice was one of the first to her feet.

When they finally got into the terminal, Beatrice scurried to keep pace with Theo's long strides. They cleared customs and emerged into the Arrivals Hall, where a man stood with a sign saying 'Beatrice Stubbs'. She did enjoy having a car sent to collect her at the airport. It made her feel valued and just a little bit superior.

Theo livened up on the drive from the airport, asking questions of the driver and observing the scenery. A familiar fizz bubbled up inside Beatrice. The land of the midnight sun, white nights, a new case and an opportunity to make a difference. Her optimism and excitement was tempered by a fear of the unknown and the constant worry she would fail, but she considered that a good thing. Overconfidence was a deadly flaw.

The driver said they would travel through the city directly to the island of Kulosaari, where their host would be waiting. Sun sparkled off the Baltic Sea as they crossed the causeway and seagulls circled in the air, giving the atmosphere an almost holiday vibe.

The approach to Karoliina Nurmi's house gave Beatrice all the information she needed regarding the woman's status. On a gentrified island filled with large, expensive properties, the majority with a sea view, Karoliina's property sat at the end, clearly the most expensive and exclusive of them all. Theo let out a low whistle.

"She's not short of a bob or two then?" he said, his head taking a slow scan of the grounds, the private jetty complete with yacht, the landscaped gardens and split-level house with floor to ceiling windows.

Beatrice had seen it all before. If not this particular piece of real estate, then something with a very similar price tag. "Put it this way, she can afford us," she muttered.

The car crunched to a halt and the driver had opened Beatrice's door before she had even released her seatbelt. A woman was standing at the portico. Beatrice raised a hand and the woman responded in kind as she moved down the path to greet them.

Karoliina wore a simple blue linen tunic over capri pants, and minimal jewellery. Her face was broad and open, unadorned with make-up and her ash-blonde hair lay in a plait over her right shoulder.

"Thank you so much for coming, Ms Stubbs. I really appreciate how quickly you arrived given such short notice. And this must be Mr Wolfe. Hello and welcome. Please, come in and have a cool drink after your travels." She addressed the driver in English. "Erik, this will take no more than an hour and then I'd like you to drive our guests to their hotel. Thank you."

Inside, Karoliina led them through the wide open spaces of the living room and out onto a terrace overlooking the sea. A tray was set with three glasses and a water jug with a sprig of mint floating in it. Their host motioned for them to sit and Beatrice eased herself into the chair, absorbing the most relaxing view she could imagine.

As she poured water Karoliina spoke. "I prepared all the documentation I thought would be relevant. But I am not a detective. If you think there is anything missing that I can provide, please say the word. The fact of the matter is that this is no simple investigation. Two people, both teenagers active in the environmental protest movement, have been missing since Saturday lunchtime. Their parents are frantic with worry, the press are pointing fingers at us and some of my colleagues believe the young people are in hiding on purpose. On top of this, we have four days before the opening ceremony of our new power plant housing a modular reactor to heat many of the homes in Helsinki. The very power plant which was at the centre of the protests this past weekend. Obviously, the police have been informed and are actively working this as a missing persons' case. The reason I contacted you is because…"

Beatrice waited for her to continue. "Is because?"

Karoliina's pale grey eyes flicked from her to Theo. "... is because I would like someone to look at the situation with unbiased eyes. I wanted an outsider, someone neutral, with no emotional investment. I need you to focus solely on the facts. My intention was originally to send the paperwork directly to your hotel, keeping myself out of it. Then I realised you would have questions and there really is no time to waste worrying about protocols. That's why I had my driver bring you here, so you can read at your leisure and I will be available for any questions you may have. I will leave you now and come back in thirty minutes. Can I bring you anything?"

Beatrice shook her head but Theo looked up at her with an easy smile. "I don't need anything, thank you. I just wanted to clarify something. You said 'the press are pointing fingers at us'. Who is us?"

"Ah, I see," Karolina said, lowering herself into her seat. "By us, I meant the three energy companies behind the nuclear power plant. That's me, at the helm of LokiEn, Ville Ikonen who is the CEO of Scanski Solutions and Jouko Lahti, currently chief executive officer at Baltic Energy Services. The project is a collaborative venture between the three of us, although as the project lead, I represent the public face and deal with the stakeholders."

Theo thanked her and she retreated into the house. The following half hour Beatrice and Theo spent in silence, turning pages, making notes and double checking their findings. The sea rushed at the walls, the gulls screeched and swooped and a fresh breeze blew across the table, provoking a contented noise from DI Stubbs. Opposite her, Theo's neatly plaited black locks formed a screen around his face.

"Should we have a chat before she comes back?" Beatrice asked. "Or aren't you ready yet?"

Theo lifted his head as if waking up. "I've read it all, but I'm going to need some thinking time. I would like to ask a few things about context. What about you?"

Beatrice gathered her papers together and took them back into the file. "No. I'd rather some digestion time first. Talking of digestion, I could do with a spot of lunch. What do you mean by context?"

"I'm interested in the principles behind this situation. What I want to know is why Finland has embraced nuclear energy with such enthusiasm. Why is it such an emotive subject and what are the key questions which divide public opinion? Obviously we should look at both sides. Right now, we've got one of the project's managers willing to give her side of the story, so why not grab the opportunity?"

Beatrice stared out to sea. "I'm not sure it's necessary to get into the whole environmental debate. Our focus is to find the missing kids. The facts are that LokiEn and two other power companies are building a modular nuclear reactor and the environmentalists disapprove. Quite simply, the protestors care about the planet. All the companies care about is profit."

As if summoned by their voices, Karoliina appeared from behind the diaphanous curtains at the French windows, followed by a large Burmese cat which sauntered across the patio and into the garden. "May I add my thoughts on the subject?" she asked.

"Yes, please do," said Beatrice, a little embarrassed and irritated her blunt assessment had been overheard.

Karoliina took her seat. "I wasn't trying to listen to your

conversation. I came to see if you were ready. Ms Stubbs, your analysis of the situation is very common, but I'm sorry to say, incorrect. Our modular nuclear reactor, along with the others in this country, is part of an effort to tackle climate change. We too care about the planet. Where the protestors and I diverge is on the best way to do that."

Before Beatrice could reply, Theo asked a question. "My understanding of nuclear power is that it has the potential to be the safest and cleanest source of energy, reducing our reliance on fossil fuels. So why do people react so strongly against it?"

"That's an excellent place to start. Rather than my repeating some bland mission statement, let's ask your partner. Do you mind if I put you on the spot, Ms Stubbs? I don't know your own views on the subject, but you stated that the protestors care about the planet. In which case, why do they object to our state-of-the-art modular nuclear reactor, which will be used to heat their homes?"

In terms of scientific data on energy production, Beatrice's grasp of the facts was sketchy at best. To stick her neck out would mean exposing her ignorance. Taking that into consideration, she doubted anything helpful would come out of such a conversation. Nevertheless, she gave it her best shot.

"I'd say young people mistrust previous generations for very good reasons. Our careless consumption of natural resources has left them with a huge problem. We've spent decades on short-term solutions and ignoring long-term risks. The reasons they object to your reactor, I assume, is part of that. Nuclear energy might well provide a modern solution, but what about the risks?"

With her open face and clear grey eyes, Karoliina bore more resemblance to a yoga instructor than the head of a multi-million-Euro company. "Your analysis seems to reflect everything I have heard from people concerned for our environment. That is the key word. Risk. Why do people think nuclear energy carries the most risk?"

She knew it was a trap, but couldn't help herself. "Umm, Chernobyl, Fukushima? One accident can decimate an area."

With a yowl, the cat leaped onto the table, took a circuit to ensure no food was on offer and jumped down again to twirl between Karoliina's calves.

Theo spoke. "I read that when nuclear power goes wrong, it's a disaster. But when fossil fuels go right, it's also a disaster. Fossil fuels go right a lot more often and its effects take longer, that's all."

Karoliina stroked the cat, her eyes thoughtful. "That much is true. But is that the best we can do? The lesser of two evils? What if I told you nuclear energy uses fewer planetary resources than even renewable forms? That the new fourth generation reactor can recycle spent fuel, using up to 90% of our existing nuclear waste? That Finland is committed to storing the limited amount of residue safely, in our own country?"

"That all sounds very reasonable," Theo agreed. "It seems the majority of Finnish people are in favour, so long as the facility is not physically on their doorstep. From what I read online, the problem with your new reactor is that it's right in the middle of the suburbs."

"It is. The best place for a heat-generating reactor. All their homes can now be warmed using locally produced energy, rather than transporting it for hundreds of kilometres and losing much of its power. Don't you think that makes sense?"

The debate had gone past Beatrice's level of comfort and she was more than a little annoyed that Theo's comprehension far exceeded hers. She shuffled her papers into a bundle. "Thank you, obviously you're a minefield of information and I've clearly got a lot to learn. My focus is on how to locate the teenagers you're paying us to find. Can I ask you, frankly, what you think happened to the two young people concerned?"

Karoliina looked out to sea, the blues and greens of the Baltic reflected in her irises. She shook her head, a minuscule movement. "I don't know. I really don't. That's why I need you."

Their hotel was situated right on the harbour. While they checked in, Beatrice gave her assistant a very hard stare. "Since when did you become an expert on forms of energy production?"

His lips curved upwards in amusement. "Since we got this job. I do my homework."

"I only told you about it yesterday afternoon."

"Which gave me all yesterday evening to do the background reading."

"Swot."

A laugh shook his shoulders. "Damned if I do and damned if I don't."

Beatrice handed her passport to the desk clerk and surveyed the scene outside. "Helsinki is prettier than I imagined. Do you fancy a wander after we've had lunch?"

"I am itching to get out there," said Theo. "I was thinking I might go for a run. I think best when I'm running. Do you mind having lunch without me?"

The clerk handed over their respective keys and wished them a pleasant stay.

"Not at all. That will give me time to marshal my own reactions to what we heard. I'll eat, you run, then let's regroup and share our thoughts."

Theo treated her to one of his thousand-watt smiles. "As bosses go, I've had worse."

Their rooms were adjoining, so Beatrice wished him a good jog, as if there were such a thing, and went to explore her quarters. First impressions were good. Spacious and light with well-stocked mini bar, sizeable bathroom and balcony with an uplifting view across the harbour. While taking in the scenery, she saw Theo loping down the steps in his shorts and taking a right towards the enormous cruise ships at the end of the dock. She scowled. She had developed quite an aversion to cruise ships since a nasty serial killer case a few years ago.

Although Beatrice's curiosity in her immediate vicinity was piqued, she decided to order room service, allowing her to spread out her paperwork and concentrate on the reason she was here. Three things nagged at her so she focused on each in turn. Firstly, the police. Conducting a shadow investigation was a delicate matter and both her experience and instinct advised her to inform the local force about her activities. Secondly, the importance of getting close to the environmental protesters was a key factor in gaining inside knowledge. She held out little hope of a warm reception for herself but had more faith in Theo's easy charm. Thirdly, Karoliina had impressed upon them the pressure of time. In her employer's view, this case needed to be resolved by Saturday. But Beatrice knew that anything not done and dusted by Thursday would be a failure. She had a wedding to attend.

Chapter 9

The windows need cleaning, thought Tanya when she parked outside her house on Monday evening. *Another job to add to the ever-growing list.* She could see Gabriel and Luke sitting at the dining table, poring over Luke's homework. She dumped her bag in the hallway and sniffed the air. No smell of cooking, she noted.

"Hello!" she called and went into the living room to give them both a kiss. Luke insisted on showing her a page of sums and Gabriel handed over a pile of post.

"Today's mail," he said, his attention on Luke's workbook.

Tanya threw the cards into the nearest armchair and stalked into the kitchen in search of a bottle of gin. She poured herself a healthy measure, topped it up with tonic and rummaged around in the freezer compartment for some ice. She leaned against the counter, glaring at the soft afternoon light throwing a tinge of pink across the clematis. The sounds of her son's laughter from the living room did nothing to improve her spirits and she took another large slug of gin.

Ten minutes later, Gabriel entered the kitchen and she had almost emptied the glass. He stood in the doorway, studying her.

"Looks like you want a top up," he observed. "May I join you?"

Without replying, she held out her glass. Gabriel took it and commenced the preparation of their pre-dinner drinks. A thump indicated Luke had left the table and his footsteps thundered upstairs.

"I told him to take off his school uniform before dinner," Gabriel explained.

"Dinner?" Tanya sighed. "I honestly can't be arsed to cook tonight. Let's get a takeaway."

Gabriel handed her a refilled glass. "No need for a takeaway. It's too hot to put the oven on, so I made three different salads. All the ones Luke likes, don't worry. Thought we'd have that with some cheesy garlic bread. It'll only take a few minutes under the grill. Do you want to eat now or chill for half an hour?"

"You're the most infuriating man," said Tanya. "I came in here, all guns blazing, dying to bite the head off someone and what do you do? Help Luke with his homework, cook a healthy meal for the three of us and mix me a gin and tonic. Now what am I supposed to do?"

He reached out an arm to pull her close. They embraced one-handed, their other hands holding the G&Ts. "How about you sit in the garden for twenty minutes and tell me all about who's rattled your cage? Then when you've got that out of your system, we'll eat and listen to Luke tell you all about the joys of multiplication tables. Are you OK?"

Tanya led the way into the tiny garden, her spirits lifting at the sight of the wrought iron table and patchwork cushions on each of the chairs. She sat heavily, releasing a deep sigh.

"I'm all right, I suppose. Just hassled, pissed off, frustrated, overemotional and probably a bit tired. Before I start bending your ear with all my woes, how was your day?"

Gabriel stretched out his long legs and rested his socked feet on the chair opposite. "Not too bad. To be honest, work is a break from all the planning and organising and discussions and endless streams of people. Just me and the trees. It's grounding."

Tanya clasped his hand, aware of what a solitary individual

her future husband was. The polar opposite to her. Gregarious, positive and outgoing, she had made a great success of her role at the estate agent. She was born to love parties and organise fun events. A scowl crossed her face. Unless it was her own wedding. The problem, as always, was other people.

"I wish I could be more like that. Instead of getting all steamed up about things and letting it spoil my day. On top of everything else, work was a bloody nightmare." She kicked off her shoes and lifted her legs so her feet shared the same chair as Gabriel's.

"One more day, that's all you have to get through. Then it's full steam ahead to Saturday. After that, just you and me and an island for one whole week. That's what I'm concentrating on. Our honeymoon. Can you imagine? Sitting on the verandah, listening to the cicadas, watching the sun go down beyond the sea with nothing to worry about. No plans other than wandering down to the beach and exploring the local restaurants before heading home for a siesta. All we have to do is sleep, eat, read, swim and enjoy each other. Bliss."

His voice lulled her into such a state of relaxation she could almost imagine herself on the island, with the scent of olive groves wafting beneath her nose. She stroked her feet against his.

"Keep talking. I especially want to hear more of the enjoying each other bit."

A window crashed open above and Luke's voice rang out. "Mum?"

"What?"

"Can I have a wombat?"

Tanya arched her neck to reply. "No, you can't."

"Why not?"

"Because I said so. Wash your hands and come down here. We're having dinner."

Gabriel stretched out a hand and his rough fingers traced the line of her jaw. "I thought you wanted to bend my ear? You may as well get it off your chest before Luke comes down."

The mushroom cloud of indignation she'd carried home had somehow transformed into a small wet puff of insignificance. "It's nothing, really. Just me getting wound up over nothing. Shall I put the grill on for the garlic bread?"

Three hours later, curled up under the quilt, Tanya lay awake, listening to Gabriel's deep, regular breaths. A small clicking sound drew her attention and she opened her eyes to look at the clock then realised it was her own jaw muscle pulsing as she clenched her teeth. She filled her lungs and exhaled through her mouth, willing herself to fall asleep as easily as her fiancé.

As if she'd mentioned his name, his breathing changed and his hand snaked across the mattress to lie on her stomach. "Tanya Bailey, I know you. You'll lie there fretting for hours if you don't cough it up, and we both have work in the morning. If you have indigestion, drink some peppermint tea. If there's something bothering you, tell me. I promise I won't lecture you on what to do or suggest how to fix it. All I want to do is listen."

She took another breath and spilled all her concerns out into the darkness. "I'm pissed off with Beatrice. I can't believe she'd choose to go off on a foreign job when I need her here. She doesn't realise it but she's my buffer. When Mum and Marianne go into full Bridezilla mode, Beatrice is my safe haven. Dad's no good as all he wants to do is keep the peace. My mother and sister want to turn my wedding into a three-ring circus, when you and I want something simple, green and meaningful to us. It's my wedding so why the hell the pair of them feel entitled to take control, I have no idea. Now the bloody hen night is turning into some kind of stupid cabaret instead of a few cocktails with my mates. If I throw a wobbler, everyone will say I'm being selfish. That's why I need Beatrice. She doesn't take any crap. But she's not here."

Gabriel's hand smoothed circles on her abdomen. "No, she's

not. She's working and probably escaping from the family tensions. If you need someone to help you fight your corner, there is an alternative. Someone else who takes no shit."

Tanya rotated her head to look at him. "What do you mean? I would never ask you to enter the fray on my behalf."

"Thank God for that. No, I didn't mean me. Tomorrow lunchtime, a London train will arrive at Exeter St David's, bringing your wedding dress and a certain straight-talking Romanian. I think Catinca Radu will add some big guns to your arsenal."

Tanya's face split into a huge grin. "Of course! My dress, my designer and my secret weapon. I love you." She leaned over to kiss him. "Do I still stink of garlic?"

"Not much. At least I've no worries about vampires. Sleep tight. I love you too."

He rolled onto his back and Tanya folded her hands on her stomach and closed her eyes. Tomorrow was another day.

Chapter 10

The appointment with the Peura family was surprisingly easy to secure. The father answered the phone, and in impeccable English assured Beatrice he was willing to talk to anyone who could help them find his daughter. He was ready to receive Beatrice and her assistant at their convenience.

Over breakfast, Theo and Beatrice planned their strategy. With so much to be achieved in such a short time, it made sense for them to split up.

Theo talked tactics. "I'm the man to talk to the environmental activists, know what I mean? Thing is, I'm not going to have a way in unless the parents can vouch for me. I reckon we play it like this. I come to the girl's parents and see if they have a contact they're willing to share. Then I'll scoot out of there and track them down. See if I can't get them onside. Meanwhile, you talk to the boy's mother. My instinct tells me she'll open up more if it's just you two."

His instinct chimed with Beatrice's. She scooped out the last of her boiled egg and ran her finger down her To Do list. "That sounds like the best use of our time. Just to let you know, I sent an email to the detective in charge of the case this morning. A matter of courtesy, really, and I hope he takes it as such. I don't expect any offers of help or deliberate obstruction, but neither do I want to trample all over a potential crime scene in hobnailed hoofs. As for the rest of the day, we have the meeting with the two bosses of the other energy companies at three and the television producer says we can buy him a drink at five o'clock. How do you see it?"

"My experience with suits in senior management ain't great, you know what I mean? Don't matter what I wear or who I'm with, I'm still a black geezer in an all-white environment." Theo drained his orange juice. "You're likely to get a better response if you go on your own. If you like, I'll meet the television news bloke. That's another macho world but one I know a whole lot better than the boardroom."

Beatrice gave him a long look, thinking about what he'd said. She had questions in abundance but now was not the time. "That sounds like a reasonable allocation of duties to me. If nothing of significance occurs, shall we regroup here at seven? Perhaps we can find somewhere to eat along the harbour and share our discoveries."

"I'm up for that. I saw some nice-looking places yesterday on my run. Tell you what else, there's a car hire place right next to the tourist office. We could do most of the investigation by public transport, but it's going to take a lot longer. Can we stretch the budget to a vehicle, you reckon?"

Beatrice patted her mouth with a napkin. "I dare say we can. On condition that you do the driving. Are you ready?"

The drive out to the Peura family's apartment was the opposite of Beatrice's scenic expectations. The suburbs of Helsinki were not sprinkled with forests and lakes, but conglomerations of commuter towns, grey and functional, with plenty of traffic on the roads. Beatrice was glad of the little Volkswagen Polo and even gladder Theo was behind the wheel. The Satnav let them down at a confusing set of roadworks but Theo did not swear or make any hasty decisions, simply working his way out of the snarl-up. Forty-five minutes after leaving the centre of Helsinki, they found a parking spot between three tower blocks.

They took the lift up three floors to find Mr and Mrs Peura awaiting their arrival. The couple seemed pleased to see them, shaking hands warmly and offering them refreshments. Theo took off his shoes and placed them on the rack by the door. With some reluctance, Beatrice did the same. The Peuras settled them at the dining-room table. After exchanging pleasantries, Beatrice began by placing her business card on the table and with a nod, indicated Theo should do the same.

"I'm aware of the fact you've been through this already with the police and I'm sorry to have to cover old ground. My assistant and I have been hired by a private individual to run a parallel investigation."

Mr Peura exchanged a look with his wife. "It would be interesting for us to know who is paying you for this investigation."

Theo caught that particular ball. "That's understandable. In normal circumstances, we'd be happy to share that information. The issue here is that we have agreed to protect the identity of our employer. I hope you understand." He gave them a warm smile.

Theo had a knack for connecting with people. Beatrice could see them thaw.

"The fact is, we want to find your daughter and her friend fast," Beatrice said, pressing on. "That's why we're here, to learn as much as we can about Valpuri so that we can locate her at the earliest possible opportunity. Can we start by talking about her involvement with the environmental activists? When did she first begin to participate?"

Mrs Peura gave a little laugh through her nose. "Valpuri doesn't participate, she instigates. She's been passionate about climate change, animal rights, the welfare of the environment and sustainability as long as I can remember. They study green issues at school and even from a very young age, she took the subject seriously. Back then, her focus was on smaller, local actions. She and her classmates gained permission to clean up an area of wasteland which had once been a scrapyard and they turned it into a community garden. It was only when we moved here and she changed schools that her attention turned outward. She and Samu were in the same class and he was more politically aware than her."

Theo asked a question. "When was it that you moved here?"

Valpuri's father answered. "Five years ago, for my wife's job. Before that we were living in Vaasa, on the west coast."

"Was Valpuri happy about the move?"

Mrs Peura looked at her husband. He shrugged. "Yes and no. She really didn't want to leave her friends in Vaasa but when she got here, she settled in immediately. Making friends, exploring the area and excelling at her schoolwork. She surprised us at how quickly she acclimatised."

"You mentioned ..." Beatrice checked her notes "... that she instigated the environmental organisation. Can you tell me a little about that?"

"Of course." Mrs Peura reached for a photograph album and flicked open the pages. Beatrice saw it was full of newspaper cuttings and printouts from news websites, detailing the activities of the Gaia Warriors.

"There were six of them, to begin with. Valpuri and Samu had the original idea. Then there was Tuula, who I would describe as Valpuri's best friend. After that, Aleksis, Risto and Ursula joined. Tuula and Aleksis go to the same school as Valpuri and Samu, but Risto and Ursula are already at university. All of them are passionate about green causes. They used to meet here a couple of times a week." She pointed to some faces in the album as she mentioned the names. The grainy print made it difficult to distinguish between individuals, and Beatrice made a note to look at the stories for herself.

"I assume the police will have spoken to all Valpuri's friends here in Helsinki," said Beatrice. "Do you think there is even the remotest chance that Valpuri would have run off to Vaasa, perhaps to stay with one of her old friends? For example, if she were shaken and frightened by the death of the journalist on Saturday morning?"

The couple shook their heads in unison. Mr Peura spoke. "We know our daughter. Of course, it is impossible to know what's really going on in a teenager's mind. That said, Valpuri would never worry us like this. She would find a way of letting us know she was safe. Your question is reasonable. The police asked the same thing. We telephoned several families that we know in Vaasa, all of whom assured us if they heard anything from Valpuri, they would contact us immediately."

"And also," added Mrs Peura. "She's not the kind of girl to run away from something. In many ways, she's too confrontational. If she thought she was in any way to blame for what happened to that journalist, she would be the first person to hand herself in to the police. This is why we are so worried. To disappear like this is completely out of character. Something is wrong, I know it."

For the first time, the calm and steady persona projected by both Valpuri's parents seemed to wobble. She closed her eyes and bowed her head, while her husband placed a protective arm around her shoulders. Beatrice waited for the woman to regain control of her emotions.

"We won't keep you much longer, Mrs Peura," Theo said. "Just one more question about her relationship with Samu."

Mr Peura nodded, as if he knew what was coming. "As I said before, it's impossible to know with any degree of certainty what's going on with a sixteen-year-old. I will say that Valpuri, her mother and I have a very open, honest relationship. She talks frankly about her emotional life and I think my wife would agree with me when I say she had a great deal of fondness for Samu. As for romantic feelings, if there were any, they only flowed in one direction."

"He had a crush on her?" asked Theo.

Mrs Peura nodded. "Yes, I believe so. Valpuri was aware of it but she made it quite clear she was not interested in getting involved. Her feelings for Samu were platonic. She saved her passion for her cause. Would you like to see her bedroom? As I told the police, I can see nothing missing other than the clothes she was wearing that day. But you might see something of significance I have missed."

Leaving Theo to get the details of Valpuri's fellow activists, Beatrice followed the woman further into the apartment, holding out precious little hope for something of significance.

In the car on the way to visit Samu's mother, Mrs Pekkanen, Theo agreed. "Parents are biased, I know, but from what they said, she doesn't sound like the kind of kid to take off in fright. Nor does it sound like she's run away with a fellow protester for a dirty weekend. So either she and her mate have gone into hiding to put the wind up the energy companies, or someone's holding them against their will."

Lawns and trees either side of the road gave Beatrice the impression of a clean suburban area, with leafy parks and playgrounds, clean schools and churches. Kidnapping didn't seem to fit into a landscape such as this.

"Hmmm. The thing is, if they've been abducted, to what end? There's been no ransom note and as far as I can see, her family are not especially wealthy. As a single mother, I suspect Mrs Pekkanen will have even less disposable cash. It's possible that someone working for the energy companies might think it a good idea to remove the figureheads from the Gaia Warriors, but for how long? Until the new plant is open? Until they've learned their lesson? How can they be sure the remaining activists will not redouble their efforts?"

Theo turned the car into a small cul-de-sac and parked at the end. "That's her house over there, with the blue door. I don't know exactly where to find the key players of the Gaia Warriors, but Helsinki's small enough for me to get around on foot or by public transport. You'd better keep the car."

"Are you sure that's wise? I'm not used to driving on this side of the road. And you might be able to get around once you're there, but how will you get back to the city?" A reluctance to let Theo go made her nervous.

"Easy. The station we passed has a line direct to Helsinki. It's only a short train ride, about quarter of an hour. Let's keep in touch, OK?"

A strange yawning sound emanated from Beatrice's stomach. "All right, if you're sure. Just be very careful and let's keep each other informed as to our whereabouts. You concentrate on tracking down those protesters and I'll see you back at the hotel at seven. Good luck!"

"Good luck to you too. Do you want to take one of my muesli bars? Just in case you get hungry?" Theo gave her a wide smile.

"I don't know where I get this reputation for having a constant appetite. It's not all that long since breakfast so I'm sure I can manage to struggle through till lunchtime."

As if to belie her, her stomach made a sound like someone trying to stifle a braying donkey.

"Whatever you say, boss." Theo jumped out of the car, not quite hiding his grin, and loped off towards the train station.

In all the photos Beatrice had seen of Samu Pekkanen, he looked like a chunky sort of chap, so his mother came as rather a surprise. She was slight, fragile-looking and so light on her feet it seemed she hardly touched the ground. Her blonde hair was twisted up into a clip and she wore a ghostly white summer dress which seemed rather too big for her. She wore no make-up and her complexion was the colour of whey. On her feet were sheepskin slipper boots and she was clutching a woolly shawl around her shoulders. Her whole appearance reminded Beatrice of a convalescent.

"I'm so sorry to disturb you. As I mentioned on the phone, I've been hired..."

"Yes, I know. Come in." Her voice was as whispery and ethereal as the rest of her. Beatrice kicked off her boots in the hallway and followed the woman across the floorboards to the kitchen.

"I will make tea. Please sit down." Beatrice did so and watched as the woman flitted from cupboards to work surface with all the grace of a ballet dancer. She spooned dried berries and herbs from various tins into a teapot, then poured boiling water on top. A pleasing fragrance wafted around the kitchen. She placed two mugs, a tea strainer and the teapot on the table between them. As an afterthought, she opened another cupboard and withdrew a biscuit tin. Inside, to Beatrice's delight, were half a dozen chocolate chip cookies the size of saucers.

"Please help yourself. I have just spoken to Olivia Peura so I know what questions you want to ask. I will tell you everything you want to know and if you still have questions, I am happy to answer. But one thing you must know before everything else. My son Samu has asthma. He needs to manage his condition on a daily basis. He carries a reliever inhaler in his bag in case he has an attack and uses a preventer inhaler every night before bed. Mrs Stubbs, his preventer inhaler is still upstairs on his bedside table. That means his health is in serious danger. His preventer contains steroids which build up over time, making an attack less likely. He has to take a dose every day. This is why it is imperative we find him as soon as possible. I'm more worried than I can say. I cannot sleep or eat or rest until I know where and how my son is."

After the woman's speech, it seemed somehow impolite to eat the cookie Beatrice had selected. She placed it on the table beside her mug. "I can promise you, Mrs Pekkanen, I will do everything I can to locate your son and his friend. That's the reason I'm here and believe me, I'm treating this as a matter of urgency."

"Please call me Nina. My name is Pekkanen but I am not Mrs." She poured the tea and pointed to the biscuit. "I bake them but I don't eat them. Although Samu tells me they are very tasty. Regarding your questions, I've made some notes. We have lived here since Samu was born. Just the two of us, his father is not part of the family. Samu and Valpuri, as I'm sure the Peuras told you, have been close friends ever since she first joined the school, around five years ago. Samu was always interested in the natural world and he has a soft heart for animals. What do you think?"

Busy making notes and eating, Beatrice looked up, puzzled by the question.

"The cookie? Would you have noticed it's vegan?"

Beatrice swallowed. "Not at all. It's absolutely delicious."

"Why don't you have another one? As I was saying, ever since he was a child, Samu took an interest in his environment."

The tea tasted of rosehips, orange peel and something else sweet and uplifting. The biscuit appeased her stomach and Beatrice continued to listen, drink and eat as Nina Pekkanen painted a glowing picture of her son.

"He sounds like a remarkable young man. Can I ask, does the fact that he and Valpuri Peura have gone missing together offer you any kind of reassurance?"

Nina's grey eyes lifted and she stared at Beatrice, her lips slightly parted as if in surprise. "I don't know," she said. "Yes, in a way I hope they are together. Valpuri knows all about Samu's condition and how to behave if he has an asthma attack. Yes, I do feel better knowing he's not alone. But I think I understand the reasoning behind your question. You wonder if there is any possibility that Samu and Valpuri have ... what's the English word? ... eloped together. It's a fair question. The answer is no. He's never told me explicitly that he has feelings for Valpuri even though everyone can see it. The problem is she does not feel the same way. They are good kids, both of them sensible, thoughtful and aware of the consequences of their actions. My son has lived with asthma for seventeen years and knows the importance of managing his health. He also knows how much I worry when he is away at a protest march or demonstration. He usually checks in regularly to let me know he is safe. Not this time. Wherever Samu is, he did not go of his own free will."

Chapter 11

Detective Sahlberg tried again. "Mrs Friman, I understand the circumstances were confusing. The problem is that your statement is not consistent. When you spoke to the paramedics, you said it was a member of the security company who pushed the journalist. The men in the black uniforms, yes? Now you say it was one of the environmental demonstrators. Our security videos picked up nothing at that spot, which means your testimony is the only way we can identify the person whose actions caused the death of Juppo Seppä. I know you're tired and it's difficult to remember, but this is vital."

The woman wiped at her eyes. "I am trying to remember. But the more I try to think, the clouds get in the way." Her beseeching expression touched Sahlberg as truthful but that still didn't help.

Officer Halme glanced at him for permission to speak. With a tiny shrug, he gave her the floor. He had got nowhere in the last 72 hours, despite interviewing the woman three times. Maybe his colleague would have more luck.

"Mrs Friman, let's not think about the incident. The shock of what happened might have affected you and your memory is trying to protect you from the detail. Can we talk more generally about the march? For example, do you remember what you were wearing? You told us you are a veteran marcher, so I'm sure you have enough experience to wear walking boots or running shoes. Marching can be hard on the feet, as I know very well."

Sahlberg could see Sanna Halme's rationale and hoped it might have the right effect, but managed his expectations. Counterbalancing Halme's forward focus, he relaxed into his chair, waited and listened between the lines.

"Yes, that's true, police officers spend a lot of time on their feet. There's a condition called Cop's Foot, you know. Good shoes are an investment. I mainly wear ankle boots, to support my joints. That day, I wore a purple pair. We all wore bright clothes, you see. A rainbow of hope." The old lady's forehead smoothed, her mind on happier topics.

"I noticed," said Halme. "The march was full of colour and music. Families too."

"Families too," agreed Mrs Friman. "All sorts coming together to make our voices heard. We owe it to the young people."

"The young people are extraordinary. The front part of the march was mostly teenagers, right? The Gaia Warriors? How far away from the front were you?"

Sahlberg could see it was working. Officer Halme was guiding her through the event, step by step and focusing on detail.

"How far? I couldn't say. I didn't have a good view of ..."

"That's fine. To be honest, we can get all that sort of information from the cameras. What we can't see is what it was like, on the ground. Listen, I'd like you to take me there, seeing through your eyes. I'm going to put my hands over my face to help me concentrate. You can keep yours open or close them if it helps. Then I'm just going to listen to your voice. Try to put myself in your shoes, the purple ones." She smiled. "Could you do that for me?"

An instinct told Sahlberg to look at his hands, as if the story were an irrelevance to his life. Mrs Friman glanced from one to the other, clasped her hands together as if in prayer and closed her eyes.

"My placard was smaller this time because holding such a big one hurts my arms. I wore purple boots, a yellow jacket and my green hat, just to show my allegiance to the cause. The tram took me to meet everyone outside the President's Palace. We marched and sang and the weather was so kind. It was like a party, a family picnic. Only when we got to Senaatintori, it was different. The atmosphere changed. LokiEn had security guards ..."

Halme did not look up, her hands still over her eyes. "I saw the news reports, Mrs Friman. Now I want to see it through your eyes."

"Through my eyes. To be honest, my eyes aren't so good. It's all right, I will try. The march stopped and many people were discussing what to do. Me and the other veterans of green groups came together to support one another. Some of us are older and being in the thick of things can be dangerous. We moved forward to see what was happening. I couldn't see much, that man with the shoulders and the loud voice was blocking my view."

Alert, Sahlberg sat up. The old lady was no longer telling a story but experiencing it. She was there. He touched the record button on the pad, convinced this might be worth hearing.

"I've never seen a man that big before, even in the Netherlands and they are all huge. He had a ponytail and nothing in his hands. I thought he was alone, but when the word came back the Gaia Warriors were denied entry to the offices, he made a connection. Just a look, I saw him. That look when you find someone in the crowd. He gave them a nod. There was one left, one right and another one behind me. The big man put his hands like this." She held up two frail arms as if they were pistols. "He pointed his fingers at the front of the march and he took off. Shoving people out of the way, shouting some chant and he snatched the papers from the teenagers. A woman with little children, one in a pushchair and another with a balloon, started to panic and ran to get away from the crowd."

She paused, her fingertips resting lightly on her eyelids. "The crowd swelled into the space, like water, and I couldn't see what was happening. Pressure from behind me was horrible and I kept losing my balance. It was time to get out. No way to go back so I aimed for the side of the square. I could hear the fight and I was so frightened and alone, I started to cry. When I reached the steps, I caught hold of a lamppost. All the people running and pushing, it was like a river, like a flood, lifting me off my feet. I held on and on, too scared to reach for my mobile phone. The men were hitting, hitting hard. All of them in black uniforms, hitting and hitting. Like this!"

She took one hand from her eyes and punched a fist downwards, her index knuckle protruding.

"The journalist man with the camera was above me, up the lamppost. I didn't see him till he jumped down and had no idea he was even there. Then two men tore out of the confusion. Someone ran into the journalist, a small man dressed in black with a hood. I thought it was an accident. The big man with the shoulders was chasing the hooded one and he pushed the journalist out of the way. That's when he fell and hit his head."

Sahlberg kept his voice soft, not wanting to break her concentration. "The small man with the hood ran into the journalist. Would you say it was a glancing blow, as if he knocked into someone on the street?"

Halme splayed her fingers at him but he could not read her expression.

"No, it was a full-on collision. The journalist was knocked backwards and lost his balance and when the big man ran past, the impact knocked him down the steps. That's when he hit his head. That's when ..." Her voice broke and she began to weep.

He hit the button and ceased recording. Halme reached across the table, thanking the witness and offering water. He gave her a nod. She'd managed what he had not. Now they had some idea of why a journalist who fell down some steps had suffered a stab wound. Now they could begin to investigate why the coroner's verdict was not accidental death, but murder.

Chapter 12

Both schools and the university had broken up at the start of June, scattering pupils and students far and wide. Mr Peura had given Theo detailed information on the two schoolkids, Aleksis Timonen and Tuula Sirkka, so he decided to start with Valpuri's best friend.

Tuula had a summer job working as a tourist guide at Luonnontieteellinen Museo, or the Museum of Natural History in English, and Theo intended to catch her on her lunch break. After spending all day indoors, she would probably avoid the museum café and get out of the building into some sunshine. At least that was what Theo was hoping. He waited at the staff entrance from a quarter to twelve, watching as small groups, pairs and individuals left the museum in search of something to eat. Three minutes after midday, the door burst open and a tall girl with blonde dreadlocks powered up the path past him, inserting white earbuds as she walked. Her momentum was such that Theo opted not to cross her path and instead eased himself from the bench to follow.

The girl paced up the main street past the parliament building, dodging tourists and lunchtime lingerers to head straight into the park. Theo had to pick up speed in order not to lose sight of her. Once she had set foot on the grass, Tuula slowed, surveyed the possibilities and plonked herself right in the centre of a large patch of sunshine. She crossed her legs, shrugged off her rucksack and pulled out a flask along with something wrapped in greaseproof paper.

Theo walked past. He kept his head facing front but looked sideways behind his sunglasses. The girl hitched up her skirt and dragged off her cardigan, exposing her tattooed limbs to the sun. She too was wearing sunglasses. She swayed from side to side in time with her music as she unwrapped her sandwich.

The only way to approach in such circumstances was from the front. Anything else would appear creepy. Theo made a wide circle, took off his shades and walked directly up to her. His shadow fell across her face. She looked up with a frown and waved him out of her light. He moved to the left and crouched down to sit opposite her. She pulled out her earbuds and stared at him, her shoulders lifted in enquiry and her jaw thrust out in a challenge.

He addressed her in Swedish. "Hello, Tuula. Sorry to disturb you on your lunch break. My name is Theo and I'm looking for a friend of yours."

She pressed a button on her phone and used her middle finger to pull her sunglasses down the bridge of her nose. Her eyes, dark with heavy make-up, gave him a blatant once over.

"What friend?" she asked.

"Two people, actually. Samu and Valpuri. Her parents tell me you are Valpuri's best friend. In my experience, friends tell each other more than they might tell their parents, which is why I wanted to talk to you. Not just that, but you were there on Saturday morning. You, Samu, Valpuri, Aleksis, Risto and Ursula, all right at the heart of things. If anyone saw what happened to your two friends, I'd say you were in pole position."

The girl didn't move, glaring at him from under her brows. "Who are you?"

"Oh, yeah. ID. Sorry, I'm new to this private detective business and sometimes forget my manners." Theo leaned to one side to pull his wallet from his back pocket. "Theo Wolfe, part of the Beatrice Stubbs private investigation agency. We've been hired as a parallel track to the police operation."

She leaned forward to read his business card.

He offered it to her. "Keep it if you want. My number's at the bottom. So yeah, Tuula, I'm sure you've already answered a ton of questions from the police and you're having a break from work. But I'd like to ask you a couple of things, if you're willing to talk. Don't let me keep you from your sandwich."

Unsmiling, she took his card and placed it on top of her phone. Then she returned her attention to her lunch, watching him as she ate.

He lifted his face up to the sun and inhaled. Then he looked over his right shoulder, rotating to gaze above her head and over to his left, taking in all the office workers, tourists, joggers and dog walkers enjoying the fleeting but intense summer. "I can think of worse places to have my lunch," he smiled.

"Why? Where do you have yours?" Her light, musical voice seemed at odds with the tattoos, DMs and dramatic make-up.

"It depends on the job. Last weekend, I had a cheese and onion pasty while standing in a graveyard, wearing a dress and holding a red umbrella. It wasn't even raining."

"Weird job," she observed, finishing her sandwich and wiping her fingers on her skirt.

Theo relaxed backwards, resting his weight on his palms. "You know what? It's the weirdest job I've ever done in my life. Guess that's why I love it. What's your weirdest job?"

"I've only ever had this one. It can get pretty weird. Most days it's regular, guiding tourists around the museum and answering dumb questions. Once in a while, I get to do the nightshift and go hunting for deadly spiders."

"Spiders? Live ones?" He sat up, genuinely intrigued.

She nodded with all the sagacity of a Tibetan monk and adopted a tour guide tone. "No one knows exactly how, but sometime in the 1960s, the basement of the museum got infested with *Loxosceles laeta,* or Chilean recluse spiders. They're incredibly resilient and have one of the most poisonous venoms of the whole genus. Left to themselves, they breed and spread and grow to scary proportions. Look."

She picked up her phone, scrolled through some images and showed him a video of a large, eight-legged beast scuttling across the tiled floor and down a ventilation shaft.

He shuddered. "Ugh. Can't stand creepy crawlies. Especially that size."

She gave him a scathing look. "I thought you said you were a private detective."

"Private detective, yes. Indiana Jones, no. Most of the creepy crawlies we track down tend to have two legs."

For the first time, she cracked a smile. "Arachnophobe. Come on then, I've got fifteen minutes before I have to get back to work. You had some questions?"

Of all the places to start, Theo had drawn the golden ticket by talking to Tuula. Not only did she give him all he needed to know about the on-the-ground view of Saturday's march, the organisation and hierarchy of Gaia Warriors and the current whereabouts of her colleagues, but she made a phone call. Just to ensure they would be there and knew to expect him. Their conversation made her late for work, even though they talked as they walked. He apologised and she waved it away.

"Don't worry about it. They'll turn a blind eye. After all, I'm the best they've got. Hope to see you around, Theo." With that, she swiped her pass against the security lock and disappeared inside the museum.

On the way to the Kallio district, Theo became aware of a hollow feeling and decided it was time for lunch. He bought himself a crab sandwich and ate it en route, replaying the recording of his conversation with Tuula on his phone.

"I don't care what anyone tells you, the security guards started it. They threw the first punches, I swear. There were a couple of guys, not Gaia Warriors, who jumped right in. They seemed to enjoy the violence, the confrontation, especially that big blond. I had never seen them before and it looked like they were only there for the fighting. Anyway, I could see Valpuri trying to calm things down. But fists were flying, people started throwing placards and the situation was out of control. The police waded in and I saw Valpuri dragging Samu away to the left, out of the crowds. Samu hates any kind of violence, it really upsets him. I caught hold of Aleksis and tried to follow them but the crowds surged away from the police. Aleksis tripped and fell backwards. He hurt his hands. In fact, he broke his wrist. We didn't know that then, obviously, he just said it hurt. When we got to the area where I'd seen Valpuri and Samu, they'd gone. That was the last time I saw them."

Theo heard his own voice, closer to the microphone. "What about the other two? Ursula and Risto. The six of you were leading the march. What happened to them?"

"I don't know, it was chaos. I remember Ursula screaming abuse when those thugs in uniform refused to accept the petition, but I don't recall seeing her or Risto after that. No one expected it to turn nasty. We just weren't prepared for that level of ugliness."

Thoughtful, Theo switched off the voice memo and considered the girl's words. He finished his sandwich and dropped the paper into a recycling bin. The Kallio district teemed with life, bars on every corner, cafés and restaurants spilling out onto the pavements, and funky shops selling some interesting gear. It was the kind of area he would have loved to explore, pottering and browsing the less touristy side of Helsinki. But not now. He had an appointment.

He checked the map on his mobile and saw the street he was looking for, Vaasankatu, was directly ahead. If Tuula was right,

Aleksis and Risto would be waiting for him outside Bar Liberté. He wasn't worried about recognising them. They would recognise him. He wasn't the only black face on the street, but there were few enough to make him stand out. Sure enough, as he sauntered towards the bar, he saw two faces staring in his direction. One older, with a mono-brow and neatly trimmed beard; the other skinny and nervous, with a cast on one arm.

Theo slowed, looked up at the name of the bar and then down at the patrons smoking outside. He lifted his sunglasses and fixed his eyes on the staring pair with a half-smile. He exaggerated his laid-back gait, arms hanging by his sides, projecting relaxation and confidence. Once at the table, he looked at the cast covering the kid's hand and forearm.

"Is it painful?" he asked in English, pushing his voice to the lower end of his range.

The kid let out a nervous laugh. "No, not really. A bit, at night. Umm, are you …"

"Yeah, I am. Thanks for meeting me, Aleksis." Instead of offering a handshake, Theo held up a palm. The kid met it with his own, in a gentle representation of a high five. Next, Theo dealt with the one more likely to be trouble.

He pointed at Risto's chest, bearing an image of the Ramones. "Cool T-shirt. Hi, Risto. I'm Theo." He offered his hand. After a pause, Risto shook it without a smile. "So I just walked all the way from the museum and I need a beer. Can I get one for you guys?" Without waiting for an answer, he tried his well-honed 'get served first' trick. He stood stock still, gathering all his presence, then focused his eyes on the harassed server collecting glasses. It worked. It always did. The man made a beeline for Theo as if summoned by a whistle.

"Hi there. Could we get three beers here, when you're ready?" Theo sank onto the bench beside Aleksis, who shuffled up to give him more room. "I like this area. It's different. It has its own vibe."

Risto stubbed out a cigarette in the steel ashtray. "It used to have. These days it's all hipsters and vegan restaurants. At least the drunks, addicts and sex workers were authentic."

It took a great deal of strength for Theo not to roll his eyes. A world-weary nineteen-year-old, cynical about urban regeneration, harking back to the good old days. Thankfully, the beer arrived, relieving Theo from the obligation of an answer.

As they drank, Theo met each pair of eyes and made a private assessment. It was obvious Risto called the tune. There would be no chance of gaining trust from Aleksis under the shadow of that mono brow. All he could hope to achieve was to give the impression of being on their side, unthreatening, understanding and open to confidences. Not that he expected to receive any in the next fifteen minutes.

"You know who I am and why I am here. My boss and I are trying to find Valpuri Peura and Samu Pekkanen. I'm starting from the point where they were last seen, the march on Saturday. I heard Tuula's side of the story and now I'm asking you to tell me anything you can which will help me find your friends." He set his phone on the table. "I don't do shorthand so this is the next best thing. How close were you two when the violence began?"

Risto lit a cigarette, inhaled and blew smoke from the side of his mouth, his dark eyes on Aleksis. "Tuula can be quite naïve. I don't mean to be rude, but I don't know who you are, who you work for and who hired you. As far as I know, you could be an employee of LokiEn or even the security services who attacked us on Saturday, trying to implicate us in the death of the journalist. It might sound like paranoia to you, but as leader of the Gaia Warriors, I've had to grow up fast."

Theo took a long draught of beer to stop himself from snorting in derision. "Fair enough. Here's my business card. I work for Beatrice Stubbs, a private investigator and ex-DCI of the London Metropolitan Police. I can't tell you who hired us, that information is confidential. Our objective is to find the two young people who disappeared on Saturday and return them to their families. You're quite right to say you don't have to trust me or to talk to me. Unlike the police, I have no authority to insist on answers. I'm dependent on your goodwill. And the fact that we both want the same thing. Samu and Valpuri home, safe and sound."

The bench beneath Theo began to vibrate slightly as if an underground train were rumbling deep below the pavement. But the motion was caused by no subterranean transport system. Aleksis was jiggling his legs up and down as if he needed the toilet.

Risto continued. "That much is true. We care very much about Samu and Valpuri. We need them to help us in our struggle. The Gaia Warriors are fighting a powerful, insidious enemy and this particular battle is one of the most strategic in the entire war. They have might on their side, might and money. On our side, we have right and conviction. We will never stop fighting for our future."

Theo looked sideways at Aleksis and jerked his head in the direction of Risto. "I bet this guy is a whole lot of fun at parties."

The kid blushed and went very still.

Theo returned his attention to Risto. "OK, listen to me. I can get all the theory and the soap box slogans from your website. That is not why I'm here. Whether I'm sympathetic to your cause is immaterial. What I want to know is where you were and what you saw on Saturday morning as far as concerns Valpuri and Samu. Are you willing to help or not?"

A burst of song came from inside the bar, puncturing the tension. Risto flicked his lighter, once, twice, three times, affecting a distant, moody stare. Theo drew on his well of patience. He'd been through the pretentious phase himself, a misunderstood poetic soul in a prosaic system devoid of beauty. At least the young adult sitting opposite him used that sense of uniqueness and teenage angst to effect some good in the world. All Theo's emotional upheavals had involved falling in love with the wrong person.

With that thought in mind, he tried a different tack. He dropped his voice, leaned forward and included Aleksis in his conspiratorial huddle. "This may be way out of left field," he said. "But I spoke to Valpuri's parents earlier this morning. They said something which made me think. Parents have more insight than we give them credit for and yet, young people are often more truthful with their friends than their relatives. To your knowledge, was there anything more than friendship between Valpuri and Samu? Is there any possibility this disappearance is something spontaneous and romantic?"

With a snort worthy of a carthorse, Risto shook his head. "That's the most ridiculous thing I've ever heard. Valpuri doesn't do romance! All her passion is devoted to the Gaia Warriors. The last thing she would do at a crucial time like this is run away for selfish reasons. Samu is different, too soft for his own good. Even so, he understands we all must be selfless when it comes to standing up for our future. No, to answer your question, no. Valpuri and Samu did not take the opportunity for a hot weekend after a journalist was killed for trying to tell the truth about what's happening. They know we must all make sacrifices as warriors on behalf of our planet."

Before Risto could take another breath in order to spout more slogans, Theo turned to Aleksis. "What do you think?"

The teenager cradled his left wrist with his right. "They wouldn't do that. They put the cause first. We all do."

"What I don't understand is why you're talking to us," barked Risto. "In whose interests is it to have two of the Gaia Warriors disappear before next Saturday's opening ceremony? Hmmm, let me think. If you remove the leaders from the most vocal and well-organised environmental activist group in Finland, the protests at your opening ceremony will be nothing more than a handful of well-meaning, shambolic tree huggers. Yes, I know what you people think of us. Why aren't you talking to LokiEn? Why aren't you talking to Karoliina Nurmi and her financial backers? These are the kinds of people who profit from a situation like this, not us." He drained his beer and evidently fired up by his own speech, raised his arm to summon the waiter. Unfortunately, the waiter ignored him and swept past into the bar.

Theo pretended not to notice. "Sorry to disappoint you, but you're not first on our list. We spoke to Karoliina Nurmi yesterday and this afternoon we will be meeting the other two CEOs. Motives for abducting Valpuri and Samu are one of our lines of investigation. Another is the starting point from when they disappeared. So to go back to my question, where were you when the violence broke out between security guards and protesters? Please be as specific as you can." He looked up and caught the waiter's eye. With a nod, he ordered another round.

It took a total of three beers to get the full story from Risto and Aleksis. Even then, Theo sensed that no matter how loose their tongues grew, the story was well practised and would never veer from its grooves. Something Risto said was bugging Theo. A clear mind and full concentration was necessary so he got on a tram to head back to the hotel. If he was going to interview the newspaper editor over a drink this evening, he needed to sober up.

In the shower, he found himself giving full voice to a soppy Elton John number, surprised he could remember the lyrics. He set his alarm and lay on the bed, hoping his mind would switch off for an hour. Before he closed his eyes, he sent Beatrice a message, choosing not to call her in case she was driving.

`Met three out of four Gaia warriors this afternoon. Possibility some marchers were plants, deliberately hired to cause` trouble. Having nap to prepare for meeting sleazy TV producer. Probably will need another shower afterwards. See you at seven.

Chapter 13

Three days. So it must be Tuesday. Whoever kidnapped them after the march had winched them down into this hole on Saturday night. She and Samu had seen dawn rise on Sunday, on Monday and once again today. The cave did not admit much light, only that reflecting off the sea as it washed in and out of the cave mouth. The opening high above their heads allowed in a small pool of sunshine.

The captors came back every night, but always at different times. They never entered the cave, simply lowering down provisions via a steel cable. On Monday night, Valpuri had been awake when the torches flickered down through the aperture. Enraged by the lack of opportunity to engage in any kind of dialogue with these people, she scrambled to her feet. In the darkness, she felt her way along the wall of the cave until she stood in the shadow below the aperture. She watched the cold box being winched metre by metre towards the sandy floor. When the box touched the ground, the cable released, ready to be winched back to the surface.

That was when she pounced. With a wild, unholy shriek, she leaped from the shadows and grabbed the steel cable with both hands, twisting it around her forearms and trying to wind it around her leg. From far above, she heard a shout and the cable lost all tension, dropping to the floor like a dead python.

Panting, she disentangled herself and saw the coils were simply the end of the rope. The remainder stretched all the way up to the opening, through which she could see distant stars.

The winch began again and the coils slithered in reverse, unwinding into a single thread upwards, outwards and leaving them alone. Valpuri howled a scream of outrage, provoking Samu to leave his nest of sleeping bags and come to comfort her. The torches went out and the cave reverted to darkness.

Exhausted, Valpuri lay on the cold sand, her tears spent and her energy non-existent. She could hear Samu unpacking the cold box, muttering to himself.

"Cans, maybe tuna. Packets, don't know. Cake? These are drinks, orange juice probably. Water bottles. What's this? Matches? Why do we need matches? This is no good for me. We told them what I need, we told them I must have my preventer. This is no good."

Valpuri sat up and made her way across uneven ground toward Samu's voice. "Matches?" she asked. "Is there anything else? Candles, wood, anything we can light? How many matches?"

In response, Samu struck a match, giving them a moment of illumination, the first in days. Valpuri saw them immediately. Right in the corner of the cold box, behind the water bottles, there were four little lanterns and a box of tea lights. Her fingers shaky, she unwrapped a lantern from the tissue paper surrounding it and inserted a tea light. Samu lit another match and set it to the wick. In an instant, a warm glow expanded between the two of them. They stared at each other's dirty faces, light bouncing off their eyes, both ridiculously emotional at being able to see. Valpuri lit all four lanterns and set them in a semicircle around the cold box.

Together, they examined their rations. Juice, water, a bag of clementines, cheese, cans of sardines, bread, milk, cereal, toilet paper, toothbrushes, toothpaste, soap, chocolate, berries and some dried salmon sticks. He was unhappy about the lack of medication, but happy at the quantity. Valpuri was unhappy at both. If they had given them this much food, how long were they intending to keep them here and when would they be back?

She encouraged Samu to drink the juice and they ate a makeshift supper of sardines and bread, huddled in their sleeping bags. But at least they could see. Valpuri took a lantern down to the sea and washed the plates and cutlery. Then she brushed her teeth, using the smallest sip from the water bottles to rinse the mouth. The joy of cleaning the fur from her mouth lifted her spirits. She returned to their little base camp on the sand and wriggled down into her sleeping bag.

"Are you OK?" she asked.

He didn't answer for a moment. "For now. They have got to bring my puffer, Valpuri. If not, I don't know how much longer I will be OK."

She reached out and squeezed his arm. "I know. They'll bring it tomorrow. I'm sure of it. Goodnight, Samu, sleep well."

Chapter 14

The journey back into central Helsinki was stressful in the extreme. Unsure of exactly where she was going and unfamiliar with the road system, Beatrice eventually made it to her hotel, having enraged at least half the drivers in the Finnish capital. Eventually, she navigated the car to the underground parking lot and was profoundly relieved to get out from behind the wheel. She only had an hour and a half before her meeting with the co-financiers of the energy project and she wanted to change into something more formal than the jeans and jumper combination she currently wore.

She was hurrying through the foyer when the receptionist called her name. "Ms Stubbs? Here are messages for you," he said, handing over two envelopes. She opened them as she rode upstairs to the sixth floor.

The first was from Ville Ikonen, changing both time and venue of their meeting. Beatrice's first reaction was relief as she had half an hour longer than she expected. That was quickly superseded by irritation. If she hadn't decided to bring the car back to the hotel, she would not have received the message and been in the wrong place at the wrong time. The second message was better news. The police detective in charge of the missing persons' case had responded positively to her courtesy email. He suggested meeting for coffee at four o'clock that afternoon.

The moment Beatrice entered her room, she opened her laptop to reply in the affirmative. Then she typed in the address Ikonen had given her and was pleased to see the offices he had chosen were in the city centre, a mere taxi ride away. Her next priority was lunch. She put a call through to room service and went into her bedroom to change into something grey.

If she had any doubts about Ville Ikonen's last minute changes being part of a power game, the second she met the man she knew she was right. The taxi had deposited her at the office address, which was covered in scaffolding and the entrance obscured by building-site hoardings, bearing images of hard hats and security warnings. Men in high visibility clothing were going in and out of the doorway so Beatrice followed. She had only taken one step inside before a man came towards her waving his arms and shouting something unintelligible. She raised her voice above the din of drilling, trying to explain she had been summoned for a meeting. He didn't understand and continued trying to herd her out onto the street. She pulled out the message she received at the hotel and pointed at Ikonen's name, the address and time. He frowned at the paper and at her. Then he jerked his head to the right and walked over to a Portakabin. Beatrice followed and he handed her a hard hat, a fluorescent orange tabard and a lanyard with the word visitor printed on it in several languages. Once he was satisfied with her appearance, he beckoned for her to follow and led her up three flights of stairs.

On the third landing, the room opened out to a huge open plan area, stretching away to what would be vast windows, when construction was complete. At present, however, there was nothing but wide open space. Mercifully, the headache-inducing sounds of metal boring into concrete had been left behind on the ground floor. Her guide said something and pointed across the room to where three men bent over a trestle table. She thanked him and made her way gingerly across the gritty floor. Her speed was partly caution and also an opportunity to regain her breath after all those steps.

It was easy to see which one was Ikonen. The workmen wore orange tabards just like hers and white hardhats. In contrast, Ikonen was dressed in a light-blue suit and his protective headgear was red. As she drew closer, Beatrice could see they were discussing blueprints of some sort. One of the workmen spotted her and straightened, saying something to the other two. Ikonen turned to give her a cold appraising look and glanced at his watch.

He raised his voice. "I'll be with you in a minute." Without waiting for her reaction, he turned back to the documents on the table. Beatrice waited, looking out across the city. The building, when it was finished, would have the most extraordinary views. She stood there for several minutes, trying to orient herself against her mental picture of the city.

A voice came at her shoulder. "Mrs Stubbs, Ville Ikonen." He held out his hand and Beatrice shook it. He did not crack a smile or apologise for relocating and rescheduling their meeting, merely turning away and addressing her as he walked towards the stairwell. "Today is very busy. I need to inspect the rest of this building site. We can talk as I continue the inspection. What do you want to know from me?"

He made no concessions whatsoever, striding away at speed. Beatrice hurried to catch up, her heart sinking. She recognised an uncooperative interviewee when she saw one. Trotting up the stairs behind him, she began her spiel. "My colleague and I are investigating the disappearance of Valpuri Peura and Samu ..."

"I know. And as I said to Karoliina, what on earth for? If those people are indeed missing, which I doubt, surely it is a matter for the police." He reached the landing and carried on up the next flight. "Bringing in a private detective seems to me both an overreaction and counter-productive. This way."

They ascended two more floors and Beatrice did not reply, mainly because she couldn't talk and breathe at the same time.

He opened a door and gestured that Beatrice should go first. Chest heaving, she emerged onto a narrow scaffolding platform, no wider than a corridor. Beneath her feet were rough wooden boards with gaps between them so she could see all the way down to street level. He joined her and closed the door behind them, pointing ahead to where a makeshift metal ladder stood. The wind flapped at her tabard and the slaps and ripples of tarpaulin sheets made her feel as if she were aboard a sailboat.

"We are going up to the roof," called Ikonen, squeezing past her. "I hope you're not afraid of heights." He tucked his clipboard under his arm and began climbing the ladder. Behind his back, Beatrice mouthed the words 'You liar', almost amused by such an obvious attempt to unsettle her. She climbed the ladder at her own pace and emerged onto the roof with a wide smile.

"What a view!" she exclaimed, disguising the bellows-like movement of her lungs as hearty inhalations. She strode past him, towards the edge of the building which had no safety rails, simply red and white tape marking tide between metal poles. Seven floors, she had counted, plus another one to access the roof. The traffic seemed insignificant from this height, not dissimilar to beetles crawling around a dung heap.

As she suspected, Ville Ikonen had no business whatsoever on the roof. He paced around, pretending to make notes on his clipboard and throwing sideways glances in her direction. Once her breathing had calmed, she walked up behind him and cleared her throat.

"Whether or not you approve of my being here doesn't change the fact that I am here and I have a job to do. I'd like to know who briefed the private security team protecting LokiEn on Saturday morning." She lifted her face to him with an expectant smile.

The man was impressive to look at, she had to admit.

Receding grey hair cropped close to his head, eyes the colour of winter sky and a large sloping nose gave him an authoritarian air, supported by his expensive-looking suit. But with that nose, sneering was not a good look.

"Not that it has anything to do with the situation, but the person who hired and briefed security was Jouko Lahti, with my approval. We both agreed Karoliina was underestimating the risks to personnel and property. I'm sorry to say we were proved right. I'm finished here. I can give you a few more minutes and then I have to leave."

Beatrice opted to go down the ladder first and took her time descending. "Can I ask, in the strictest confidence, if you or Mr Lahti hired anyone else to attend the protest march? Did you have any plants amongst the activists, perhaps?" She waited for him to step off the ladder. It wasn't his most dignified angle.

"Certainly not. As far as I'm concerned, the less attention we give these people, the sooner they will go away. Their actions will change nothing, apart from making them even more enemies than they already have." He strode away towards the door, then stopped at the sound of her voice.

"One thing you should know, Mr Ikonen, is that Samu Pekkanen has asthma and if he suffers an attack, his health is in grave danger. Anyone holding these young people should be aware that an abduction gone wrong could lead to a murder charge."

He flared his nostrils. "Rightly so. This detail does not concern me."

"Not even out of human sympathy? You really don't care what happens to two young Finns whose opinions diverge from yours?"

He stormed across the rough wooden boards in her direction, mouth pinched and his footsteps kicking up dust. "They won't listen to our opinions. We have tried to explain. We extended an invitation to come to an existing plant, to meet the scientists, to ask questions, to learn something. It was a waste of time. These people don't do dialogue, only slogans. How can you rationalise with someone who shouts the same three words at you, no matter what you say?" He shook his head in exasperation and Beatrice knew it was the only genuine emotion she had seen thus far.

In contrast to Ikonen's blatant status games, Jouko Lahti was positively genial. He welcomed her into his office, offered refreshments and engaged with all her questions. He confirmed that he had selected and briefed the private security organisation, denied hiring any stooges to infiltrate the march and posited his own theory that the young people had gone into hiding in order to cause maximum news coverage in the build-up to the opening of the Neljä modular reactor. Beatrice believed his first statement, suspected his second and could see the argument behind the third.

"It's possible, I suppose. Though having spoken to the parents, I find it hard to believe their children would put them through such agonising uncertainty in order to make a political point. If it could be proved they had vanished on purpose, they would certainly be charged with wasting police time."

"Not just the police!" Jowly of feature, Jouko Lahti wobbled when he got animated. "You as well, no? I have every respect for what you do, Mrs Stubbs, but I do think Karoliina made a mistake in hiring a private investigator for this case. It's not an effective use of resources, I promise you."

Beatrice tilted her head in understanding and took a sip of mint tea. "Perhaps. Let's look at another possibility. Someone in the senior management structure behind this collaborative venture decided to remove the Gaia Warriors' ringleaders, thereby ensuring there would be no more protest marches leading up to your big day on Saturday. You must admit, as a theory, it makes as much sense as yours."

Lahti did not seem in the slightest bit offended, nodding with enthusiasm. "The double bluff, yes? It is obvious that the enemy of these … what did you call them? Gaia fighters? It is obvious that their enemy is us, the evil energy corporations. Of course it is in our interests to put a stop to all the marching, protesting outside our offices, signing of petitions and attempts to hack our website. But that is the first thing the police will check, no? So we make sure we have an alibi and arrange for the teenagers to be kidnapped. The most obvious suspects would never attempt such a thing because the finger of blame would immediately point at them. That is why it is a double bluff! The most obvious suspects really are the kidnappers!"

The man's glee puzzled Beatrice somewhat. He seemed to be enjoying testing various theories, as if all the world he were participating in a murder mystery weekend, rather than devoting his attention to the missing youngsters. She asked a direct question. "Mr Lahti, do you have any information which might help me locate Ms Peura and Mr Pekkanen?"

He sighed, his body sagging into a slump. "None at all. Not even to support my own hypothesis. They will either turn up next week or the police will work out where they are hiding by watching the CCTV cameras. Something boring like that, no?" His eyes lit up. "I have an idea! The double-double bluff! What if the person who hired you to find the kids is actually the person who took them? Karoliina is the figurehead of this project and attracts most of the criticism. She kidnapped the teenagers and then hired a private detective to find them, sure the last person you would suspect is her! That's a good theory, yes?"

"Do you think she sent herself death threats as well?"

His face fell and he chewed his lip. "No, that doesn't make sense. But the death threats could be real. Someone else came to the same conclusion as me and is letting her know they are onto her. Oh, but Ville and I also had letters."

Beatrice looked at the clock. Her appointment with Detective

Sahlberg was in under forty minutes. "One last question, Mr Lahti, regarding the collaboration between yourself, Mr Ikonen and Karoliina Nurmi. Have you worked together before?"

He shook his head, and his cheeks flapped. "No. Normally my company works on joint ventures with international companies. This is the first time we've been involved in an all-Finnish exercise. Probably the last, to tell you the truth. Even without the protests, it has been a long, hard struggle to get this far. It will definitely place us at the heart of European power generation for domestic usage, that is not just marketing. The problem is my colleagues are difficult people to work with. I am a simple man, uncomplicated. At heart I am a farmer. Karoliina is inflexible and insistent on business buzzwords like 'transparency' and 'stakeholder buy-in'. Ville, well, you met him. What did you think?"

Beatrice chose her words carefully. "He seemed very busy and important."

"Ha!" Lahti pointed at her. "Brava! This is exactly what Ville wants people to think. You have an expression in English: 'up his own backside'. That is a very good description of Ville Ikonen, yes?"

Beatrice kept her mouth shut but couldn't quite hide her smile.

In the taxi to the police HQ, Beatrice picked up a message from Theo.

`Leaving hotel now. Had a rest between beers with activists and beers with editor. Such a lightweight! Hope to be back by seven. Good day?`

She replied briefly.

`Lots to discuss. I'll book a table somewhere close for half seven. Let me know if you're going to be late.`

If Ville Ikonen had been uncooperative and unfriendly, and

Jouko Lahti had proved amiable but no use whatsoever, Detective Sahlberg was the best surprise of the day. Younger than expected, he had strawberry blond hair twisted into a quiff at the front and sported a gingery beard. He reminded her of Prince Harry. He was waiting for her in reception and his china-blue eyes crinkled in greeting as he got up.

"Ms Stubbs, I'm Timo Sahlberg. Pleased to meet you."

"Likewise. It's kind of you to spare me the time, detective."

"I appreciated your email. In such circumstances, we'll be more effective if we work together. There's a staff area on the roof where we could talk. Our office is noisy and crowded and doesn't smell too good."

Beatrice hesitated. What was it with the Finns and their obsession with roofs?

She gave him a wary look. "Do I have to walk up the stairs?"

His forehead creased in surprise. "Of course not. We have two fully functioning lifts. Come this way."

Rather than bare concrete covered in cement dust, the police roof garden had a pleasant ambience and a reasonable view across the city. Tables and chairs were scattered around the space, divided by artificial plants and latticework screens. Detective Sahlberg indicated the table in the centre and placed his briefcase on the seat between them. Before Beatrice had even opened her handbag to retrieve her notes, a young woman placed a tray in front of her, with two coffees, a bottle of water and a bowl of grapes.

Sahlberg placed his hands together. "I want to be honest with you, Ms Stubbs. There are lots of things about this case which are new for me, including the presence of a private detective. I had to do my homework on the protocol. I also did some research on you. As someone who held a very senior position with the London Met, you probably understand far more than I do about how this works."

"That's not strictly true," said Beatrice, warming still further to the man. "Each case differs and every police force has its own way of dealing with interested parties. The reason I'm here is to assure you that I will not get underfoot, withhold information or try to use anything I learn for personal benefit instead of solving this case."

His eyes crinkled once again. "Thank you. Can we start with what you've discovered so far? I know you've been here over twenty-four hours and I doubt you wasted any time."

With every attempt to be concise and factual, Beatrice related the contents of her meetings that day, adding the theoretical leads she and Theo were pursuing. While she spoke, Sahlberg nodded and made notes, but his expression said he was learning nothing new.

"As an ex-police officer, Detective Sahlberg, my mind immediately reaches for police resources, an option that is no longer open to me. For example, if this had happened in London, I would have a team examining the CCTV footage to see if there are any clues as to Valpuri Peura and Samuel Pekkanen's movements after they left the demonstration. I've spoken to both families and thanks to Karoliina Nurmi, put some questions to her co-financiers. My assistant has spoken to a few of the Gaia Warriors and in about an hour's time, he will be talking to the producer of Channel 6 news. So far, all I've managed to dig up is a bunch of theories and the extremely concerning information that Samu Pekkanen has asthma. You're very generous to offer me the floor, but to be completely honest, nothing I've learned will be of any use to you."

Sahlberg opened his briefcase and pulled out two grey paper folders. From the first, he withdrew a plastic sleeve, containing a document. "Protocol differs from force to force, that is correct. Here in Helsinki, we are open to working with journalists, private investigators and members of the public. The only requirement we have is a confidentiality agreement. Whatever information I share with you must remain private. By that of course, I mean private between you and your assistant. Are you willing to sign?"

Beatrice had a pen in her hand before he'd even withdrawn the paper. "Absolutely. You must understand how important it is for me to find, or help you find, these two young people. I have no interest in working with the press or earning anything more than a good reputation. Karoliina Nurmi thought I could add something. I'm not yet convinced she's right, but I am determined to keep trying. There, signed and dated. I can get my assistant to do the same, if you wish."

Sahlberg replaced the document in the plastic sleeve and opened his grey folder. "That's a good idea. I will make arrangements to leave a copy downstairs at reception. Perhaps he will find time to pass by the station tomorrow morning. I am able to share a limited amount of information with you. You asked about the closed circuit television recordings. They do reveal a lot about what happened at the centre of the violence. I can say no more about that as it is an active part of our investigation. What is no longer of interest is the footage showing Valpuri and Samu leaving the area. We were able to locate them leaving the square and turning into Unioninkatu. Unfortunately, the street has many cafés and bars all with, how do you say that in English? Like a screen overhead?"

"Awning. You mean to protect the customers from the sun? Yes, that's called an awning."

"How do you spell that?" he asked.

Beatrice obliged and watched him write down the word in his careful hand.

"Awning," he repeated. "Rhymes with morning. Thank you. The street has awnings which block the view of the pavement. After they left the square, it's impossible to see where they went. We do have people watching the apartment block where some of the Gaia Warriors live. We are 95% certain none of them returned on Saturday."

Now it was Beatrice's turn to request a spelling. "Could you tell me the name of the apartment block, and maybe the address? It's possible my assistant already discovered that information but… belt and braces, you know."

The blond head looked up from his scribbling. "Belt and…?"

"Braces. It means taking no risks if you want to keep your trousers up. Can I ask if you are making any enquiries with the security firm hired by Jouko Lahti?"

Sahlberg gave an immediate shake of the head. "As I said, some elements are still confidential. What I can tell you is that we are looking closely at two people present at the protest on Saturday morning. They are not members of the Gaia Warriors and neither registers on any database we have of environmental activists. We believe they may have been employed to cause trouble at the event or even shadow the missing teenagers. It's possible they may lead us to where they are being held. I can say no more, Ms Stubbs, but I will keep you informed. I hope you will do the same for me."

Beatrice drained her coffee and nodded emphatically. "You can count on that. I have your details and if I find something I believe to be significant I will most certainly share it with you. Thank you for your time and your trust. I wish you all possible luck in this case and if I can help at all, I would consider it an honour."

On the walk back to the harbour in still-bright sunshine, a recognition of mutual respect lifted her spirits. She would consult with Theo this evening and throw everything she could into solving this case. She meant what she had said to Detective Sahlberg and hoped very much she could take him at his word.

Chapter 15

The Great Western service from Paddington pulled into Exeter St David's almost exactly on time. Tanya's head bobbed from side to side, trying to spot Catinca as passengers disembarked and flowed along the platform. Being a mere five foot two, Catinca was easy to lose in a crowd. Tanya need not have worried. Her attention was drawn to a Great Western Railway employee wheeling a baggage trolley laden with suitcases, accompanied by a miniature version of Holly Golightly, guiding his progress with a constant stream of instructions.

The little Romanian looked up at the ticket barriers and saw Tanya waiting for her. She waved a hand like a cheerleader and her worried frown relaxed into a smile. Once the overloaded trolley was squeezed through the luggage barrier, Catinca squealed and embraced Tanya, the poor man she had cajoled into helping her forgotten. Tanya widened her eyes at the number of cases and bags on the trolley. She had rarely seen so much luggage unless accompanied by a family of five through Heathrow Airport.

"What on earth is all that?" Tanya asked.

"Everything I need!" Catinca replied. "Let me look at you." She drew a circle in the air with her index finger, indicating Tanya should turn around.

Tanya obeyed, with a sense of skittishness.

"Looking hot, mate. This dress is gonna look one million dollars, no kidding. Oi, you been using cream I told you? What's with the worry lines?"

Tanya took the helm of the trolley and began wheeling it towards the exit. "Long story, I'll tell you in the car. Good job I brought Gabriel's Land Rover, we'd never get this lot in my Fiat."

En route to the village, Tanya explained how her best laid plans for the week before her wedding had spun out of control.

"I understand why Mum and Marianne are doing it, I really do. In their minds, they are offering to help and upping my game. Except they are not. Everything Gabriel and I wanted has been dismissed as not good enough for our guests. We wanted a basic ceremony at the registry office, followed by a marquee for the reception on the village green with a simple supper of cheese, biscuits and fruit. The whole idea was to be as eco-friendly as possible, not just in an environmental sense, but reflecting Gabriel's work, the village, the forest. Oh, you know."

Catinca faced Tanya, her hair scooped up into a style reminiscent of a Walnut Whip. "Yeah, I know, mate. It is how I designed your dress. Simple, elegant, perfect foil for green background. Don't tell me they've been messing with the decor." One fist rested on her hip.

"Not just the decor, the music, the wine, the table decorations and even, can you believe it, the hen night. My family have made everything ten times more complicated than I wanted it. And every time I try to rein them in, they get hurt and resentful because they think they're doing me a favour. It's driving me mad, Catinca. And now Beatrice has taken off to somewhere in Scandinavia to escape from it all. Gabriel's not interested in the planning phase, Dad is keeping his head down and I'm fighting for the wedding I want, all on my own."

Catinca reached out to clutch Tanya's shoulder. "If you're gonna cry, can we pull over? We got very precious treasure in the back."

Tanya laughed and shook her head. "I'm not going to cry. Scream, shout, punch something, perhaps, but no tears. I'm so glad you're here. I need someone in my corner who'll stick up for me and tell them that I'm not deluded. The other reason I'm happy to see you is I'm wildly excited to try on the dress."

For several minutes, Catinca did not respond. She leaned back in her seat, drawing her knees up to her chest and wrapping her arms around them. "The dress is centrepiece of whole ceremony. You and me planned colour scheme, atmosphere and whole look. Nobody, and I'm serious, nobody messes with that. We've been planning this for half a year now and we know what we want. Listen, Tanya, I've been mixing with designers and fashion people and creative sorts so I know how to throw artistic tantrums. Leave it to me. Stop worrying, I got it."

Despite her assertion, tears welled in Tanya's eyes and she reached for Catinca's hand. "Thank you. That means so much to me."

"You're welcome. Eyes on road now."

For the duration of the wedding celebrations, Catinca was booked into The Angel, along with several others of the inner circle. Before checking her guest in, Tanya drove to Matthew's cottage in order to drop off the majority of the boxes and bags. Then the moment of truth: trying on the dress. Just Tanya, Catinca and the dream they had envisioned.

As always, Matthew was delighted to see Catinca and welcomed her with open arms. He assisted in lugging bags and boxes into the spare room and offered to fetch Luke from school to give 'the ladies some time alone', as he put it. Tanya leaped at the offer and bustled upstairs with the most special delivery of them all.

Catinca unzipped the garment bag and unwrapped the contents as if she were revealing gold bullion. She removed the protective cover, peeling it away from the dress beneath. Tanya clasped her hands to her clavicle, her lips parted in anticipation. Catinca held up a hand for patience.

"If you've got your bridal shoes and undercrackers here, you can try it on now. If not, we wait till tomorrow. When you put this on, it has to be perfect. No grimy bras or scabby trainers, we gotta get this right."

Tanya gulped. "Everything is here. I brought it all because this is where I'll be getting ready on Saturday morning. We're ready, so may I? May I try it on?"

With a regal nod, Catinca gave her assent and with nervous giggles, the two of them began assembling the accessories. It took them a quarter of an hour to dress the bride-to-be and only when she was completely satisfied did Catinca remove the throw she'd chucked over the mirror.

Tanya blinked at her reflection, scarcely crediting the woman in the mirror was herself. She could hear Catinca's voice but paid no heed to the words. She looked, as Catinca had promised, a million dollars. Champagne-coloured silk clung to her body, creating a flattering hourglass shape. The neckline was off-the-shoulder, with frothy layers of lace interspersed with tiny red rosebuds and green ivy leaves. At the knee, the dress flared out, falling in folds to her ankles. She looked like a champagne flute, bubbling over and decorated with wild strawberries. It was more than she could have hoped.

She held out her arms to embrace Catinca. "You are a genius! I can't believe you took my scrappy ideas and turned them into this!"

Catinca returned the hug and stood back with a critical eye. "It works, I reckon. Don't forget, this is without hairdo, flower circlet and bouquet, but we can get the idea. Shows off all the curves and lights up your complexion. You look beautiful, Tanya. My first bridal gown and I knocked it out the park!"

"You did, you really did. I don't want to take it off, but I'd better put it away. If Luke comes charging in here with Monster

Munch dust all over his sticky fingers ..."

Catinca locked the door. "No one comes in here. Nobody but me and the bridesmaids can see dress before ceremony. Quick, let's put it away. You sure there's nothing you wanna change, now? Last chance, mate."

Smoothing her hands over the fabric, Tanya shook her head. "Nothing. It is perfect and actually really comfortable. Unzip me, then, and we'll hang it in the wardrobe till Saturday. What about your dress?"

Catinca gave her feline smile and put a finger to her lips. "Surprise, innit. But don't worry, it will complement theme. No upstaging from me. Or any-sodding-body else, I will make sure of that."

A door slammed downstairs and Tanya could hear Matthew whistling. They packed up all the bags and boxes and made their way downstairs, discussing the evening ahead.

"Ah, there you are. How did it go?" he asked.

"This woman is the best designer in the world. I couldn't be happier," sighed Tanya.

"What marvellous news! Shall we celebrate with a cup of tea and a cream cake?" Matthew switched off the boiling kettle and stood looking around for the teapot.

Catinca pointed at it on the counter behind him. "Yeah, I got time for a cuppa, then I better get to The Angel. Gotta prepare for tonight. Where's Trouble?"

Matthew poured hot water into the pot and replaced the lid. "In the garden, gnawing on a bone. At least I hope she's only gnawing and not burying the thing. She makes a dreadful mess of the flowerbeds. Tanya, would you pass the milk?"

Tanya did so, puzzled by her father's remark. "I think Catinca meant Luke, not the dog. Is he in the garden as well?"

Matthew looked at her, his expression blank. A jolt of fear shot up her spine. "Luke, Dad! You went to get him from school. Where is he?"

"Oh, good heavens!" Matthew exclaimed. "Luke, of course. I was supposed to be making him a sandwich. He must have gone into the garden."

Tanya raced across the hallway and out through the conservatory. Digging a hole in the flowerbeds with the dog was her son, his face dirty and uniform showing evidence of grass stains. Her heartbeat slowed to normal and she reached down to stroke his hair. "You pair of mucky pups. Luke, come wash your hands and say hello to Catinca."

His head snapped up and he scrambled to his feet. "Where is she? Did she bring Beatrice back? Are Will and Adrian here too?"

"They'll be here tomorrow. Probably with Beatrice," she said, without much conviction, but Luke had already pelted away into the house.

While Catinca was being led into the garden by a small boy in school uniform, Tanya accepted a mug of tea from her father. She refused the gingersnaps.

"I'm not putting on another ounce now I've seen that dress." She softened her voice. "Dad, did you know Luke was in the garden? Or did you just forget?"

A frown of concentration flitted over Matthew's face. "I got back to the house, picked up the post and gave Huggy Bear a bone, then I started to make a sandwich for Luke but must have got distracted making tea and clean forgot about him. Very poor behaviour on my part and I apologise. Juggling too many things at once, I'd say. Won't happen again, promise."

She kissed him on the cheek. "Not to worry. It happens. Are you two going to be OK this evening? When I asked you to babysit for my hen night, I thought he would keep you company because Beatrice would be coming with us. Have you heard from her at all?"

"Not in any detail. A few brief messages to assure me all is well, but as yet, no estimated date of return. She always does this when she doesn't want to answer questions. Texts or emails but no phone calls. Still, it's only Tuesday."

A shriek of laughter caused them both to peer out into the garden. Catinca was attempting a move of some kind which Luke found hilarious. Tanya had no idea what they were doing and judging by his bewildered expression, neither did Matthew.

"Granddad, look! Catinca is rubbish at cricket. Even worse than you!"

Tanya was pleased her fiancé was having dinner with his mother. Gabriel was completely relaxed about her going out with the girls, just as she was happy that he'd have his boys' night tomorrow. But with Luke staying over with Matthew, she didn't want her future husband to spend the evening at the cottage alone, especially as she had booked a room in The Angel.

She finished her make-up, put on her denim jacket and checked the playlist she had assembled on her phone. Tonight was all about the 90s and remembering the party girl she used to be.

He whistled when she came down the stairs. "That's exactly how you used to dress when I first had a crush on you." His fingers traced her face. "All those years we wasted."

"Believe me, in those days I was a horrible little cow. It would never have lasted. These days, I'm more mature and have better taste in music, not to mention fashion. Only now do I deserve someone like you. If you like, we can have a once-in-a-blue-moon date night? I'll dress up in stonewashed denim and we can listen to the Spice Girls. Whatever turns you on."

"I can honestly swear I have never been turned on by the Spice Girls. But even in stonewashed denim, you are my dream woman." He kissed her. "Are you ready, Lady Lip Gloss? I'd like to drop you off a bit early so I can buy some wine for Mum."

En route to the pub, she charged him with delivering her love to Heather and promised to be home by lunchtime tomorrow.

He pulled up outside The Angel and wished her a fun evening. She blew him a kiss goodbye, so as not to leave more sticky gloss on his face and hopped out of the Land Rover. He drove away with a toot of the horn and she turned to the pub. *Let battle commence.*

The landlady, Susie, had followed Tanya's instructions to the letter. The function room was all set for a girlie party of cocktails, music and a trip down memory lane. A slide show was all prepared to play on the white wall at the end of the room. It would show pictures of Tanya from bald pudding in a pram to the day she got engaged. Everyone present was included in at least one photograph and even some absent, such as Beatrice Stubbs.

The minibus arrived at seven-thirty, announced by whoops and squeals and gales of laughter. Tanya met her guests at the door, kissing and hugging and exclaiming over their outfits. Friends from school, from work, from the village, her babysitter, her sister and finally, her mother all ascended the stairs and filled the room.

The atmosphere was giddy, as guests helped themselves to glasses of Prosecco. Marianne immediately buttonholed Tanya. "Where's the stage area? I told you we planned a little performance. I specifically asked Susie to leave a place for ..."

"I know what you said. But this is my night and I have chosen the tone. Sorry. No performance, no surprises." Out of the corner of her eye, she saw her mother approaching.

Pam hovered at Tanya's elbow? "What's up, girls? Do we have a problem?"

"Yes," said Marianne.

"No," snapped Tanya.

The door opened and Catinca walked in. All heads turned to stare at the vision in the doorway. In a pink tutu, pink tartan bustier with exposed midriff and bright red Converse All-Stars on her feet, Catinca had styled her hair into a cascade of black ringlets, threaded with electric pink streaks. The room erupted into spontaneous applause.

She swept into the room and embraced Tanya. Then she clasped Pam's hands in both of hers and whispered something in her ear. Pam nodded, all earnestness, and motioned to Marianne. The three of them snatched up a glass of Prosecco each and retreated to a window seat, deep in discussion. Curious as Tanya was, she trusted Catinca to handle things her own way. Now it was party time and first track on the playlist was Britney Spears.

At half past eleven, Susie came upstairs to let guests know the minibus had arrived. With much groaning, emotional farewells and a final few selfies, the room emptied. Tanya and Catinca followed them out into the car park, waving and blowing kisses. Once the bus had departed, they returned to the pub. Seated at a table covered in glitter and feathers, they toasted a successful evening.

"What did you say to my mother and sister? They've been as docile as lambs," Tanya asked, draining her glass.

"Truth, mate. Told them your wedding is not just your special day, but also a Catinca Radu showcase. Got a photographer coming, gonna put selected pictures into catalogue and whole event is stage-managed by me. Nothing, and I mean nothing, happens without approval by me. I am wedding designer and I need two smart women to make sure everything I say goes. Anyone tries to change one tiny detail, they tell me. Them two are my Rottweilers, innit?"

Tanya rubbed a hand over her face. "But the only people trying to change details are my mother and sister."

"Not anymore, mate." Catinca blinked her eyes like a cat. "People will fall over themselves if they think pictures will end up in gossip magazine. You gonna have the wedding you want and rest of your squad got your back."

Tanya held out her glass and Catinca filled it with the dregs from a Prosecco bottle. "You are amazing, Ms Radu. What would I do without you? You know what? I wish Beatrice was here."

"Me an' all. Sodding off to Finland just before wedding? Me and her gonna have words. And I'm kicking Theo's arse too."

"Kick his arse? I thought you fancied him."

Catinca snorted and ran her fingers through her ringlets. "Of course I fancy him. Who doesn't? He's sexy as hell. That don't mean I can't kick his arse. Trouble with Theo, he's way too willing to please. Beatrice says jump, he jumps. With forceful personality like Beatrice, you gotta be strong. Otherwise she always gets her way. Tell you what, Matthew deserves a lot of respect."

"Is there any more Prosecco?"

Catinca placed an arm around her shoulders. "Not for you, mate. Big glass of water and bed or you ain't fit for nothing in the morning."

"I'm getting married on Saturday," said Tanya, as Catinca heaved her to her feet.

"I know. And it's gonna be sodding spectacular."

Chapter 16

At that precise moment in time, Catinca wasn't the only person who wanted to kick Theo's arse. Wide-awake and alternating between annoyed and amused, Beatrice lay under the duvet, wondering if she was likely to get any sleep.

With one look at her assistant when he had arrived back at the hotel bar at twenty past nine in the evening, she gave up on having any kind of intelligent conversation. For someone who rarely drank, Theo must have consumed an entire week's worth of alcohol in one afternoon. His eyes were glassy and his coordination was suspect. On top of that, his usually soft-spoken voice had turned into a foghorn.

"Beatrice!" he boomed. "Sorry I'm late. Didn't get a chance to send you a message, sorry. Have you eaten? I'm starving. Let's have dinner and I'll tell you what I found out from the..."

Beatrice slipped from her bar stool and guided him towards the lifts. "Hush now. Not here. Let's get you upstairs and order you something from room service. You need to eat, wash your face and get some sleep. We'll talk about this in the morning, when you're sober."

Theo weaved his way into the elevator and turned to Beatrice with a finger to his lips. "Ssshh. You never know who might be listening. Walls have ears," he said, with a giggle.

Beatrice pressed her lips together and pushed the button for floor six. "I assume you've been drinking with the television producer since five o'clock this afternoon. No wonder you're three feet to the wind. The question is, did you get anything useful out of him?"

The lift ascended and Theo blinked at her, apparently concentrating hard. "Out of who?"

"The producer. The person you've been getting drunk with all afternoon. Did he tell you anything useful?"

Theo looked over his shoulder as if checking for eavesdroppers. Where he thought they might be hiding in the lift containing two people, Beatrice had no idea. Theo leaned in to whisper in her ear. "He's not a he."

Fortunately, at that moment the lift opened onto floor six, because Beatrice was on the point of strangling her incoherent assistant. His breath certainly should not come into contact with a naked flame. She marched him down the corridor to his room. Theo found his key card after some pocket searching and let them both in. Beatrice switched on the lights and located the room service menu. When she turned to suggest burger and chips might be the ideal way to soak up all the beer, Theo was on his hands and knees, looking under the bed.

"What are you doing?" Beatrice asked, exasperated.

"Checking for bugs," Theo replied, in a stage whisper.

"God give me strength," she groaned and picked up the phone to make her order.

She all but forced him into the shower where he sang lustily about what sounded like red ribbons and a motorised tortoise. When the water stopped, she knocked on the door, opened it a few inches and handed him a bath robe.

The food arrived and Theo fell on it as if he hadn't eaten in weeks. Between mouthfuls, he spouted some gibberish about the news programme of which Beatrice could make no sense. Finally, his head began to droop over the remains of his dinner. She opened the balcony door just a touch for some fresh air, made him a cup of coffee, placed a bottle of water beside his bed and left him to sleep it off.

Despite her conviction she would lie awake all night, Beatrice did fall asleep in the wee small hours and awoke just shy of eight o'clock, feeling rather fresh and ready to tackle the day. She suspected Theo would be feeling precisely the opposite and decided to let him sleep another hour while she checked her emails and sampled the delights of the breakfast buffet.

She had just sat down with a plate of scrambled eggs, potato cakes and sausages when a sorry-looking sight hove into view. He sat down opposite with a mumbled "Good morning".

"And good morning to you too. Dare I ask how you're feeling?"

"Better than I deserve to. On a scale of one to ten, how embarrassing was I last night?"

Beatrice gave him a compassionate smile and gave him her orange juice. "There, drink that. You were on the tipsy side, it's true, but I bundled you out of the bar and upstairs before you could say anything indiscreet. You're not a big drinker, are you?"

Theo shook his head. "No, I'm not and she knew it."

"She?" Beatrice gave him a puzzled look. "Is that what you were trying to tell me last night? The TV producer is a woman?"

He nodded and took a slug of juice. "Päivi Aho is definitely female. Not only did she get me pissed, but she came on to me when I was trying to leave. I was lucky to get away with my innocence intact," he said, with a sorrowful shake of his head.

"You poor lamb," said Beatrice, cutting into a sausage. "Had I known I was sending you after a man eater, I might have gone myself. Go get yourself something to soak up the booze and then I want a full debrief."

"So did she," said Theo. He finished the juice and headed to the buffet table.

Considering he had spent four hours drinking with the woman, the information he had gleaned from the television producer was patchy and inconsequential. Nothing Päivi Aho had said incriminated herself or her staff, but she had told Theo the editorial angle was to fuel the divide between environmental protesters and supporters of the new nuclear facility. Not only that but the journalist who died at Saturday's march, Juppo Seppä, had been sacked by Aho herself for his overly sympathetic attitude towards the Gaia Warriors. The third piece of information, which the editor had hinted at but not directly confirmed, was that the violent elements who confronted the security guards had been paid for by 'parties with an interest in balanced news'.

"Theo, what you've given me is supposition, possible fact and unverifiable allusion. What do you mean when you say she hinted at those plants being on the TV station's payroll?"

"If you'd been there, you'd think the same as me. When I mentioned the idea that some protesters were there merely to cause trouble, she batted her eyelashes, did the wide-eyed innocent look and said 'who would do a thing like that?' in a little girl voice. She was basically telling me she knew who'd hired those thugs. She's a nasty piece of work, I'm telling you."

They finished their breakfast, both deep in thought.

Finally, Beatrice broke the silence. "Find out who funds Channel 6. See if you can link its parent company to anyone in government, private enterprise, or any other organisation with influence."

Theo made a note on his phone. "On it. Now we've both shared all our discoveries from yesterday, where do we go next?"

"My key concern is Samu Pekkanen's health." Beatrice dropped her voice. "We need to ramp up the pressure on anyone and everyone who might have the smallest inkling of where those teenagers are."

"And that would be...?" asked Theo.

"And that would be the CEOs of Scanski Solutions and Baltic Energy Services, as the key people most likely to want protesters off the streets. I also think it possible that if Päivi Aho is dirty enough to stir up trouble at the march, she's certainly capable of having two genuine protesters kidnapped. In the guise of an exclusive and with police permission, we could give her the information about his illness. That might trigger an attack of conscience."

Theo looked sceptical. "I honestly don't think she has one. Whatever. If you think it's worthwhile, we could try pressing the emotional buttons of the money men and the TV news management. Something else occurred to me. For some reason yesterday afternoon, I was singing an Elton John song in the shower."

Beatrice peered into his face. "I think you need more black coffee."

"No, hear me out. This is typical when my subconscious is trying to attract my attention. When I talked to the Gaia Warriors yesterday lunchtime, one of them used an interesting expression. He said Valpuri and Samuel understood the importance of sacrifice. A sacrifice. I wonder …"

Beatrice studied his face. "You think those young people are actually in hiding? Making a sacrifice in faking the disappearance?"

"Could be. Although I get the impression not all the Gaia Warriors are in the same place, in terms of political activism. Some come across as more extreme than others. What if the extreme element decided to hide Valpuri and Samu in order to throw suspicion on the energy companies?"

"That's a long shot," said Beatrice. "But if we are pressing buttons, let's press them all. Why don't you take Samu's mother to meet the activists? I can think of no more compelling person to explain the dangers Samu is facing. Meanwhile, also in the spirit of double bluffs, I will talk to Karoliina again. If she takes the threat to the young man's life seriously, she'll pass that on to her financial backers. As for the telly people and other media, I'll need the detective in charge to release that kind of information. There may be a very good reason why they have not yet done so."

Theo scratched his chin. "You managed to get the cops on your side? How?"

"Charm, obviously. That reminds me, I had to sign a confidentiality agreement and they want you to do the same. Otherwise, they will not be able to share their findings with us. Could you swing by the police station at some point today?"

"Yeah, no worries. Is it OK if I take the car to collect Mrs Pekkanen?" Theo asked.

"Absolutely. I never want to get behind the wheel of the bloody thing ever again. My track record with driving in foreign countries is the stuff of nightmares. It's all yours. After I've spoken to Karoliina, I'm going to check the street where the missing teens were last seen. Ask a few questions, that sort of thing. When you speak to the Gaia Warriors, will you find out how they got to Saturday's march? Mode of transport, whether they travelled together, how they carried their placards and so on?"

"Sorted." He gave her a sheepish look. "Umm, it's Wednesday. No stress but should we be thinking about flights home tomorrow? There's a storm forecast for the afternoon."

Beatrice folded her napkin and stood up. "Let's just see how we get on today, shall we? Right, I'm off to brush my teeth. Check in with each other at lunchtime?"

"You're the boss," said Theo, with a helpless shrug.

Chapter 17

Normally when the Helsinki police called a surprise press conference, Päivi Aho watched it live with her team, barking orders at her news gatherers the second any new information came to light. Today, a gut feeling told her to watch it alone. All news is good news, her mentor used to say. Somehow, she had a premonition this was the exception to that rule. She gave her deputy instructions to act on whatever information the police released and locked herself in her office.

It was a wise move. As she listened to Detective Sahlberg describe the death of Juppo Seppä as premeditated murder by suspected infiltrators of the protest march, the colour drained from her face. A witness had given them a good enough description to create a photofit of the two men they were seeking in connection with the journalist's death. Instantly, her phone rang.

On seeing the name on her screen, she hesitated, fighting the urge to disconnect the call, in the full knowledge she had no choice but to answer.

"Change tack. Major feature expressing shock, sympathy, outrage at the loss of a colleague. Get footage of his reports, eulogies from anyone who worked with him and focus on his integrity. Send a cash donation to his widow on behalf of the whole company and arrange a huge wreath to be delivered to the funeral. The tone should be deep sadness and journalists all over the world should be entitled to do their job without fearing for their lives. As for the…"

Päivi interrupted. "Really? That's going to look like we're making a U-turn so fast we're burning rubber. I sacked Juppo because the stupid bastard had genuine integrity. On top of that, you paid those thugs to stir the shit. Isn't there the slightest whiff of hypocrisy here?" Her deputy rapped on the glass door and she sent him away with an aggressive hand gesture.

The voice continued, ignoring her points completely. "As for the missing teenagers, we offer a reward. If murderers have wormed their way into a well-meaning group of young people, those passionate young voices cannot be silenced. Throw the weight of the entire channel behind this and from tomorrow, make them the main story. We get the whole of Finland rooting for them."

She thought about his words. "Ah, I see. Then miraculously produce them like rabbits out of a hat?"

"We could only do that if we knew where they were. And I don't." There was a long pause. "Do you?"

She placed her palm over her eyes. "Of course I don't know where they are. Unlike you, I report the news, I don't make it. You should know there's a private detective sniffing around."

"Yes, I met her already. Nothing to worry about there."

"Her?" Päivi released her grip from her temples. "I'm talking about a young black guy, British and wet behind the ears. He tried pumping me for information last night."

"Presumably he was unsuccessful."

Päivi flushed, thinking of the unsubtle pass she had made and the clumsy hints she'd dropped. If the guy was any good, he'd join the dots and connect her to the paid protestors and therefore to the death of Seppä. "I gave him Finnish vodka and pinched his arse. He got nothing more than a reminder never to try winkling a story out of a hard-nosed journo. What now?"

"Do as I told you. More instructions after I see the evening news. Päivi, make sure your entire staff stick to the editorial line. Have a good evening."

The phone buzzed the second she rang off. Activity in the corridor caught her eye. A gaggle of people demanding her attention. She picked up the wastepaper basket and hurled it at the door. Her deputy and two junior reporters recoiled and hurried away.

A smile lifted her lips and she answered the call. "Do you have any idea how insanely busy I am? I can't talk to you now." Her honeyed tones belied the message in her words. "Give me a few hours. Can you go for a jog around three this afternoon? I know you have a lot to tell me."

His voice was breathless. "Three o'clock? The usual place?"

"The usual place," she purred. "I deserve a little rest and relaxation."

Chapter 18

The best way of arranging a meeting with the Gaia Warriors was definitely through Tuula. Theo called her from his hotel room before leaving to collect Samu's mother. This time, he decided, he needed to meet all the leaders of the movement and ideally, somewhere that did not serve alcohol.

Tuula was doubtful she could gather the whole team at such short notice, but she promised to try. She gave him the name of a café near the museum where they could meet in relative privacy. Theo thanked her, took another swig of sparkling water and deemed himself sufficiently recovered to be able to drive. Due to the sheer embarrassment factor, he'd been unable to ask Beatrice the questions which were nagging at him. He had very little recollection of the night before. He wanted to know exactly what he had said to his new boss, who had undressed him for his shower, why there was a half-eaten burger on the end of his bed and how come the pockets of his bathrobe were stuffed with handfuls of chips.

On the road to Haaga, he opened the window and allowed the fresh air to fill the car and his lungs. Since he hadn't managed to get himself fired for drunken behaviour last night, he had to put every effort into making sure it never happened again. One way to get back in his boss's good books would be to make some sort of progress today so they could both fly home in plenty of time for the wedding. Where that progress would come from, Theo had no idea.

Nina (not Mrs) Pekkanen spoke very little on the journey into Helsinki. Theo explained the importance of impressing the dangers of Samu's condition on these young people. He told her it was a strategic move so that they would spread the word, hopefully getting back to the people who were keeping Valpuri and Samuel hidden. He also asked her to bring Samu's preventative inhaler, just in case. She did as she was asked and posed no awkward questions. When they arrived at the café, good as her word, Tuula had gathered the other three remaining members of the Gaia Warriors' leadership.

The only one Theo had not seen before was Ursula. She was the complete opposite to her friend. Whereas Tuula was all tattoos, piercings and torn black fabric, Ursula was completely unadorned. Her long straight hair hung down her back, her face was free of make-up and she wore a simple white T-shirt, denim shorts and ballet flats. She seemed like the youngest in the group and Theo couldn't get his head round the fact she was a university undergraduate.

He made the introductions and watched with some amusement as Risto tried to keep up both his sneering posture with Theo and respectful humility towards Nina Pekkanen. She spoke to them in Finnish, so Theo was excluded, but that was not a bad thing. These kids had to keep their full attention on this softly spoken woman, so Theo trained his focus on the table in front of him and breathed himself into stillness. He did not look up, nod, make noises of encouragement or move a muscle while she spoke. At one point, she placed the two inhalers on the table. No one moved to pick them up.

Once he sensed their attention was completely held by Nina's words, he risked lifting his head a few millimetres to take in their postures. It made for interesting viewing.

Risto leaned back, his arms folded and brow hooded over his eyes. His focus on his friend's mother only wavered occasionally as he flicked a glance towards Aleksis. Ursula was the picture of sympathetic concern, her brow creased in understanding as she murmured her comprehension at every statement. In contrast, Tuula seemed tense and fidgety, her attention divided between a worried mother and the brooding figure of Risto beside her. It was almost impossible to get a good look at Aleksis because he sat the other side of Ursula, shrinking back so far Theo thought he might fall off the bench.

In his stillness, Theo noticed every tiny movement. Tuula fiddling with the fringe of her top and biting at her lip. Aleksis's hunched shoulders and downcast gaze. Ursula, placing her hands either side of her legs, while making little noises to express compassion. The slight creak of his jacket as Risto folded his arms still tighter. Theo looked past the three people sitting opposite him; Nina Pekkanen and Ursula. Behind them was a long brushed steel counter, the kind you might find in an American diner. The reflections of the mismatched party were clear and he realised he could see a rather different angle.

To his surprise, Ursula's hand snaked along the bench towards Aleksis. The young man was curled forward as if to stare at his navel, his injured left hand resting in his lap. Ursula caught his right wrist and he winced, but did not look up. All the time, the fresh-faced pretty blonde kept her head turned towards Nina Pekkanen, still nodding, still saying 'mmm'.

When she finished her speech, Mrs Pekkanen thanked them for listening and asked them once again if they heard anything to go to the police. She repeated it in English, for Theo's benefit.

Risto cleared his throat. "I mean no disrespect, Nina, but we don't have a lot of faith in the police. Even less after Saturday."

Theo saw Ursula's hand release Aleksis and she twisted her body to place a hand on Nina Pekkanen's arm. "Please don't worry. We will be sure to do the right thing."

"And if you don't feel you can trust the police, contact me," said Theo, his eyes taking in the sight of Aleksis rubbing at his wrist and pulling his sleeve down to cover his hand. "I'm going to give each of you my card and you can call me on this number any time, in confidence." He passed his business cards around the table and everyone except Tuula took one. The inhalers remained where they were.

"I've already got one of your cards," said Tuula, with a knowing smile, playing with the earring in her left ear.

Ursula shot her a sharp look and the girl's smile faded.

"Tuula, I'm sorry to take up your break like this and I want to thank you all for taking the time to listen to what Nina had to say. I have one last question. Can you tell me how you travelled to Saturday's march? I'm just curious how you transported all your placards and so on."

Theo kept his face bland and open, making eye contact with them all, but intensely aware of Aleksis in his peripheral vision. No one spoke for a second and Theo could sense the tension. Each of them was waiting for Ursula.

She took a long drink from her water bottle and screwed on the cap. "Same way we always travel to events. In our minibus. We parked it at EuroPark because it's only three minutes' walk from the President's Palace. Then we marched to Senaatintori and LokiEn's office."

"Right, thanks. Who travelled in the minibus?"

Risto spoke. "The six leaders of the Gaia Warrior Movement. I'm the only one old enough to drive it, so I pick everyone up and take everyone home after the event."

"At what time did you decide to leave without Valpuri and Samu?"

Risto's eyes hardened. "We don't always travel together if we're close to home. People have other things to do. We sent them a text, saying we'd be leaving at one. Neither of them replied so we figured they'd gone off somewhere and would get home by train. We left just after one."

"You travelled in together, but went home separately," Theo repeated. "So they hadn't left any bags, coats or anything else in the bus?"

Ursula shrugged. "Obviously not."

Theo thanked them again and walked outside with Nina Pekkanen. Once the café door had closed behind them, he spoke.

"Nina, I appreciate your doing that. Who knows if it will make any difference, but it was worth a try. Would you like me to drive you home?"

"No, thank you. I have a few errands I need to run in the city. I'll take the train home when I'm ready. Thank you for all your help and please give my regards to Beatrice Stubbs." She held out a delicate hand for Theo to shake. "I wish you luck. I have a good feeling about you." With that she turned and walked away in the direction of the park. He watched her go, so light and fragile he could almost imagine her being whisked away with the wind.

"Mr Wolfe?"

Ursula stood at his shoulder, her long brown limbs awkward and gauche. "We wanted to show you something. Do you have a minute?"

Theo followed her as she led the way around the side of the café and down towards the car park. As they drew closer, Theo saw Risto leaning up against a motorcycle. Aleksis sat on the pavement, his arms wrapped around his knees. There was no sign of Tuula.

Ursula stopped and held out a hand to Risto. It took a second, but Risto reached inside his jacket to retrieve an envelope. Ursula took it from him with a solemn look and handed it to Theo.

He looked at the envelope which had three words typed on it. The Gaia 'Warriors'. Theo noted the sardonic inverted commas. He didn't touch it but looked at Ursula.

"What's inside?"

She pulled out one sheet of paper, again, typed, and held it out for him to read.

`You have blood on your hands. Today, the blood of three people. From Saturday, the blood of millions.`
`You must be stopped. You must be killed.`
`You will be killed.`
`For the benefit of Finland.`

Theo looked at the two expectant faces in front of him. Aleksis kept his head bowed.

"You should take this to the police," he said, still careful not to touch the paper. She shook her head.

"As Risto said, we don't have any faith in the police. But we wanted someone to see the evidence. People should know we're being threatened. We think whoever has Samu and Valpuri sent this. Some powerful people want us dead."

Chapter 19

Look at me, thought Valpuri. *Little Miss Green, environmental activist, Gaia Warrior, defender of the planet and here I am throwing plastic into the sea.* She waded deeper, until the waves began to splash around her thighs. The current was strong and she dared not lose her footing for fear of being tossed against the rocks. She steadied herself, picked up the first of the bottles and threw it as far as she could out to sea. It landed a pathetic two metres in front of her. That was better than her first attempt when she hadn't even managed a single metre. Despite the cold, she flushed with embarrassment, recalling the hysterical weeping fit which had followed.

This was a new iteration. She and Samu kept all the water bottles their captors had given them. Valpuri drained and dried each one, dropped a small pebble into the bottom and inside each, she stuffed one of the many messages she and Samu had scribbled on lined paper.

HELP!!! SOS!!! MAYDAY!!! Samu Pekkanen and Valpuri Peura are in a cave on this coast. If you find this message, contact the police urgently. Samu is asthmatic and needs medical help. EMERGENCY!

Every bottle she hurled at the waves provoked a surge of embarrassment at the futility of the exercise. But what else could she do? Since helping her write the messages, Samu had retreated into his sleeping bag, uncommunicative, lethargic and constantly complaining of thirst. Of the six bottles in yesterday's cold box, only one remained to last them until the evening when their captors should return. *Will* return, Valpuri chided herself. *They will return, they will bring water and they will bring his puffer.*

In addition to the messages for the bottles, Valpuri had composed a third letter to those holding them hostage. Every time the winch came down to collect the empty cold box, Valpuri inserted a note, the tone of which grew increasingly hysterical. Firstly, she warned of Samu's condition and the importance of regular medication. The second time, her words were less measured and she demanded they either provide him with his medication or release them to seek medical attention. This time, she used the most potent language at her disposal. So far, he had managed his one and only attack with the reliever, but the cold, damp and stress of their confinement would only lead to more.

The people holding them had to be in the employ of the energy companies. They didn't give a shit about the planet, about people or even about Finland. The only thing that made them happy was profit. So she had to hit them in the wallet. Her carefully composed letter explained that Samu's breathing had now become laboured and wheezy, a potential threat to his life. If he died or suffered brain damage as a result of their incarceration, the company's reputation would never recover. Neither would the profits. According to the Geneva Convention, even war criminals were entitled to basic medical care. Should anything happen to Samu or her, her friends, family and colleagues would ensure the energy companies would carry full blame.

The light was fading and Valpuri was chilled to her bones. On a hot, sunny beach, the Baltic Sea might seem refreshing. Not so in a dank cave with almost no natural light. At least while wading as far as she dared, she had managed to urinate, so as not to pollute the cave any further. For the first two days, she and Samu had meticulously buried their waste deep in the sand. Yet the smell crept out, increasing in intensity as time went by. And now Samu had lost all interest in basic hygiene, merely crawling out of his bag to urinate a few paces from their base camp area.

Each day, Valpuri tried to drag their sleeping bags closer to the gap in the roof and further from the soiled sand. That strategy backfired when a rainstorm hit the coast, waking them with fierce fat raindrops pelting their faces. All their fleeces, sleeping bags and blankets were wet and they had no means of drying them. That was when Samu started to cry, broken, defeated sobs racking his large frame. She dragged him away from the opening to the elements and found a dry spot of sand. She wrapped them both in a groundsheet and curled her body around his.

Now, she dried herself as best she could with the brown paper bag which once held bread rolls. The thought of the bread triggered a twinge in her stomach accompanied by a desperate thirst. She dragged on her jeans and crawled over to where Samu lay on his side. Her heart plummeted when she saw the empty water bottle by his side. She had hidden it behind the cold box, rationing the last precious drops. But he had obviously found it and finished the lot.

For a second she knelt there, battling with her rage at his selfishness. Then she sat back on her heels and blinked away tears. She reached into her sleeping bag for a fleece which had dried overnight. She sat cross-legged on the groundsheet, releasing her hair down her back to keep her ears warm. She closed her eyes and began to turn her gaze inward, focusing on the strength of her breath and the power of her mind. It wasn't easy to direct her thoughts while her physical body sent signals of discomfort; cold, hunger, thirst, desperation. Her eyes snapped open as if a sound had disturbed her but the aural landscape of the environment was unchanged. Waves rushed in and out, Samu wheezed from the depths of his bag, and the wind howled angrily across the aperture above. Breathing steadily, ignoring the frequent wafts of urine and faeces, she drew on her strength, chanting silently 'I will prevail', until she almost believed it.

There was another sound, so much part of the background she had failed to identify it. A dripping. A slow steady dripping of water which flowed down the walls of the cave, gathering in a trickle across the rocks, towards the sea. Water. She uncurled her legs and waited for the blood to flow back to her extremities. She took out a candle from the cold box, lit it and eased the empty water bottle from Samu's grasp. First she unscrewed the lid and scooped up no more than a sip from one of the tiny pools which formed part of the rocky route towards the sea. She looked at the water for a long time, weighing up the chances of getting sick. Then she made a decision and took a sip with great caution, fully aware of what salt water would do to a body as dehydrated as hers.

It tasted of limescale and dank greenery but it was fresh. Fresh water. Sweet water! She drank capful after capful then forced herself to stop. A little would keep her going but if it made her sick, she would be unable to help Samu through this ordeal. Tilting the bottle on its side, she managed to fill it halfway and making sure Samu did not see, hid it in her sleeping bag. She got inside and lay down to wait. Nothing else to do but hope for mercy from their abductors.

Chapter 20

The key to effective detective work was adaptability, Beatrice told herself. Karoliina could not make time for a conversation that morning and offered to meet Beatrice after lunch. That worked out equally well, so Beatrice rearranged her plans, informed Theo and used her free morning to do some poking around. Once all her emails and messages had been either dealt with or deflected, she left the hotel to retrace the marchers' route and explore the central government and business district of Vironniemi. Happily, it was within easy walking distance, the sun was shining and she was comfortably full of top quality *pulla*, a sort of Finnish cinnamon roll.

Last Saturday, peaceful protestors had gathered outside the President's Palace with its gold-tipped fence and imposing courtyard. Beatrice took a couple of photographs through the bars and a few more of the Sky Wheel in the distance. She checked her map and set off up Mariankatu at a steady pace. It was a long time since she'd been on a protest march, but from memory, large crowds of people tended to move incredibly slowly. A little park caught her attention and she was just crossing the road for a closer look when Theo rang.

While she had been clearing her emails, making a few calls and organising her schedule, Theo hit the streets. Not only had he put the Gaia Warriors under the cudgel, but he'd gleaned their means of transport, parking place and time of departure. She sat down on a bench to make notes and located EuroPark on her map.

"Excellent work! That's not far from where I am now. I'll pass by on my return journey to the hotel. What is your plan next? I want you with me when we meet Karoliina at two o'clock."

The line was silent for a moment. Beatrice smiled at a young chap with a man bun walking a dachshund. "Theo, are you still there?"

"Yeah, I'm here. Sure, I'll come with you to talk to her. Makes sense for us to share what we found from both angles. After that, I can't help thinking I could get more info from the Aho woman. With your permission, of course. If she hired those fake protestors, that could prove an interesting lead. What I'll need to do is offer some kind of carrot."

Beatrice snorted.

Theo tutted. "I meant information, as you well know. You've already had me wearing a dress in an entrapment sting and I have no intention of graduating to gigolo, at least this early in the job. I just feel I behaved unprofessionally last night and want to make it right."

Beatrice got up from her bench and resumed walking. "Listen to me. If you got drunk and blabbed anything indiscreet to that woman, then I would consider you unprofessional. As far as I understand it, you got merry and engaged her trust. No harm done. Any way you can get more out of that horrid female, be my guest. As a friend of mine used to say, just hang onto your ha'penny."

"My what? Never mind, I can work that one out for myself. If she can't get into my pants, the next best thing is a story to chase. She might be in a generous mood and chuck me a few crumbs. Quid pro quo. What could I tell her?"

Beatrice ran the possibilities through her mind. Once as a seasoned copper and once as a private investigator. "You cannot tell them anything the police have not yet released. We have to stay on their good side. You could allude to the fact 'certain sources' are keeping an eye on the town of Vaasa, in case Valpuri fled to her home town. I can't see that getting up anyone's noses but the locals of Vaasa itself, who will shut any journos down."

"Great idea. I'll try that. Thanks, Beatrice. OK, I'll let you get on with your trail sniffing. How long will we have with Karoliina?"

"About half an hour. She's leaving today for the new nuclear plant to rehearse the opening ceremony and check security. We get a window of her time while she packs. Not ideal, but she's a busy lady. A car is collecting us from the hotel at half past one."

"See you there."

The Senate Square was a huge space, perfect for large gatherings whether political or celebratory. Along with all the other tourists, Beatrice took photographs, paced around the perimeter, admired the Senate building and studied her map. What marked her as different from the rest of the holidaymakers was her interest in an unobtrusive office building on the right-hand side. LokiEn's presence was so discreet and understated, one could almost miss it altogether. As Beatrice watched, smartly dressed men and women swiped in and out of the building using security badges. Visitors spoke into an intercom and once their credentials were verified, were permitted into a glass holding area until someone came to claim them. A uniformed guard noticed her attention and stared at her through the window. When he bent his head to speak into his lapel, Beatrice decided it was time to move on.

The sun beat down on her head and she stopped at a café on Aleksanterinkatu for a fizzy water and a think. She faced up to the facts. Unless she stumbled across a day-glo set of footprints marked Valpuri and Samu, she was unlikely to discover anything pertinent to the whereabouts of these young people. All she could do was present Karoliina with the information they had discovered, such as it was, and book a return flight tomorrow. She had promised, in all sincerity, she would report for wedding duties on Thursday. As that was tomorrow, it was growing increasingly difficult to avoid querulous demands from her nearest and dearest. Decision taken, she made up her mind to go through the motions of asking questions at the cafés near where Samu and Valpuri were last seen, to check out the car park where they had left their minibus and then to return to the hotel for lunch to await Theo.

As expected, she drew a blank at every café and restaurant on Unioninkatu. Most proprietors and waiting staff spoke English well enough to comprehend her questions, but shook their heads regretfully as she showed the photographs of the missing teenagers. She persevered, turning right along Pohjoisesplanadi and making the same enquiries at a rather posh eatery, only to get the same response. With a resigned expression, she tucked the photos into her handbag and went in search of EuroPark. From the end of Fabianinkatu, she could see the sign indicating the parking lot and crossed the road to walk on the sunny side of the street. Two doors down from the underground garage, she spotted another little café with cartoon vegetables dancing in the window. The menu, written on a blackboard outside, made a big feature of being vegan.

Beatrice hesitated. Ethical, conscientious activists were far more likely to drop into a place like this for falafels and oat milk lattes than the high-class restaurant she had just left. *No stone unturned*, she told herself, and opened the café door. A tubby little fellow greeted her and waved a hand at all the empty tables, inviting her to seat herself. She was about to protest and explain her mission but caught sight of the dishes warming on the counter. Instead, she sat and read the menu, translated from Finnish into both Swedish and English. She opted for a summer ragout with *härkis* and a glass of pomegranate juice, feeling positively virtuous.

When the young man returned, Beatrice gave him her order and withdrew the photographs, asking him if he had seen either of the two people pictured last Saturday. He studied them for a moment and turned her with a smile.

"Yes, I know these guys. They came in here on Saturday, after the demo in the square."

"Really?" Beatrice asked. "You know them?"

He shook his head. "Not as friends, I see them sometimes, when they come in here. They were here on Saturday, sitting over there with the others." He pointed at a table towards the back of the room.

"The others? They were in a group?" Beatrice scrabbled in her bag for photographs of the newspaper clippings of the other Gaia Warriors. "Were any of these people there?"

He squinted and pulled an apologetic face. "Maybe, but it was a busy day ... him, yes." His finger pointed towards Risto. "And definitely her." He tapped the picture of Tuula. "I remember because I liked her. Pretty girl."

"That's extremely interesting. I'm sorry to take up so much of your time but do you happen to remember what time they left?"

His round face wreathed into smiles. "Happy to help. Not much else to do today. What time they left? They came here just after twelve, I know because that is when we open. They stayed for one drink, all very nervous, and left when the bus came."

"When the bus came," echoed Beatrice. "So they stayed, what, half an hour?"

"Half an hour maximum. Like I say, just one drink. That Goth guy left first and came back a few minutes later with a minibus. Parked outside. The little blonde girl paid the bill and they all left together to get on the bus. Oh, there was a young guy who was injured. Hurt his hand, I think, because he held it like this." He demonstrated by putting his left hand on his right shoulder and cradling his left elbow.

"This is more helpful than you know. I'm a private investigator. Beatrice Stubbs. Here's my card. May I ask your name?"

"Lauri. I work here every day from eleven till five. I'm very observant, you can ask me anything. Do you still want your fava bean ragout?"

"I most certainly do. I'm very glad I stopped here. Thank you, Lauri." Beatrice opened her notebook and began writing down every last detail of her breakthrough.

One delicious ragout later, Beatrice visited EuroPark and found precious little of interest. Not that it bothered her one iota. After her conversation with Lauri, she had the most promising lead yet and according to their agreement, intended to share it with Detective Sahlberg at the earliest opportunity. She messaged Theo and ensured he would accompany her to the meeting with Karoliina Nurmi. Their individual findings looked limp in isolation, but together they had a line of enquiry which merited serious attention. As far as Beatrice was concerned, they hadn't found the kids, but they had learned something the police had not. She would dearly love to stay on a few days to pursue this angle but that was out of the question. She had simply run out of time.

By the time she got back to the hotel, it was one o'clock and a LokiEn car was scheduled to arrive in thirty minutes to take her and Theo to Karoliina's home. She called Helsinki police station and asked to speak to Detective Sahlberg. He was unavailable. Annoyed at not having the opportunity to discuss the implications of her findings, she spent twenty minutes composing an email. It would be poor manners to share a discovery with her employer and not the police.

She changed her clothes to look less like a tourist and more like a professional investigator, then waited in the lobby until her assistant arrived.

The ping of the lifts attracted her attention and she looked up to see Theo emerge. It was impossible to ignore the number of heads turning as he sauntered across the carpeted floor in her direction. He wore an odd-coloured suit, not grey, not green but the material seemed to change its mind every time it passed beneath a sunken spotlight. His shirt was purple and around his neck was a tie in a shade of green Beatrice had only ever seen on a mallard. The hungover wreck of earlier that morning was a distant memory. This individual oozed confidence and, as even an ancient dowager such as herself could observe, sex appeal.

His dark lashes dipped as he took in her sober slate-grey suit. "Should I change? I didn't realise the dress code was funeral."

"Less of your lip. This is my intimidation gear although it obviously doesn't work on you. Quick now, before the car comes." She stood up and linked her arm in his as they walked towards the revolving doors. "Judging by the outfit, you wangled an appointment with that woman. Ooh, I have to say, you do smell rather nice."

He bent closer so she could sniff his neck. "You like it? Catinca bought it for me from your old mates at Parfums Parfaits. All about forests and nocturnal predators, so she tells me. I just like the fact that it doesn't make me choke in the lift. What did the police say?"

A man in a chauffeur's uniform stood just inside the front doors; Erik, the same man who had collected them from the airport. He gave a brisk salute.

"Good afternoon, Ms Stubbs, Mr Wolfe. The car is right outside. Shall we go?"

Conversation regarding the case was clearly inappropriate under the circumstances. Behind the driver was a glass partition but Beatrice had no way of knowing if there was a microphone picking up every word they said. As the car purred along the coastline, Beatrice decided to pursue a different line of investigation.

"Do you know, I don't think anyone in the world has ever bought me perfume. Which is perfectly understandable as I rarely wear the stuff and have such pernickety tastes. Even Matthew, who's been with me several millennia, still would not presume to buy me scent. Either Catinca is supremely confident in her tastes or you two are closer than I thought."

"Subtle as a brick." Theo shook his head, his smile flashing in the sunshine. "The answer to your question, Inquisitor Stubbs, is no. Catinca and I are not together. I think she's lovely, I really do, and I'm well glad she gave me this job opportunity. But we're not right for each other. At least not yet."

"Well, obviously it's going to take more than a brick to beat the gossip out of you. I'm pretty sure you're not gay, I know you're not married as I happen to be your employer and everywhere you go, you leave a trail of smitten females in your wake." She dropped her voice. "Have you taken a vow? You know, celibacy or some such? I won't judge you. I did something very similar at one time."

Theo threw back his head and laughed. The gesture reminded Beatrice of Matthew in a way.

"My only vow is to be the kind of person I can live with, leave alone with anyone else. Now, will that satisfy you or do I have to make up an entire saga of personal histories just to keep you quiet?"

Beatrice settled back in her seat and looked out at the multi-coloured façades along the shoreline. "Each to his own," she said. She waited a beat and added, "Although it is an awful shame."

Once again, Karoliina was waiting to meet them on the doorstep, but unlike the last meeting, her husband was present. She introduced him by his first name – Heikki – and them by their full titles. It soon became clear the man was going to stay for the meeting, which of course was Karoliina's prerogative.

They refused tea and Beatrice got straight down to business.

"The first thing I should say is that Theo and I are here to hand over our findings because we will be leaving Finland tomorrow. I appreciate the fact we have not completed the task with which you charged us, but we have another obligation to fulfil. That said, we have discovered a discrepancy we believe points you in the right direction. I'm only sorry we are unable to take this further."

The brown-black cat stalked into the room and brushed past Beatrice's leg. Cats, in her experience, made a flea-line for anyone who detested them. The more she ignored it, the more attention it would try to demand. She tickled it behind the ears.

"I see," said Karoliina, her complexion wan. "I hoped we might persuade you to stay until the weekend."

"Unfortunately not. Believe me, if I could, I would. In summary, Theo and I have been researching parallel lines of enquiry and it seems one particular angle requires a closer look. I should tell you I have shared our findings with Detective Sahlberg, as per our agreement."

"And are the police pursuing it?" asked Heikki, leaning on his forearms.

Beatrice gave the man her attention, noting his neatly trimmed stubble and cap-sleeved T-shirt, revealing muscular biceps. "That remains to be seen. I hope to have a conversation with Detective Sahlberg before we leave in the morning. The theory we are pursuing is that the young people are willing participants in their own abduction."

Karoliina exhaled in disappointment. "That's what Jouko Lahti said. I can't believe that flabby old fool is right."

"On the other hand," interjected Theo, "the alarm surrounding Samu Pekkanen's health is less of an emergency. There is no way he would have participated in a fake kidnapping without sufficient medication. We believe he must have taken a second inhaler without his mother's knowledge. If we are correct in our assumptions, and we can't be sure of that, Samu and Valpuri are alive and well."

Heikki shot a meaningful look at Karoliina and bounced up from his chair to pace into the kitchen. "I need a beer. Can I get anything for you, detectives?"

Beatrice did not need another distraction and drinking on duty was not a professional look. "Not for me, thank you, Mr Nurmi."

"Heikki, please. I'm not Mr Nurmi. My wife and I kept our own names. What about you, Theo? Join me in a beer?"

Theo gave him a friendly smile. "Thanks, but not when I'm on duty."

Internally, Beatrice added another tick to her assessment of his performance.

"Very wise," said Karoliina. "Can we get to the details of the matter? I'm sorry to hurry you but I have to leave at three o'clock. I have a dinner with our sponsors tonight and a full tour and inspection of the facility tomorrow. Everything needs to be perfect before Saturday's opening. Including some good news about those missing teenagers."

Heikki returned from the kitchen and resumed his place, drinking from a bottle of beer and carrying a plate of dried meat slices. He offered them around the table. Karoliina and Theo refused, but Beatrice took one. It was very strong and chewy but not unpleasant. She wondered if the gamey flavour might be reindeer and decided not to have another.

Beatrice withdrew some papers from her briefcase and handed them to Karoliina. "The detail is all in here. But in a nutshell, Theo has been in conversation with several members of the Gaia Warriors movement while I made enquiries in the neighbourhood where they went missing. The leaders of the protest told Theo they returned to their minibus and left the city without Valpuri and Samu at just after one o'clock in the afternoon. My enquiries, on the other hand, indicate that all six of them were in a café on Fabianinkatu between twelve and half past. After that, one of them collected the minibus and they all drove away together. This leads us to believe the protesters arranged the 'disappearance' of two of their members, hoping to capitalise on the negative publicity. From now on, prosecuting this angle must be down to the police."

"Do you think the same people are responsible for sending both my partners and me those death threats?" asked Karoliina.

"Of course they are! A bunch of kids stirring up a shit storm and trying to frighten you. I hope the police throw the book at those little bastards," Heikki exploded. "In fact, they should be out there now, arresting these so-called Gaia Warriors and piling on the pressure until they get the truth. Then they can find this pair of losers and expose the whole scam by Friday. That way, Saturday's opening will be 100% positive." The cat bounded onto the table with a demanding miaow and Heikki offered it a piece of meat. It accepted, taking the dried flesh from his fingers and jumped off to devour it elsewhere.

Theo cleared his throat. "I should tell you the Gaia Warriors themselves have received a similar letter. That could be a smokescreen, deflecting attention, or it could be there is someone else involved. Whatever happens, we're handing all we know over to the police and returning to the UK."

The four of them sat in silence for a moment, the only sound the bubbles fizzing in Heikki's beer. The cat returned.

"Got a kiss for Papa?" Heikki placed a piece of meat between his lips, pushing his face towards the Burmese. With delicate jaws, the cat took the meat and sprang off the table.

Karoliina's telephone rang. She glanced at the screen and refused the call. "I have to go. I will be unavailable for the rest of today and tomorrow, because I will be spending most of the time underground. Thank you for all your efforts. I will pay you in full, as per our agreement. I intend to settle your invoice as soon as it arrives. It was a pleasure to meet you, Beatrice. You too,

Theo." She shook their hands and got to her feet.

They said their goodbyes to Heikki and left him in the kitchen with the cat. Karoliina followed them to the car and handed Beatrice a card.

"Please keep me informed if the police decide to act on your findings. I'm not completely off grid for the next two days. If anything occurs between now and when you leave, please call my deputy with an update. Astrid's handling the public-facing side of this so I would prefer it if any sensitive information goes to her first. She's the person I trust above anyone else." She glanced behind her at the house.

Beatrice met her eyes, picking up the hint. The LokiEn business card read Astrid Falk, Personal Assistant to Karoliina Nurmi. She placed it in her purse with a nod. After Karoliina waved them off, Beatrice and Theo remained silent the whole journey, until Erik drew to a halt outside the hotel. They thanked him and made their way to the revolving doors. Theo stopped.

"Are we officially off duty?" he asked. "Because I still want to seek out Päivi Aho."

Beatrice's interest in the case had waned. As long as she'd passed everything relevant to the police, the self-inflicted kidnap was no longer her problem. "If you wish. Did she agree to another meeting?"

"No. She didn't answer my email and she's not taking my calls."

"So how do you plan to talk to her?" Beatrice demanded.

"Turn up at her office and use every ounce of whatever I've got to persuade her to talk to me."

"Watch your step and good luck. While you're stalking her, I'll book our flights home tomorrow morning. Be very careful."

"I will. See you back here for dinner. Promise not to turn up shitfaced again."

Beatrice tried to laugh but a cloud coloured her mood. "Theo, please don't drink at all. I'm not talking alcohol, I mean don't drink anything she gives you. Especially if she presses the point. Claim a hangover, carry a water bottle but do not imbibe anything you did not purchase or prepare yourself. Call me an old fusspot, but I am deadly serious. Play it like a choirboy."

He exhaled a low whistle. "Got it. See you later."

Chapter 21

For someone who couldn't keep her hands off him last night, it seemed Päivi Aho had changed her mind. Theo got the brush-off at reception – 'she's in meetings all afternoon' – and she blocked his number so he couldn't even leave a message. Very weird. He walked away from the TV station and wandered around the block until he found the bar they'd visited the night before. He went inside, scanning the clientele for her face. She wasn't there.

The idea of sitting outside in the sunshine with an orange juice appealed, but he wanted to be unobtrusive. If she did come here for a drink and saw him, she might well leg it. But she would have to come out of the TV station at some time, and when she did, he'd be waiting. He surveyed the street for a likely observation point. Cafés, an expensive-looking hotel, a mobile-phone shop, a sandwich bar, a place selling Scandi-style furniture and the ubiquitous chain-store clothing outlets. He stood still as a monolith, waiting for the pulse.

It didn't always happen, but when it did, he listened. Rotating his head to study his environment, Theo listened to his instinct. One turn over his left shoulder. Another over his right. Return to centre. He closed his eyes and concentrated. Once again, he looked over his right shoulder. From a first-floor window of the furniture shop, the end of white curtains blew in the wind, like handkerchiefs waving farewell to a steamboat. It was nothing, but the only tiny pulse in this atmosphere-void shopping area. Theo responded, walking along the pavement and into the shop.

On the first floor, he wandered around beds, wardrobes and mock-up interiors. There was one young man at the cash desk who didn't look up from his computer screen. That gave him enough peace to stand at the half-open window, watching the street. The pulse grew to a buzz. Theo relaxed, taking long slow breaths and waited. He was good at waiting.

Fifteen minutes passed. Theo didn't move, his stillness blending into the background. He'd been standing there over half an hour when he saw Päivi Aho hurry up the street, power-walking and talking into her mobile. She walked right past the bar and with a sense of purpose, bounded up the steps to the hotel.

A hint of a smile crossed his face. *I knew it. She had to come out sometime.* The question now was whether to confront her inside or when she came out again. He debated the pros and cons for several minutes while watching the hotel doorway.

A man crossed the street, heading in the direction of the hotel. Theo recognised his face: Heikki Mäkinen, cat lover and husband of Karoliina Nurmi. Theo reached for his phone and selected the camera mode, catching a shot of Heikki as he entered the hotel portico. Theo zoomed in and got several shots of him greeting the doorman and entering the lobby. As Beatrice often told him, there was no such thing as coincidence. Time to find out what was going on.

He left the pine-scented store, put on his sunglasses and walked with a confident stride towards the hotel. Neither Heikki Mäkinen nor Päivi Aho were in the lobby, the bar or the restaurant. They must have taken a room. Theo had no way of observing so ordered tea and retreated to the darkest corner of the lobby. It took him over an hour to finish his pot of peppermint, his focus apparently on his phone. It was nearing six o'clock before Päivi Aho swooped down the carpeted stairs and rushed across the lobby, her cardigan flowing in her wake, reminding him of the hankies he'd seen earlier. The sunlight worked in his favour, shining into her eyes and making him a silhouette. He practised his stillness, barely breathing, not moving and dropping his gaze. She didn't see him, enabling him to take several surreptitious shots of her hurrying back in the direction of the TV station.

Shortly afterwards, Heikki Mäkinen strolled down the stairs and rather than going out through the revolving doors, he meandered into the bar, sat on a stool and ordered a beer, chatting to the barman like an old friend. Theo leaned into his wing-backed chair and waited. It was essential he left without being seen.

Heikki turned his attention to the TV screen on the wall, so Theo left a few Euros to cover his bill and got out into the fresh air. He hit the pavement with a long steady stride. Top priority, tell Beatrice what he had just seen.

His boss had the opposite of a poker face. Her expression altered as she pondered his information, her face changing from sunny to thunderous like a summer sky dimmed by clouds.

They sat in the hotel restaurant, eating a fish pie with kale and trying to agree on a theory. Theo refused wine, so Beatrice ordered a half bottle for herself.

"The question is, what relationship do these two have? If lovers, I can see what's in it for her. Beefy body and inside source. What about him? Why leak stories about his own wife? The man is so bloody minted he can feed top quality cuts of meat to his cat. Is it a perverse kind of loyalty? Protecting her company by selling crappy misdirection to the media? I don't get this."

Theo saw the same problem. "I don't know what their game is, but I strongly suspect they are orchestrating this whole drama. Each for their own reasons but ... and this is important

... for their own ends. They want stories or success or whatever. The last thing they care about is the missing kids. The kids themselves are expendable."

"Not to us, not Karoliina and not to the police."

He swallowed some water. "That's true. Anyway, this is a matter for them to sort out. I'm ready for home. Did you book flights already?"

Beatrice chewed another mouthful. "I did, but there's a horrible storm about to hit the coast. If we get out tomorrow morning, it will be nothing short of a miracle."

Theo put down his cutlery. "Let's hope for one. Whatever Päivi Aho and Heikki Mäkinen are up to, that's their problem. We got better things to do."

Chapter 22

For such a big man, Karl moved with surprising grace. He passed the building site on the opposite side of the street, familiarising himself with the layout, and walked all the way around the block before returning. There was no one around at this time of night, but he wasn't taking any chances. He slowed, taking a 180° scan of his environment. Only when he was convinced the area was empty did he slip behind the scaffolding and through the gap in the hoardings.

The door was closed, but as agreed, the padlock had been taken off. He moved with great care through the darkened building, aware of the dangers of loose electric wires, trip hazards and rubble. There was enough twilight for him to ascend the stairwell to the third floor at something like normal speed.

The view was pretty impressive, he had to admit. The lights of the city stretched out like stars until they met the blackness of the sea. He stood in the doorway, waiting for his contact to make himself seen. It didn't take long. The man appeared at the other end of the huge space, silhouetted by the city lights. He made no move to approach and Karl knew it was up to him to cross the distance between them.

No handshake, not even a nod of greeting, he simply turned away to look across the semi-darkened city. Karl stood beside him, waiting for the reason he had been summoned. Eventually, his employer spoke.

"You were supposed to make it look like an accident."

"I did. I knocked the guy down the steps. The other idiot added the knife."

"I hired you to work as a team. I'm disappointed with the results."

"So am I. Far too stab-happy, these southerners. I can't stand people who won't follow orders. That's why I got rid of him."

"He's left this country?"

"He's left this world, my friend."

"I see."

"Once things have calmed down, I intend to disappear for a while. The witness statement puts me in an awkward position."

"I'll make sure the media focus remains on the other guy. I need you here for a little longer."

"What for?"

"An irritation has arisen. A private investigator from Britain is trying to find the missing kids. She and her assistant are circling uncomfortably close to my operations. She's getting under my feet."

"What do you want done?"

"Nothing yet. I want you to watch and report their activities to me. It may be necessary to hasten their departure from Finland."

"Just from Finland?"

"That remains to be seen."

Chapter 23

It might have been because she was in a strange bed, the relief of knowing Catinca was handling her family or possibly the copious amounts of Prosecco she had drunk the night before, but Tanya slept better than she had in months. She woke late, and instead of flinging herself out of bed to attack her To Do list, she luxuriated under the sheets until someone knocked.

"Just a minute!" She got out of bed, pulled on her dressing gown and opened the door. There was no one there, but at her feet lay a breakfast tray, with orange juice, coffee pot, a basket of croissants and a red rose in a vase. Bless Susie. She must have realised Tanya was not going to make the eleven o'clock cut-off point for breakfast service. She picked it up and took it back to bed. Exactly what she needed before tackling all the messages on her phone.

She had no more than half a glass of juice and one bite of pastry before her calm was shattered. Two messages from the caterers, one confirming the change of menu and another informing her of the revised price. The florist called to apologise for the fact they were unable to double the number of red rosebuds at such short notice and offered a mixture of yellow, pink and orange as an alternative. One of her cousins left a cryptic voicemail, asking why Tanya had forgotten to mention the big news over last night's cocktails. Finally, Luke's form teacher let her know that he had arrived at school without his gym kit, so would be unable to take part in sports day unless Tanya could deliver the necessary items by lunchtime.

She swore with considerable vehemence and checked her watch. It was ten past eleven. She had forty minutes. Without bothering to shower, Tanya dragged on jeans and a T-shirt, stuffed her clothes and hen night presents into her suitcase and called Matthew's landline. When she couldn't reach him, she dialled Gabriel. His phone went straight to voicemail. In a panic, she tried her mother, but the line was engaged. She bit her knuckle in frustration. Freshly laundered gym clothes in a kitbag were hanging on the coat rack at Matthew's cottage. The question was, how to get in, pick up the gym bag and get it to Luke's school in the next half an hour? If he missed sports day, he would be inconsolable.

With great reluctance, she dialled Marianne, always a last resort when it came to domestic crises. To Tanya's amazement, she rejected the call. Where the hell was everyone? She yanked her hair into a ponytail, washed and dried her face, zipped up the suitcase and clattered down the stairs, close to tears of frustration. She dumped her bag in the hallway and burst into the bar, in the hope of persuading someone to give her a lift.

To her immense relief and delight, Will and Adrian had just arrived. They stood with their suitcases talking to Catinca at the bar. She cut short their effusive greetings and explained the urgency of the situation. As she had hoped, the police officer in Will came to the rescue.

"All right, Tanya, we can sort this out. Does anyone else have a key to Matthew's place? Have you checked your text messages in case your dad or Gabriel let you know where they were going? How far away is Luke's school and does he have only one set of gym clothes?"

Catinca handed Tanya a glass of water. "Keep calm, mate. Drink this."

After a soothing swig, Tanya released a shaky breath. "Beatrice has a key but she's in bloody Finland. No spare keys, as far as I know, which is ridiculous, if you come to think about it. No, I'll check WhatsApp and texts now. The school is about ten minutes from here, fifteen from Dad's cottage. He has a spare gym kit, but that's in the laundry. I told Dad at least three times not to forget the gym kit this morning."

She went ahead to scroll through the various apps on her phone, vaguely aware of Adrian talking to Susie about nearby school uniform shops and Will suggesting the possibility of breaking a window to gain access to the cottage. Then she saw it. A message from Gabriel.

School just phoned. Luke forgot gym kit. Washed and dried spares. Dropped them off just now along with his old trainers. Forest clearing this morning, i.e. chainsaws. Call you at lunch. Hope last night was fun. G X

"Panic over," said Tanya. "Gabe already fixed it. I'm so sorry, creating a drama over nothing. That's a Prosecco hangover for you. Can we start again? Hello, you two!"

Adrian and Will embraced her and she looked at them properly for the first time since she burst into the room. Next to her husband, these were the best-looking men she knew. Adrian, graceful, chiselled and dark with eyelashes she would kill for, had a natural elegance and a smile to make anyone melt. His husband was taller and more muscular with the kind of chest often seen on the cover of romance novels. She adored them both and knew without question their arrival meant her team now held all the winning players.

"I cannot tell you how pleased I am to see you both. You look gorgeous. Have you eaten?" she asked. "I didn't manage any of my breakfast and I'm absolutely starving. The thing is, I need your help." She made a pleading face at Catinca. "Our strategy has backfired. Mum and Marianne have dropped all pretence and simply taken over. While I was sleeping off the effects of last night, they changed into fifth gear. Not only that, but I have no idea when Beatrice will turn up. I need her right here, right now! What the hell is she playing at?"

Catinca put her left hand on Will's shoulder and her right on Adrian's. "We need an emergency meeting with our Gay Diplomacy Squad. Let's sit down and make battle plan. Susie? What is lunch special today?"

Four portions of tomato and basil soup later, everyone had their duties. Adrian and Catinca were promoted to official wedding planners aka trouble-shooters. Adrian would nobble Marianne and Pam, requiring their help with a series of themed surprises, each of which had been not-so-secretly approved by Tanya and Catinca. Meanwhile, dress designer and wedding stylist herself, Ms Radu, would visit all service providers to deliver her business card and insist that any wedding-related enquiries be directed to her. Will was in charge of Matthew.

"He's stressed to the eyeballs about the speeches." Tanya met Will's kind gaze. "As father of the bride, he's expected to say a few words but it doesn't need to be anything special. Then I asked him to help Luke. It was a lovely gesture from Gabriel to ask my son to be his best man and even if he is only seven, Luke can do most of it on his own. It's just the speech. We should have had a wingman but it's too late now. Could you mind him, Will? Actually, could you mind both of them? Dad manages well most of the time, but that's because he's got Beatrice." She released her hair from her ponytail and scratched her scalp. "Well, at least he usually has Beatrice."

Will opened his mouth to respond but Adrian spoke first. "I know that woman has a way of cutting it fine, but the wedding rehearsal is on Friday evening. How much finer can she cut it? Ow!" He winced and frowned at his husband.

Catinca rolled her eyes. "I would kick you too, but can't reach from here. Shut up, Adrian, you're making things worse. We gonna sort this out. First priority, take pressure off Tanya. I got the wedding, Adrian has got the relatives, Will is minding Matthew and Luke. We better get to work, stag night is this evening." She gave them a supercilious smile. "Ain't no way you old farts are going to have better time than we did last night. Still, give it your best shot. Will, take Tanya home, drop me and Adrian in Crediton and you go and find Matthew. Your job is help him write that speech."

Will finished his half of ale. "At your service, ma'am. Is it too much to ask that we can check in first? I promise to be back in five minutes."

After the men had left the bar, Tanya leaned forward to clasp Catinca's hand. "What are you doing this evening?"

"Dunno. My plan was maybe me and Beatrice could have dinner together. Give you one last mother and son night with Luke, but she went and sodded off to Finland. Why? You got an idea?"

"Could you come round to my house? I'll cook and we can go over a few details. Luke will be in bed by eight so we can make a pot of tea and finalise battle plans while the blokes are downing a few pints at The Star."

"Great idea. Between you and me, I think Adrian wishes he could come with us. Blokes' nights aren't really his thing. Listen, while we are waiting, let's call Beatrice. I just want to know what time she's arriving."

Tanya watched as Catinca's thumbs flew over her screen. She pressed the handset to her ear and smiled at Tanya. Her hair was twisted into a French roll and her silk jumpsuit made her look like a glamorous version of Rosie the Riveter.

She shook her head. "She ain't answering."

"What about Theo? Could you call him?"

Catinca placed her index finger on her forehead, her gaze on her mobile. She traced a line down her nose, over her lips and brushed her chin. "Theo. Yeah, I could, but I don't want to mucky the waters, know what I mean?"

With a laugh through her nose, Tanya gazed at her friend. "Thousands wouldn't, but I think I understand. Do you ever think you've been spending too much time with Beatrice Stubbs?"

Chapter 24

VALO: The only independent news site to shed light on the truth

'MISSING' PROTESTORS – PUBLICITY STUNT?

In a national exclusive, this morning's programme can reveal new evidence indicating the so-called missing environmental activists may have staged their disappearance and are currently in hiding. Their objective is to draw attention to their cause and to create maximum disruption to the LokiEn small reactor nuclear energy project.

Helsinki police has made no progress in ascertaining the whereabouts of Valpuri Peura (16) and Samu Pekkanen (17) who have not been seen since a protest march turned violent on Saturday 13 June. However, a trusted source confirmed that a private investigation company has had more success. The British team, hired by the business consortium behind the Neljä nuclear project, say they have sufficient proof that the apparent abduction is nothing more than an elaborate hoax. Six of the protestors were seen leaving a café and entering a vehicle together shortly after violence broke out at Senaatintori. At the time of going to press, the two youngsters have not appeared in public.

Detective Sahlberg, the senior officer in charge of the investigation, refused to speculate. 'In a hunt for missing persons, the police receive hundreds of tip-offs per day. There is no reason to believe there is any more truth in this allegation than any of the other so-called explanations in the past few days. We urge the public to remain vigilant and report anything they believe to be significant to the police.'

If the allegations can be proven, this will be the latest in a long line of increasingly desperate attempts at attention-seeking by the Gaia Warriors and similar environmental groups. In 2019, a group calling themselves One Minute to Midnight staged a protest using drones at Stockholm airport, which resulted in flight cancellations, delayed holidays and the cost to the business community of over half a million Euro. In April this year, teenage demonstrators brought the city of Tampere to a standstill, endangering lives of civilians and police officers, as they threw themselves in front of moving vehicles.

Citizens of Finland have grown increasingly impatient with this small but noisy minority, intent on promoting their pessimistic agenda at the expense of a progressive, long-term environmental policy. The government insists well-planned collaboration with the business community is the best way to ensure Finland's self-sufficiency in terms of meeting its energy needs.

Junior Education Minister, Kari Summa, speaking after the launch of a new youth sports centre in Espoo, said, 'This country has the best informed and fully engaged younger generation when it comes to global planetary concerns. The vast majority are aware that the way to achieve change is by working with all sectors of the community'.

The financial backers behind the long awaited new nuclear facility, LokiEn, Baltic Energy Services and Scanski Solutions have been approached for comment.

Chapter 25

Beatrice was awoken by the noise of her phone. She reached for it with a glance at the window, wondering what time it was. Impossible to tell, as the light summertime nights in this country could be deceptive. Her handset told her it was twenty minutes past seven. Her alarm was set for half past eight so who on earth would be ringing her at this hour? Unless it was an emergency.

"Hello, Beatrice Stubbs speaking."

"Ms Stubbs, this is Detective Timo Sahlberg."

Beatrice heaved herself up to sit against her pillows. "Ah, good morning, detective. I hoped to speak to you before I leave. Although I wasn't expecting you this early."

"I'm sorry to disturb you but this is a matter of some urgency. Yesterday, I shared police information with you on a quid pro quo basis. I also asked you to sign a confidentiality agreement and not to reveal any information you might discover without sharing it with us first."

Beatrice reached for a glass of water, giving herself time to think. "Yes, I know. That's why I sent you an email, explaining what we found. Detective, is there something wrong?"

"I got your email, among many others I only had a chance to read this morning. At no point did you mention the urgency of a reply. Neither did you tell me you would be going to the press.

I find your behaviour unprofessional and worse, potentially destabilising to this case. I would have every reason to charge you with obstruction of justice."

"Obstruction of justice? Hang on a minute. There was no urgency regarding your reply and I didn't go to the press. In what way is my behaviour unprofessional?"

"I understand. You see this as a matter of semantics. It may not have been you personally who spoke to the journalist, perhaps it was your colleague. The one who *didn't* sign a confidentiality agreement. I have to tell you that my first interaction with a private investigator has been a very disheartening experience."

"Detective Sahlberg, you have me at a complete loss. My assistant and I have followed best practice. When we found some relevant information, we informed you first and secondly our employer, Karoliina Nurmi. While I would like to stay on and see this case to its conclusion, I have run out of time and handed over my findings to those best placed to follow the map. What does the press have to do with this?"

"My question precisely. I suggest you watch this morning's report on Channel 6. It's in Finnish so ask someone to translate. Did you say you were leaving today?"

"Yes, that's correct. We have a flight out at lunchtime."

"I'm very glad to hear it." He hung up.

Beatrice stared at the handset with wide eyes. How incredibly rude! The complete opposite of his behaviour the previous day. She got out of bed and paced the room. Channel 6 was the broadcaster whose editor Theo had met. She called reception and asked if they had anyone who could translate something urgently. The receptionist confirmed they had and offered to send someone up to her room along with some coffee. While she was waiting, Beatrice scanned the online version and saw the photographs of Valpuri and Samu front and centre. She put the article into a translation engine and managed to get the gist.

When the young hotel employee delivering her latte macchiato arrived, she persuaded him to convey a slightly more sophisticated rendering of the report. With some embarrassment and apologies for his English, he obliged. As she listened, the reason for Detective Sahlberg's exasperation became clear. She tipped the waiter ten Euros and dialled Theo's room. There was no reply. Where the hell would he be at this hour of the morning? An acidic sensation in her stomach made her call his mobile.

After several seconds, he answered, his breathing heavy. "What's up?" he asked.

"Where are you?" Beatrice demanded.

"On my way back to the hotel. Just been for a run. Wish I hadn't. Man, this wind is wild! You want to go down to breakfast already?"

"No. I'm ordering room service for us both. Get back here, have a shower and I'm coming next door in quarter of an hour. We need to talk." It was her turn to ring off without saying goodbye.

Twenty minutes later, she had showered, packed and calmed her agitated thoughts. She stomped next door to Theo's room and arrived the same time as the breakfast trolley. She thanked the maid and rapped on the door. It opened to reveal Theo wearing a dressing gown and a concerned frown.

"What is it? You sound pissed off."

Beatrice glared at him as she wheeled in the trolley. "I am pissed off. Shut that door. You didn't sign that confidentiality agreement at the police station yesterday, did you? Channel 6 ran the story this morning, made the police look like idiots, disrespected the Gaia Warriors and all but christened you and me Batman and Robin. The truly shitty thing is that we know where they got the information, but cannot prove it. If you'd signed the damn thing, we would have a pretty good chance of convincing Sahlberg it wasn't us."

Theo stared back at her and shook his head like a pendulum. "I forgot the confidentiality agreement, I'm sorry. It just slipped my mind. But I have photos of Päivi Aho meeting Karoliina's husband – the only other person who knew what we found out."

"Circumstantial. A couple of photos showing them entering and leaving the same building. Not even one of them together. Nowhere near hard evidence. Oh bloody hell! Why didn't you sign a confidentiality agreement? The police called me first thing to call me an unprofessional backstabber or something similar. They're convinced it's us!"

Theo sat down at the writing table, his expression thoughtful. Beatrice poured him a coffee and shoved the plate of pastries in his direction.

"Right, listen to me for a second, Beatrice. I'm new to this game but I swear I played it by the book, apart from me getting drunk and forgetting that agreement. Stupid mistakes and I'm sorry. Apart from us, the only people who know the details are that copper you emailed, Karoliina and Heikki." He selected a croissant. "That management geezer you spoke to, the Lahti guy, he had the same theory. Maybe he fed it to a journo to take the heat off Saturday's opening."

Beatrice sat opposite him, tore open a croissant and began adding butter and jam. Something about the word 'fed' triggered something in her mind. A picture formed, Matthew sneaking bits of bacon from his breakfast plate to feed Huggy Bear or Dumpling, thinking she couldn't see his reflection in the oven door. Yesterday, at Karoliina's house and that big brown-black Burmese with its dainty jaws. Her gaze rested on Theo, who was dunking his croissant into his coffee.

"That's an appalling way to eat a croissant," she observed.

Theo's eyes flicked to the sticky mess on her own plate but he said nothing.

"The thing is, why would Heikki Mäkinen go to the press?"

asked Beatrice. "Karoliina would never have endorsed that."

"I don't think Karoliina would endorse her husband meeting a woman in a hotel room while she's away, either. I have a hunch it's not the first time those two have used that place."

"Hunches will do nothing to change Sahlberg's mind about ..." From her handbag, Beatrice's alarm rang, reminding her they had a flight in a few hours. This latest development was embarrassing and unfortunate but she could do nothing about it at this stage. She hated to leave Helsinki with an unfinished job and on a sour note with the local police, but she and Theo had to return to Britain.

"We need to get to the airport. I'll check online to make sure flights are still leaving in this weather. Are you all packed? If so, I'll book a taxi for ten o'clock," said Beatrice.

Theo took his cup to the trolley for a refill, the little beads at the end of his plaits creating a little seashore sound as they brushed past each other. "So we're really leaving then?"

"We're leaving. What else can we do? The police aren't talking to us, Karoliina is out of reach and there's no way of proving her shitty husband let the cat out of the bag. Let's face it, what we found indicates those kids are in no real danger. So I say we leave them to it and get back to the wedding. Have you decided what you're wearing? Because I think that greeny purple combination you had on yesterday is a real winner."

To Beatrice's irritation, Theo wasn't listening. He was staring at something on the breakfast trolley. Something about the intense focus of his body language made Beatrice stand up to see what had caught his attention.

"What? What are you looking at?"

He pointed at the envelope lying beside the jug of orange juice. A plain manila envelope with two words typed on it. `Theo Wolfe.`

Beatrice held up a finger. "Wait." She dug around in her handbag, pulling out plastic gloves and a pair of tweezers. She slid open the flap and withdrew the single sheet of paper, unfolded it and held it so they both could read what it said.

V and S are not hiding. They are in danger. Where they put them, the place at Malmen, it's not safe. They need your help. Please do not share this information with the police.

Beatrice read the message twice and then locked eyes with Theo. "Sorry, what was your question again?"

"I asked if we were really leaving."

She chewed her lip. "No, I don't believe we are. Not while we've a job to do. Find out where Malmen is and I'll get a message to Detective Sahlberg. We'll postpone the flight until tomorrow and tell everyone it was cancelled because of the weather. It's not ideal, but it will have to do. Quick now, look sharp."

Chapter 26

Theo did a search for the name Malmen and found a small hamlet around thirty kilometres outside Helsinki. It was on the coast, near a golf course and seemed to have nothing remarkable about it whatsoever. If there was the slightest chance the two people they been searching for were in the vicinity, he had to get there and see what he could find.

While considering how to handle his mystery message, he half listened to Beatrice's conversation with the Helsinki police. It seemed the detective was not taking her call, so she left a message with his team. Beatrice put down the phone. "I'm going to deliver this note in person. That will be faster. Do you have any idea who your mystery messenger might be?"

"Maybe, I'm not sure. Whoever it is, I reckon we should take this tip seriously and at least check it out. There's a place called Malmen under an hour's drive away. Should we go and have a look?"

Beatrice looked into the middle distance. "We do need to take it seriously, you're right. What I'm concerned about is that it might be some kind of trap, throwing us off the scent or putting us in harm's way. Who do you think sent you this and more importantly, why?"

"My gut says it was from one of either two people, both of them members of the Gaia Warriors. Tuula, Valpuri's best friend, helped me out when I needed to talk to them as a group. She seems to wear her heart on her sleeve and I think she kind of likes me. But my instinct says it's the younger guy with a broken wrist, Aleksis. He's obviously terrified of the others and just does what he's told. Both Risto and Ursula bully him into silence. This might be his moment of rebellion."

"What do we know about him? Is there any way we could make contact?"

Up until this morning's newspaper report, Theo had kept Tuula in mind as a possible ally. It was clear the girl was attracted to him and who knows what she might reveal in the course of a harmless flirtatious conversation. But now? She would be unlikely to take his calls and he did not dare ask for Aleksis's contact details. He could not alert anyone that Gaia Warriors' tight ship had sprung a leak.

"Theo, if this young lady is sweet on you, that might be your route in. I know, I know, you're bound to have principles about this kind of thing. But let's say, for argument's sake, you call her to say goodbye, apologise for the newspaper article and assure her they didn't get it from you. Then say something like you couldn't bear to leave Finland with her thinking badly of you. Do you see what I mean?"

Theo gave a sideways glance, suspecting she'd been reading his mind. "And in the course of that conversation, I ask her to pass on my regrets to the rest of the crew and ask for Aleksis's address?"

"That's the sort of thing. Of course one needs years of experience to pull off true subtlety, but I'm sure you'll manage. You can make the call here if you don't mind my earwigging or perhaps to spare your blushes, you might want to go out on the balcony. Do you want that last croissant?"

"I speak to her in Swedish so you wouldn't understand a word anyway."

"True, but I am fluent in body language."

Theo sighed, wondering how this woman managed to twist him round her little finger. He took the croissant and his phone, stepped onto the balcony and closed the door behind him. In the fresh air, he took a couple of minutes to compose himself, gazing around the wind-buffeted harbour, pulling his robe tighter against the morning chill. Then he dialled Tuula's number.

She answered on the second ring. "What do you want? More made-up stories to sell to journalists?"

"Tuula, they didn't get it from me. That's why I'm calling. I couldn't bear…" He looked over his shoulder to check Beatrice was not standing with her ear to the balcony door. "I couldn't bear to leave Finland with you thinking I was some kind of grubby hack. I really am a private detective. I really am trying to find Valpuri and Samu. I swear to you, I didn't give that story to the journalist."

There was a long silence before she replied. "You're leaving?"

He closed his eyes, aware of the wistful note in her voice. "Yeah, today. Whoever gave the press that story has trampled all over my investigation. There's nothing else I can do here, just leave it to the police. Anyway, I just wanted to say goodbye and thank you for all you did."

The pause didn't last as long this time. "Right. You know, I couldn't believe you would do that to us. I mean ... well, anyway. Thanks for calling. It was nice to meet you."

Theo bit his lip. "You too, Tuula. I want you to know that I really respect what you're doing and admire your commitment to your beliefs. When I get home, there's something I'd like to send you, if you don't mind."

"I don't mind."

"Thank you. I hope you'll like it. It reminds me of you." He kicked at the balcony wall in self-disgust. "In fact, I have something I'd like to send each of the Gaia Warriors. The Peura family gave me everyone's addresses except Aleksis. Do you know where I can send him a little something? I think it might make him laugh."

Tuula snorted. "That would be a first. I've never seen that kid laugh in my life. You can send it in the same package as Risto's and Ursula's. He's staying in their student house over the summer. They wanted me to move in too, but I've got a life, you know what I mean?"

"I know what you mean. Tuula, I'm really grateful, for everything. Take good care."

"You too. Bye, Theo, and if you ever come back, look me up."

He ended the call and chewed his croissant as if it had personally insulted him. This forked-tongue fakery did not sit well. It was different when catching out scammy fraudsters, but he hated lying to innocent teenage girls. Raindrops spattered onto his face and a fierce wind made him shiver.

The door opened and Beatrice brought him another coffee. "Don't go all hair-shirt and self-flagellation. All's fair when it comes to getting what we need to know. Unless you've declared undying love, which I presume you have not, she'll have a couple of moony weeks and forget all about you. Now, do you have a phone number for Aleksis or not?"

He accepted the coffee. "An address. Turns out he's living with Risto and Ursula, a fact that makes me feel uncomfortable. I'm the one who should go round there, because they know me but at the same time, I'm the last one they'll allow to speak to Aleksis. What about getting out to that Malmen place?" His napkin blew off the table and stuck against the balcony door.

"The weather's on the turn and you need to put some clothes on. Come indoors and let's make a plan."

Once he was fully dressed, he came out of the bathroom to find his boss waiting, arms folded and mind made up.

"I'll give you three reasons why you should not go dashing

off to some unspecified place in Malmen. One, the message you received was exactly the same format as all the other death threats. OK, it wasn't a threat but how do we know we can trust the sender? Two, we need police support. To go searching for people by the seaside, one needs specialist equipment, dogs, wet weather gear, heat-seeking sensors." Beatrice waved a hand airily. "Three, if that letter came from one of the Gaia Warriors, they are the best possible people to lead us and the police directly to the location."

"They said not to contact the police," Theo reminded her.

Beatrice gave him a look over her specs. "They always do. I suggest a dual plan of action. Firstly, we need the police on our side or failing that, listening to us would suffice. To that end, I intend to prove it was Heikki Mäkinen who spilt the peas to the newshounds. All I need to do is feed him a juicy little titbit which not even you know about because I haven't even made it up yet. Then I warn Detective Sahlberg and we sit back and watch when it surfaces. Once he runs his mouth off again, you and I are sitting pretty and the police have no choice but to support us."

Theo shifted in his seat, wanting to believe her. "There are a whole lot of ifs in that plan. If you meet Heikki Mäkinen, if he swallows your fake news, if he sells it to his girlfriend, if he does it in time for us to take action and if Detective Sahlberg will even listen to you. I don't want to rub it in, but he's given you the cold shoulder this morning."

"Who can blame him? He doesn't trust me, or should I say, us. What I intend to do is prove to him the leak came from a different direction. The only issue is how quickly I can pull this off. That, I grant you, is a worry. Which leads me to our second string."

Wind rattled the French windows and the drops of rain pelted the glass. The bright room grew gloomy and Beatrice got up to switch on the lights.

"As I was saying, second string. You seek out Aleksis. Think like a sheepdog, you will need to separate him from the others. Presuming it was him who sent this note, he has enough of a conscience to respond to a guilt trip. He was there to listen to Samu's mother so he must understand the dangers of this situation. We need to get a precise location before we go haring off into the wilds of Finland on a wild coots' chase. There is one other thing."

Theo waited and when she did not speak, he noticed an awkwardness in her demeanour. She seemed to be casting around for the right words. Theo understood.

"You want me to call Matthew and lie to him that we've been delayed for a day by this storm."

She looked up at him, her eyes beseeching. "It's above and beyond the call of duty, I know that. But teenage environmental activists are not the only ones who respond to guilt trips. They'll blame me, Theo, and I need all my faculties to focus on this case."

"For such a hard-headed woman, you can be a right coward," he said, with a grin to soften the impact of his words.

She grinned back and he realised his words would have no impact whatsoever, as long as he did what she wanted. "OK, you'd better go. I'll make your excuses and then I'm heading over to the student house. Do you want the car?"

Beatrice wrinkled her nose. "No, you can have it. I'll take a taxi to the police station. Keep in touch and update me whenever you can." She hefted her handbag onto her shoulder and picked a strawberry from the breakfast trolley. "Theo?"

He lifted his face.

"Thank you. You really shouldn't let me use you as a human shield, but I'm awfully glad you do. Good luck and I'll see you later." She popped the strawberry into her mouth and was gone.

Chapter 27

Last night, no one came. No puffer, no food, no water, nothing. That was not great for her and really bad for Samu. The water she collected every couple of hours had not made her sick. She judged it as a risk but decided to give it to Samu. The alternative was a whole lot worse.

Since yesterday evening, he had been in and out of consciousness and his breathing ragged. Valpuri was unable to keep him awake and upright, no matter how hard she tried. She couldn't keep him clean any longer as he kept soiling his sleeping bag. Figuring the sun would hit a patch of the cave for a few hours in the morning, Valpuri removed the stinking fabric from around his body and washed it in the sea. She stretched it out across the rocks beneath the aperture, using ties from their hoodies to string it from two stalagmites and prayed for sunshine. For the first time in her life, she actually prayed.

Meanwhile, she covered Samu with everything warm and dry they had and dug a channel so that every time he relieved himself, it flowed away towards the sea. The stench was probably nauseating, she thought, but she had long since ceased to notice. There was nothing left to eat and even the emergency apricots she'd saved for Samu had gone.

She tried to conserve energy, wrapping herself into a ball, hands between her thighs, hood pulled up around her head and her feet in the cold box. The insulated vessel kept heat in as well as out. She concentrated for hours on her breath, reassuring herself that she had the strength to get through this. The sun would shine on Samu's bag, drying it, warming it and making it clean again. They would come tonight, bringing food, water, dry clothes and most important thing of all, Samu's inhaler. If not ...

She closed her eyes and dozed, dreaming of light, of motion. While her body lay shivering and tense on the damp sand, another Valpuri stood up and stretched, glowing with energy and warmth. She shimmered like an animated heroine and bent to brush sparkling hands over Valpuri's fake fur hood. Her arms arced backwards as if she were a seagull about to take flight. Her head rose to the glimpses of the sun reflecting from the waves and she took off at a run. Across the sand without making a footprint, taking huge strides to leap over the rocks and flying out from the cave, diving into the sea, her glowing silhouette undulating beneath the waves. A dolphin. A mermaid.

Her stomach cramped and her eyes flew open. *I'm not sick. Just hungry. I'm not sick. I'm strong, I'm healthy, I will survive this. We will survive this.* Her stomach cramped again. The wind blew in from the sea with unusual force, knocking the soggy sleeping bag to the ground. Valpuri uncurled and crabbed her way across the cave with the intention of fixing her makeshift washing line. As she stood beneath the aperture she realised there was no sunshine, and a storm was heading in their direction. The waves grew bolder, not just tiptoeing in but swelling, thrusting and crashing into their pathetic little refuge.

In a moment of brutal clarity, Valpuri could see what would happen if they remained where they were. One glance at the raging sea told her the fantasy of a glowing mermaid was nothing more than the onset of delirium. A storm, if not a hurricane, was about to hit the coast and their cave would flood, battering her and Samu against the rocks as if they were blueberries in a blender. She fell onto her knees and covered her face with her hands. She would not give in to tears or despair. She had a fine mind and now was the time to use it.

Someone at some time had climbed down here. Maybe they had ropes, torches and back-up but somebody had to be the first one down into this cave. If someone climbed down, someone could climb up. She had none of the right gear, simply trainers, jeans and a sweatshirt. The only thing she could count on was an instinct for survival. She took a long breath in through her nose, willing herself to identify ozone rather than faeces, and tilted her head back, peering up at the aperture. The cliff walls seemed unassailable, smooth and wet as marble. If she climbed, she might get stuck, injure herself or fall. What was the alternative? To sit listening to her friend's struggles to breathe until the waves came to claim them? If there was any way to save Samu, she would have to get help.

Valpuri unzipped her jacket and tied it tightly around her waist. She stood beneath the aperture, avoiding the rain and studying her limited view of the ascending walls. Illumination was poor and she would be feeling her way. She assessed the metre or so she could see clearly and chose her route.

A voice whispered in her ears. '*Don't leave me, Vappu. Please don't go.*'

Her head snapped around to stare at the comatose lump on the sand. She crept around to look at his face. Eyes closed, breathing painful. She patted his cheek.

"Samu? Can you hear me? Just open your eyes if you can, OK?"

His eyes didn't flicker and his breathing continued, a dragging thready snore that sounded painful. She cast a fearful glance behind her at the encroaching waves, halfway up the cave. Whether she made it out or not, the sea would not wait. Her only hope was to drag him as far as she could up the sand, beneath the aperture. Away from the roiling sea but directly beneath the pounding rain.

Sweating and tearful, she hauled the deadweight of her best friend as high as she could. She covered him with a groundsheet, tucked it around his body and kissed his forehead. Maybe there would be more oxygen here?

"I'm popping out for a coffee. Can I get you anything?"

She pressed the heels of her hands to her eyes and began to climb.

The only way to get through this was to look at the next step and no further. Valpuri had ascended around three metres in what seemed like hours. Every time she found a hold for a hand or a foot, she had to be sure there was another within reach. Otherwise, she would have to descend and find a different path. Her muscles in her forearm screamed as she clenched onto the crevice, fumbling to find the tiny ledge she sought with her foot. Water slipped down the walls of the cave, numbing her fingers and clouding her sight.

She repeated her mantra. *I'm strong. I'm healthy. I will survive this. We will survive this. Hold on, Samu, I'm coming back.* As she ascended, the curve of the wall sloped over her head. If she climbed any further, she would be crawling like a beetle across the roof. Her body weight would pluck her like a rotten fruit and she would fall, onto the sand, possibly onto Samu, and would inevitably damage some part of her weakened frame.

In the gloom of the afternoon, she tried to see another way of getting closer to the rim. All around the aperture, the walls ballooned outwards and then down. Nothing but an insect could ascend these walls and in this weather not even a cockroach would survive. Tears of frustration added to the water in her eyes and with infinite care, she started the terrifying journey down.

Chapter 28

Beatrice could evade scrutiny from most people by keeping busy and focusing on the task in hand. Except her counsellor. James had repeatedly asked her to check in via phone or video call and she had ducked each slot. Today, she resolved to tackle that responsibility, regardless of how much she had to do.

In light of the deteriorating weather, she took a cab to the police station, with the anonymous message in its bag. At reception, she emphasised the importance of speaking personally to Detective Sahlberg. Once again, he was unavailable. Beatrice had no choice but to leave the note at reception, stating three more times how vital this information would prove to the investigation. Then she waited out of the buffeting wind and whiplash rain until she could get another taxi back to the hotel. The sky was the blackest she'd seen it since arriving. Even when she'd been awake at one am on Theo's night of excess, the night retained a hint of light. Beatrice would not describe it as white, but one could have jogged along a remote beach with no need of a torch. If that was the sort of thing one did after midnight. A taxi came to a halt and Beatrice began rehearsing her excuses to James.

In her hotel room, she decided to do a face-to-face meeting for a change. Her usual habit was to hide from the camera, a factor

James always accepted as her choice, but never failed to note. Today, she would be open and on camera and look into his eyes.

"James Parker?"

"Hello, James, it's Beatrice. Thank you for finding time for me. Are you well?"

"Beatrice." The way he said her name felt like a hug. The screen flickered and she saw her face come up in the corner. She cringed at the sight of her windswept hair, but did not switch off the camera.

"Oh, you're doing visuals today? In that case, I can say in all honesty, it's lovely to see you. I am well, thank you. How are you?"

"Busy. I have to solve this Finnish case by tomorrow or I'll be in hot water when I get home. Tanya's wedding is this weekend."

On the screen, James rested his fingers on his temples. "Yes, I thought as much. How realistic are the chances of you making sufficient progress in the next few hours?"

"We have a long shot and we're taking it. My new assistant is working out well, you'll be pleased to hear. His skill set differs to mine but it's complementary. There's another person I think I can rely on, so to answer your question, the chances are slim, but I have a great team behind me."

His blond hair shone in the lamplight. "That sounds optimistic. How about you? No regrets about leaving Devon at such a vital time for the family?"

She had regrets, mostly about putting herself on camera now, because she dearly wanted to wrinkle her nose. "All fine there. Plenty of hands on deck and I'll be home tomorrow, come hell or high horses. They can manage."

James cupped his chin in his hand. "That wasn't my question. The wedding situation is not my primary concern. You are. So I ask again. No regrets?"

She looked at his image and caved in. He'd get there in the end. He always did. The only question was how long it would take.

"I postponed our return because some new information has come to light. I don't regret that per se, but I was cowardly enough to ask Theo to make the call and blame it on the weather. Matthew will see right through such a ruse."

James waited for her to continue. She knew what he was going to ask, and answered the question without him needing to open his mouth.

"I don't really know why, to be honest."

"You don't know why you chose to lie about the weather or you don't know why you asked Theo to tell the lie?"

There was really no need to keep referring to it as a lie. It was possibly even true, although it wouldn't be difficult for someone to check Arrivals at Heathrow Airport. "The weather is dreadful, James. But that's not why I wanted to stay, you're right. As for Theo ..." She tailed off, unable to avoid the obvious.

"Two questions, if I may. Why did you decide to tell me your choice of action when I asked if you had any regrets? Secondly, how would you describe your behaviour?"

She sighed. "Because that's the thing I feel guilty about. Staying on another day, telling lies about why and getting Theo to do my dirty work. My behaviour is bloody typical. Evasive and irresponsible. At my age, it really is time I grew up."

"How do you think your assistant felt when his boss asked him to lie?"

Beatrice was stung. "Theo doesn't mind. We have a very good relationship like that."

"Good for whom?"

She thought about it. Due to Theo's remorse over getting drunk, she had taken advantage of his willing nature, bullying him into a situation he did not enjoy. He didn't want to profit from Tuula's crush on him, but he did it anyway. He would not have enjoyed delivering unwelcome news to Matthew either.

"Theo's too good-natured and tends to go along with

whatever I say. I've been domineering and manipulative. God, every time I talk to you I feel like a horrible person."

"Beatrice, a horrible person does not perceive her behaviours as horrible. I am doing nothing more than asking you to examine yourself in the mirror. Because if you don't acknowledge that you sometimes act in a way that makes you feel guilty or ashamed, those feelings will weigh on your subconscious. It's like sweeping dust under the carpet. You can't see it but you know it's there. Then what?"

"Then sooner or later I'll have a down cycle and the negative feelings will multiply because there's another pile of them under the rug. So how do you think I should deal with this?"

"Let's switch roles. I've just told you that I've been treating my new assistant unfairly and not being honest with my partner. How would you advise me?"

"All right, I get it. I'll confess to Matthew that it's reluctance to leave this case unfinished that keeps me here another day. And I will apologise to Theo. On top of that, I will consciously check my behaviour towards him."

James smiled. "An excellent start. I would add that relationships are a two-way street. You might find time for a conversation around the subject of assertiveness. You have a strong character and I can imagine some people find it hard to say no. Theo will need to take his share of responsibility and you can start by giving him permission to do that. Do you remember the 'No, but' exercise we tried when I was encouraging you to stand up for yourself at the Met? Softening a refusal by making a concession. Why not try that? It could benefit both of you."

"Good point. Theo's work history has been quite chequered and I think he really likes this job. So he might be overcompensating in order to keep it."

"So what else do you need to do when modifying your working relationship?"

"Reassure him that I'm pleased with his work. He's made a

few mistakes but learnt from them and I can't fault his enthusiasm."

"You see? You're perfectly capable of thinking this through and making wise choices on your own. All I do is prod you to start. Shall we address the medication question and your mood diary before summarising this call before we finish?"

When Beatrice ended the call, she experienced a rush of positive energy, as if she had averted a collision. Adrenalin pumped through her and she found she was smiling. For the millionth time, she wondered what she would do without James.

Chapter 29

The decent thing to do when intending to expose one's client's husband for both leaking to the press and having an affair was to let the client know. However, she did not have that option. Karoliina was off grid until tomorrow, but she had told Beatrice where to place her trust. Time was of the essence. She dug around in her purse until she found the card she was looking for and made the call.

Astrid Falk responded to Beatrice's request without a second's hesitation. "Yes, of course I can meet you. Karoliina said you might call with developments. If you want to talk face to face, you can come to the office unless you prefer somewhere more public?"

Beatrice was ready with her suggestion. "Given the inclement weather and the urgency of the situation, how about the cathedral? Not far from your office and near where I need to be."

"I can be there in twenty minutes."

"Perfect. I'll wear a red scarf so you can identify me."

"I will identify you, Ms Stubbs, don't worry."

Beatrice ended the call, curious how the woman could be so sure.

Twenty minutes later, Beatrice was regaining her breath and drying herself off after ascending the steps to the imposing white edifice towering over the city. She made directly for the nave, but doubled back to leave her sopping wet umbrella in the stand. As she shoved the brolly in amongst all the others, she reminded herself not to forget it. The big church door opened and a huge man blocked out all the light. His stature was such that she wondered how he would fit in a normal room. He walked past her and into the vaulted space within.

Once inside, she avoided the organ, pulpit and relics where the tourists gathered and parked herself on a pew. An Amazonian goddess walked up the aisle and held out a hand. Almost as impressive as the cathedral and with similar colouring, Astrid Falk had a presence one could not miss. She held out a hand.

"Hello, Beatrice Stubbs. I'm Astrid. Good choice of location. For the most famous building in this city, it's usually pretty quiet. Did you get caught in the rain?"

"Just a bit. Thank you for meeting me. Karoliina says I can trust you. You're her PA, correct?"

Astrid sat beside her, straight-backed and elegant in her trench coat. "Karoliina is right. I'm her PA, her right hand, bodyguard, confidante and friend. I know she hired you and why. Last thing she told me is that you had completed the job and were returning to England."

"Things have changed." Beatrice interlaced her hands and bowed her head as if she was at prayer. "What I am about to tell you is in complete secrecy."

"I understand." Astrid mirrored her move.

Beatrice explained her concerns regarding Heikki in the briefest terms and waited for a reaction before proceeding.

"I wish I could say that is a surprise. But it is not. Not at all. Heikki and Päivi were a couple before he met Karoliina. Several of us suspected that relationship wasn't over and it seems we were right. He's still screwing his ex and screwing his wife by leaking stories. I'm guessing you plan to shine a light on that loser."

"Yes. I want to feed him fake information, record him sharing it with his fancy piece and show the police I can be trusted. Sadly, that means showing Karoliina that Heikki can't."

Astrid rested her right temple on her knuckles, her eyes so green she looked like a hologram. "Why do you think she told you to call me and not him? In her heart, she knows her husband is a faithless little shit. I don't know why she didn't kick him out years ago. What can I do to help?"

"OK, here's the plan."

Bugging was not Beatrice's speciality. As she waited for Heikki to arrive at the hotel, she recalled previous experiences of trying to plant a listening device on a human being. In that situation, she had an opportunity, an expert, and most importantly, a translator. If, as she expected, Heikki Mäkinen would go right to the point of assignation as soon as he had seen Beatrice depart, he had to be carrying a discreet recording device. Placing something in his pocket was risky as she might not have an opportunity and even if she did, he might easily find it. Her best chance was to give him some paperwork in a file containing a hidden bug. If he believed what she was about to say, he would be desperate to share the information. Naturally, he would take the documents to show Päivi. If Astrid got to the hotel ahead of them, if she managed to identify the room and if she wasn't spotted ... she squeezed her eyes shut. As Theo had pointed out, there were a whole lot of ifs.

Nevertheless, she had the equipment and the expertise. She had to give it her best shot. She reassured herself by patting the brown paper folder on her knee, which contained a fake statement, a meaningless set of timings and some grainy photographs she'd printed in the hotel's business centre. Sealed inside the metallic clip on the spine was a voice-activated microphone with transmitter.

Across the lobby, she saw Heikki coming her way. She stood up to shake his hand, leaving the folder on the table. *Performance time, PI Stubbs, and you'd better make this plausible.*

"Beatrice! I came as quickly as I could."

"Heikki, I'm most grateful to you. As I mentioned on the phone, I need to contact Karoliina with maximum urgency. I have vital information to share with her and I cannot make contact on her mobile phone. I know she's at their facility and off the grid, but I assume you as next-of-kin would have a way of reaching her in an emergency. This is very irregular, I understand, and I would not ask if it were not of the most extreme importance. I simply cannot share my findings over the airwaves."

The waiter brought Beatrice's coffee and Heikki ordered a beer. It was not yet lunchtime, but Beatrice raised no eyebrows. Their conversation was on hold until the waiter returned to the bar.

"Karoliina is inspecting the facility, as you know. That means the majority of the day she will be out of reach. I understood that you had finished your job, Ms Stubbs, so I wonder why you need to speak to Karoliina again so soon? None of my business, of course, but I feel a personal interest in this case."

"It's perfectly understandable that you do," said Beatrice. "And I would happily share this latest development except my agreement was to inform Karoliina before everyone, including the police. Although if there really is no way of reaching her, I will have no choice but to take my findings to the force in Helsinki. Do you think she might pick up her messages at lunchtime?"

The waiter delivered the beer bottle, opened the lid and went to pour it into a glass. Heikki said something in Finnish and the man left them to it.

He took a slug straight from the bottle. "Karoliina receives a lot of messages and she doesn't always listen to them all. She just hasn't got the time. One thing she always does is call me, just to check in. So if there's something she urgently needs to know, maybe I'm the fastest means of communication?"

No way on earth would Beatrice capitulate so easily, even though she wanted the man to take the bait. She had far more style. "That's exactly the kind of thing I was hoping to hear. So perhaps if she does call you this lunchtime, you could ask her to contact me at her earliest convenience. I do believe this is information she would like to know. I appreciate your willingness to pass things on, but my contract is with Karoliina and I'm a stickler for the small print. Thank you for meeting me and now I really should leave to go to the police." She took the folder in a protective gesture and tried not to look at her untouched coffee.

His eyes clocked the move and fixed on the file. "I understand. What you should know is that Karoliina and I are a partnership. We made a joint decision to hire you. We want to find those kids and we're doing all we can to help the police. What I'm saying, Ms Stubbs, is that anything you need to tell Karoliina, you can tell me."

Beatrice hesitated, delivering an Oscar-worthy performance of Miss Indecisive, shooting glances into Heikki's intense eyes. "I'd prefer to speak to her. Please understand, I'm not being evasive, but neither can I break my contract."

"Your contract is underwritten by me and my wife. In her absence, I'm your point of contact. She should have made that clear."

Beatrice sat down again, recalling exactly who Karoliina had nominated as her second-in-command. "In that case, I have no choice. Karoliina needs to know that the children are no longer in Finland. We believe they are in Tallinn, Estonia. This means the investigation now involves two national police forces. Rather than returning to Britain as I expected, I will be flying to the Estonian capital in a few hours' time. The situation is far more complex than we first assumed and I will need Karoliina's say-so before I go any further. Please ask her to call me as soon as she can. These young people's lives hang in the balance."

His eyes widened. "Do you know who has them? I mean, are they safe?"

Beatrice shook her head with immense sadness. "When dealing with organised crime, there is little point in negotiation. All we can hope for is that the young people represent enough bargaining power to keep them alive. I must go. Time is of the essence. Obviously, what I have told you must remain in the strictest secrecy. In this file are copies of a statement from a witness, the timings of their departure and photographs of the youngsters boarding a ferry from Helsinki to Tallinn. I share this with you as a trusted partner, as the person who can convey the message to Karoliina the fastest. Would you ask her to call me anyway? Unless I can make her understand the seriousness of the situation, I fear all is lost." She flared her nostrils, appalled by her own theatrics.

Heikki held out his hand for the folder. "Thank you, Beatrice. I will pray for them. You can trust me to tell Karoliina the moment she makes contact. Please, do whatever you can to bring them home. Do you need a lift to the police station? This weather ..."

She shook her head. "Thank you, but that's not necessary. My assistant is waiting for me upstairs. Goodbye and thank you so much for all your help."

He left with almost indecent haste and the second he was out of sight, Beatrice picked up her phone.

"Astrid, he has the file. Now make your move. Good luck!"

Ten minutes later, when she was sure Heikki had definitely left, she crossed the lobby and exited the hotel into the wind. She hailed a taxi and instructed him to take her to the train station. Hotel Kuu was a few minutes' walk from there and even if she was soaked by the time she arrived, she preferred no one to know her business. A movement caught her eye as the taxi driver waited for a break in the traffic. A huge blond man came out of the hotel and got into the cab behind her. Something niggled at her. She'd seen him before. A chap of that size drew attention even in a space as large as ... the cathedral. That's where she had seen him, coming through the cathedral doors like a Nordic giant. A fellow tourist, probably. Just coincidence they happened to be at the same location twice on the same day. Her own voice echoed in her ears. *Theo, I've told you before, there's no such thing as coincidence.*

Once she located the hotel, she chose a café chain opposite and sat in the window, drying off for the second time that day. Her attention was fixed on the street, watching for any sign of oversized blond men. For a change, her nerves overcame her appetite. So she drank a camomile tea and watched passers-by dashing out of the rain. The first person to catch her eye was a woman pelting out of the revolving doors as if she'd just robbed a bank. Beatrice recognised her instantly from Theo's photos. She hailed a taxi, her mobile clamped to her ear and a brown buff file under her arm. Päivi Aho had taken the bait.

She snapped several pictures as the producer scrambled into a cab. With a glance at her watch, she saw the tryst could have lasted fewer than thirty minutes. The cynic in her wondered if they ditched the romantic element of the rendezvous in favour of her story making the six o'clock news. Moments passed and no one of interest emerged.

A text message buzzed on her phone.

`She left, he's drinking in the bar and I'm just coming out of the underground car park. Where are you?`

Beatrice sent a hurried reply.

`House of Coffee, across the street. Did you get it?`

She gnawed on a thumbnail as she waited for a reply. The café door opened and in strode Astrid, dressed in black jeans and a rain-slicked jacket. A slow smile spread over her face.

"Mission accomplished. All on here." She reached out a fist to drop the tiny recording device into Beatrice's palm. "I deserve a drink." She called something to the guy at the counter.

Beatrice closed her fingers over the little box and stared in admiration. "No wonder Karoliina is such a fan of yours. How on earth did someone with no previous detective experience manage to pull this off?"

Astrid took the shot glass from the barista and downed it in one. "By following instructions. The second I got your call, I put on my costume and waited till he turned up. Squeezed into the lift with him and alighted on the same floor. From there, it was easy. I saw which room he went into and found the nearest stairwell where I set up the receiver."

"No one saw you?"

"No one uses the stairs. I recorded their whole conversation and even got a couple of pictures, time and date stamped, of them leaving the room separately. It's exactly as you said. He's feeding her everything he knows, confident he won't be found out because he can blame you."

A cramp convulsed Beatrice's stomach. She had proof the man was leaking to the press but it involved throwing a bomb into Karoliina's marriage.

Astrid looked into her face, as if reading her thoughts. "It's better that she knows her partner is betraying her. Not only romantically but professionally."

"Oh dear. I hope you didn't have to hear anything embarrassing."

Astrid swung her rucksack onto her back. "No, they didn't have time for a quickie as she needs to take the story back to the station. The pair of them disgust me. When I get home, I want a long, hot shower."

"Astrid, I don't know how to thank you. This is ..."

Astrid held out a hand. "I like you, Beatrice. You're honest. But the truth is I did this for Karoliina. If there's anything else I can help with, you have my number."

"I'm deeply grateful to you. Just one question. Heikki has met you before. Plus the fact you're ... quite distinctive. What kind of costume did you wear as a disguise?"

"A hijab. That's all I need. People see the scarf, not the face, and look away. Easy. Gotta go. Goodbye and good luck!"

The barista and Beatrice gazed after her as she strode through the door, across the street as if the foul weather meant nothing, and slung a leg over a large black motorcycle. She wound her hair into her helmet and roared away into the traffic.

Chapter 30

The rain was Theo's friend. Had it been a sparkling summer's day, his loitering on the street outside the student accommodation would have been much more noticeable. The vicious gusts of wind and ceaseless rainfall curtailed all curiosity. People ran from tram stop to shop doorway, from front door to car, collars up, heads down and vision blinkered by umbrellas. The second advantage was that Theo was able to conceal his face with the hood of his jacket, just like everyone else trying to protect themselves against the storm.

He passed the address Tuula had given him three times; once on the other side of the street, once close enough to cast a glance at the ground-floor windows and the final time in a diagonal line, as if he were simply crossing the road. It was an unremarkable building, around four storeys high and in need of some care and attention. The door was scuffed and dirty, litter lay in the porch and the walls were streaked with grey where something had leaked. Lights shone on the first and second floors, but Theo could see no signs of movement. He walked as far as the tram stop, intending to wait and watch before making his move.

A few people waited in the shelter, each with the withdrawn attitude of a miserable traveller. When Theo joined them, no one even gave him a glance. He settled on the bench, far enough from the other passengers to be inconspicuous, and turned his attention to his breath. Long slow inhalation, steady calming exhalation, both part of the same mindful cycle. His intention was to breathe and watch for thirty minutes, repeating his intention as a mantra in his mind. Then, when he was calm and focused, he would cross the street and knock on the door.

Except he didn't get the chance. The tram arrived, masking his view of the house, and every other traveller boarded. Once the vehicle hummed away, his view looked quite different. Two vehicles had pulled up outside the student house; the first a plain sedan, the other a police patrol car. A man in a raincoat got out of the unmarked vehicle and waited for two uniformed officers to join him. In formation, detective first, uniform second, they approached the door.

Theo needed to get closer. He pulled his hood tighter and crossed to the other side of the street, dodging puddles until he found himself almost directly opposite the building that interested him. There, he stood in a shop doorway, sheltering from the rain. The police had gone inside and the façade of the building was bland and innocuous. Moments ticked past and Theo stayed absolutely still, his attention on the other side of the street.

The lights on the third floor went out, shortly followed by those on the second floor. The front door opened and Risto and Ursula emerged, each guided by a police officer. The detective opened the back door and ushered Ursula inside. The police officers, with the minimum of fuss, put Risto in the back seat of the patrol car. Doors slammed and both vehicles splashed away down the street. Maintaining complete stillness, Theo watched the building they had just left, now in darkness. He withdrew further into the shadow of the shop doorway, took out his phone and informed Beatrice of the latest developments.

Then he switched his phone to silent, zipped his jacket right up to his chin and loped over the road. Without hesitation, he strode up to the door and eased his box of tricks from his inside pocket. He put his finger on the bell, but did not press it, looking up to check his assumption this place had no security camera. He pressed once. No voice came through the intercom. He pressed again. Silence. In his head, he heard Beatrice's voice during his training sessions. *Push the door away to maximise any kind of space between lock and jamb. Press the card between the door and where the lock lies. Pull the door closer, turn handle and open. On a bog standard Yale lock, that will get you in.*

She wasn't wrong. Theo was not the kind of person to learn a skill and hope he would never need it. After every session in which Beatrice introduced him to the equipment he would need, he had spent several days practising. He broke into his own flat, and with permission, his neighbour's flat, Catinca's house and Dionysus, the wine bar where he used to work. He knew both theoretically and in muscle memory, how to open a locked door.

The door opened with a whine. To Theo's ears, it seemed a negligible creak, but he knew regular residents would be attuned to such a sound. He closed it behind him and pressed himself against the wall to listen, steam rising from his wet clothes. A student house, with three rooms on each floor, could house up to twenty-four people. Yet they were on their summer break, the vast majority returning to parents, holidaying with friends or working summer jobs outside the city. In most cases, the fact that two residents had just been arrested would be a cause for much discussion, gossip and consternation. Theo could hear nothing. While he waited, he slipped on a pair of plastic gloves.

He paced on tiptoes along the corridor and found the kitchen. Nothing like the student house he remembered, with cornflakes on the floor, spilt milk on the work surfaces and mugs so stained and chipped, they should have been growing culture in a scientific laboratory. This was clean, almost military in its organisation. Some washing-up still in the sink and a few open packages beside the hob. Theo touched nothing apart from the handle of the back door. It was locked and spattered with raindrops, as was every window in the room.

He checked the living room, crept cautiously up the stairs and tried each door on the first floor. All locked. He could break in, of course, but he chose to explore the rest of the house before intruding. His instincts told him the place was empty. There was a deadness and absence of energy, but relying on instinct was the attitude of an idiot. He checked the bathroom and silently made his way to the second floor. Same story, although the humidity and scent in this shower room told him it had been recently used. None of the bedroom doors gave any indication as to which belonged to whom. The last flight of steps was an iron spiral, more like the ascent to an attic than a regularly used stairwell. Each step announced his presence with a light metallic clink. He paused after the first, waited thirty seconds and stretched to take two steps in one stride.

The house creaked and groaned under the onslaught of the weather, the drumming on the roof like a frantic samba band. Theo took three cycles of breath and eased himself up four more steps until he could see the landing. There was only one door and the bare minimum of light from the floor below. He allowed his eyes to adjust and could see a heap of cardboard boxes stuffed into the corner where the roof sloped downwards. In front of him, there was enough space to stand upright for whoever wanted to enter the top room.

He reached out to check if the door was locked but some internal warning system stayed his hand. Breathing regularly and calmly, Theo crouched and with a crablike scuttle, retreated into the shadows between the cardboard boxes. Minutes passed. The howls and clatters of the storm grew to a crescendo and kept on going. Then another sound, closer, joined the unholy symphony.

Above Theo's head, a trap door opened. The flap swung backwards, blocking Theo's view of the space above. For several seconds, nothing happened and then a metal ladder slid to the ground in stages. After a long pause, someone began climbing down. Even if Theo's suspicions had not already taken that direction, he would have guessed who it was by the awkward, one-handed descent. He waited until Aleksis had reached the ground and was peering down the stairwell before he made his move.

"Hello, Aleksis."

The kid gasped and stumbled backwards, then launched himself at the stairs. Theo was faster, grabbing Aleksis's uninjured arm.

"Be realistic. You're going nowhere. Is there anyone else apart from you in this building?"

Aleksis shook his head but said nothing.

"What say you and I go downstairs, have a cup of tea and a nice little chat? Why don't you lead the way?"

Aleksis turned to him, face stricken. "There's no time," he said in a voice barely above a whisper. "We have to help them."

"Help who? Do you mean Risto and Ursula?"

Aleksis shook his head again, this time more vigorously. "No, not them. I mean Samu and Valpuri. They're in danger."

Theo narrowed his eyes. "Where are they, Aleksis? Tell me. I know you sent that note."

The words came tumbling out in a rush. "They're in the caves, the caves at Malmen. We take them food and water every day, but yesterday we couldn't go. And today the storm.... it's dangerous. The cave is safe in the summer but in this weather, I don't know, they don't know. Samu needs his inhalers. Ursula says Valpuri is exaggerating but I think he could be sick and we didn't go yesterday. We couldn't go because Risto said the police were watching us after the news report. It was too dangerous and we couldn't go. I'm worried about both of them and really worried about Samu. We have to help them."

"How far away are these caves?"

"Half an hour, maybe forty minutes. I can't drive. But I have his inhalers and we have supplies, up there."

Theo gave the kid a 'do you think I'm stupid?' look, but Aleksis's face showed nothing but concern. "Right, and I go up there leaving you to do a runner? I don't think so. You are going back up this ladder to pass supplies down to me, then we need to call the police…"

"No!" Aleksis shouted. "No police! If you call the police, I can't take you, I won't. We have to help them, but not police."

The kid seemed panicked, like a bird caught in the net. Theo listened to his gut feeling and decided the welfare of the missing kids came first.

"I'll make you a deal. You take me to where they are so we can help them. But, Aleksis, if Samu needs medical help, I must call emergency services. Do you understand?"

Aleksis's eyes darted from left to right and in a murmur, he said, "Yes, I understand. I'll get the stuff." One-handed, he dragged himself back up the metal ladder and into the attic. Theo heard him dragging boxes and moving heavy objects about over his head, so he took the opportunity to send Beatrice a rapid text message.

Think I know where V and S might be. Aleksis (Gaia Warrior) says they're in some caves in the Malmen area, thirty mins from Helsinki. Going there now, don't call me in case this kid panics. I'll let you know as soon as I find anything.

He put the phone in his pocket and climbed the ladder to give Aleksis a hand.

Chapter 31

The entire journey to Helsinki police station, Beatrice was preoccupied with how she might entreat Detective Sahlberg to listen to what she had to say. In the past, she had used some extreme measures to come to the notice of European law enforcement officers, including crashing a BMW into the wall of a Spanish police station. She looked at the back of the taxi driver's head and allowed herself a smile as she imagined trying to persuade him to do the same.

Her attention was distracted by an incoming message from Theo. Her instinct on reading it was to call him back instantly but he had expressly asked her not to do that. She took a deep breath and told herself to keep faith. Her priority right now was to gain a sympathetic audience with Detective Sahlberg. After all, hers was the first concrete lead in finding Valpuri Peura and Samu Pekkanen. If he wouldn't listen to her, she would go over his head and throw herself on the mercy of his superior. She steeled herself for a fight.

As events turned out, she needn't have worried. On requesting a meeting, the receptionist told Beatrice that Detective Sahlberg would join her in around ten minutes. Her pent-up sense of injustice had nowhere to go, so she sat quietly in the interview room, using her phone to research the area of Malmen. In a few days, she had seen very little of the countryside and found it hard to believe there was an area sufficiently remote within half an hour's drive where you could hide two teenagers for almost a week.

When Detective Sahlberg opened the door, Beatrice was taken aback. The man looked five years older than the last time she had seen him, his eyes weary and his shirt in need of an iron.

"Hello, Ms Stubbs. You're still here, I see. I'm sorry I did not reply to your message. I'm afraid things have been rather stressful since we last met. Let me tell you that I did read it and the note you shared with us. As a result, I took appropriate action."

Beatrice dispensed with niceties. "By appropriate action, what do you mean?"

"We have taken two of the Gaia Warriors in for questioning, but they're not talking. You mentioned the area of Malmen. I sent a patrol car to search any abandoned buildings in the area. They found nothing, so far. The receptionist tells me you have new information?"

"Yes, on two counts. I just received a message from my assistant. He is with one of the Gaia Warriors, who says the missing young people are hidden in a cave in the Malmen area. He is going there now. You should point your officers in that direction."

Sahlberg raised his eyebrows. "Which Gaia Warrior? Aleksis Timonen?"

"That's correct."

A light entered Sahlberg's eyes. "And he's talking? That is good news. Sorry, you said a cave? Can you be more specific?"

"That's all I know. Theo sent me a message and asked me not to call back in case I throw the kid into a tailspin." She read out the text from her phone and Sahlberg reached for his own handset. Beatrice waited while he spoke.

After ending the call, Sahlberg looked directly into her eyes. "Thank you. We will take the information into account. Was there anything else?" He placed his hands on the desk as if he were about to push himself to his feet.

"Yes, there is!" Beatrice was prepared to wrap her arms around his ankles before she would let him leave. "Before I say anything else, I want you to know that you can trust me. I did not sell our findings to the press and neither did my assistant. Your next question will be how I can prove something didn't happen. The answer is, I can't. But I can prove that someone else is feeding information to Päivi Aho and Channel 6. Someone who knew exactly what I had found. Obviously this is deeply unethical and against police best practice, but please remember I'm not a police officer. Today, I went to see the person I believe released those details to the media and fed him a great steaming pile of bullshit. Then a colleague of mine hid near a hotel room and recorded what he did next. Listen to this."

Sahlberg sat back in his seat and folded his arms, his expression wary. When the recording began, a frown crossed his forehead but he leaned forward. Resting on his elbows and listening intently, he heard the whole thing without speaking. When it ended he met Beatrice's gaze.

"This guy is Karoliina Nurmi's husband?" he asked, shaking his head in disbelief.

"Yes. His name is Heikki Mäkinen. He is the only other person who knew what Theo and I had uncovered. Apart from you and Karoliina Nurmi. I can't see any reason why she would leak the story to the press and you certainly wouldn't. In your shoes, the obvious people to suspect would be me and my assistant. This is why I had to prove to you it was someone else. I don't know why he's doing this and obviously I can only guess at a motive. That said, you can see he is the leak. Not me, not Theo, but Karoliina's own husband."

Sahlberg rested his chin between thumb and forefinger. "I need to hear this again, but the sound quality is poor. Can I give this to one of my engineers? I miss a lot of detail."

"You can do what you like with it. I know it's not legally admissible evidence, but prosecuting Heikki Mäkinen is not in my remit. The only reason we recorded this is to convince you to trust me. My options were limited."

The detective made another phone call, his gaze resting on Beatrice. He ended the call and leaned forward.

"You lied to Heikki Mäkinen about the missing teenagers being abducted by an organised crime network in Estonia, planted a bug on him and recorded his conversation with the TV producer in a hotel room. That is hard to believe. Please be honest with me. You didn't hack his phone?"

Beatrice was outraged. Phone hacking in her opinion was the practice of unscrupulous tabloid journalists, and she condemned the practice wholeheartedly.

"Absolutely not! That would be a despicable thing to do. Underhand, sneaky and invasion of a person's privacy. I may bend the rules occasionally, detective, but I would never resort to such filthy tricks."

Sahlberg interlaced his fingers and rested his chin on his hands. "In that case, may I ask how you managed to come by this recording?" A smile was playing at the corner of his lips.

A knock came at the door and a young woman came into the room to collect Beatrice's recording device. Judging by the brief conversation and Sahlberg's glance at his watch, he was asking how long it would take.

He returned his gaze to her. "The engineer estimates it will take her an hour or possibly two. She'll clean up the original material. I suggest you return to your hotel, wait and watch the news. If Aho swallowed that story, it will be one of the top three items on this afternoon's news. I will keep you informed if anything turns up in Malmen and please make contact with your assistant. We need to know his precise location in order to offer support. Ask the receptionist to call you a taxi and I will speak to you later this afternoon."

"Is that it? I hand over all my findings over to you and have to sit fiddling my thumbs in my hotel room?"

"No, that is not everything. You didn't answer my question. May I ask how and with whom you recorded Heikki Mäkinen having that conversation?"

Beatrice got to her feet and yanked her handbag onto her shoulder. "I bugged the file of fake information because I knew where he would take it and to whom. As for my colleague, a good PI always protects her sources. Good evening to you."

Detective Sahlberg watched her leave, shaking his head.

Chapter 32

This whole situation set off alarms in every area of Theo's brain. Aleksis insisted they take the minibus out to Malmen. It was an unfamiliar vehicle, the weather was chronic and Theo had no experience with driving this route. He capitulated mainly because the minibus contained all the equipment they needed, including a tail hitch for lowering and raising items from the cave. Despite the young man's agitation, Theo refused to be hurried and made sure they had everything they could possibly need. He knew little about asthma but Aleksis retrieved Valpuri's messages and explained what she had demanded. They stopped at a pharmacy for some first-aid materials, just in case. Eventually, provisions packed, emergency gear procured and a hot flask of tea stashed between the front seats, Theo programmed the Satnav as best he could and they drove off into the summer storm. Its biting winds and lashing rain seemed almost like a punishment after the clear Nordic skies of the previous days.

The motorway crossed a wide body of water, spray and rain pelting his windscreen and sudden gusts blowing him off course. Theo kept his speed steady, hands gripping the steering wheel, his neck tense. Exploring a coastal path in this weather was an alarming prospect. He had no serious wet-weather gear and his trainers were not intended for Finnish paths, more

Finsbury Park. Even though traffic grew less congested as they crossed the city, driving conditions were a nightmare. He breathed, in a conscious effort to relax his shoulders and prepare himself for the unknown. This was unfamiliar territory in every sense, yet he could handle himself. His eyes were open, his body primed and his mind flexible. He was ready for this, whatever it was.

Once off the bridge, they drove through an apparently endless suburb. In order to be fully prepared for what he was about to face, he needed more detail.

"Aleksis, I want you to understand something. I'm a private detective hired to do a job. I have no vested interest because my motivation is professional. I want to find Valpuri and Samu or I don't get paid. Why they are in a cave, who put them there and the finger-pointing of blame? That stuff doesn't interest me in the slightest. You want me to help them and I'm flying blind here. Can you at least give me a rough idea of what I can expect?"

Curled up in his wet weather jacket with his hood up, Aleksis looked like a hermit crab. They continued through the grey streets, windscreen wipers on full speed, the heater blowing like a hairdryer and Theo's patience extending like the road ahead.

"What she said, his mum, I think that's true." Aleksis's voice was only just audible above the sound of splashing tyres and the rumbling engine.

Rather than snap questions at the kid, Theo stayed silent, his focus on the traffic.

"Risto and Ursula…" He took several deep breaths, his voice catching in his throat. "Risto and Ursula are strong, mentally strong. They analyse everything and they understand the big picture. I don't. This is why they decide Gaia Warrior strategy. The rest of us, Valpuri, Samu, Tuula and me, we have passion. They have vision. Sometimes, I'm too emotional. I didn't want to do this."

Traffic lights ahead changed to red and Theo turned down

the heater a notch. He was tempted to repeat his speech on not giving a shit about why and trying to focus the boy's attention on what. He didn't, simply leaving a space for Aleksis to fill.

"What we do at grassroots level is a personal choice."

The lights changed to green and Theo drove away, trying not to cross his eyes at the repetition of a mission statement.

"On a bigger scale, when we were trying to address a global problem, we agreed on a more extreme path of action. We can't communicate a message without using the media. Somehow or other, we have to attract attention, get people talking, start a discussion. It's not enough to change our own behaviours, to talk to our friends and families, we need a wider platform. We need to pull people's focus on to us and our message." He paused. "Sorry, you said you weren't interested in why."

Theo kept his voice gentle. "I want to hear your story. You can start at whatever point you like. All I'm doing is listening."

Signs overhead indicated another bridge and Theo tensed himself for the inevitable onslaught of winds from the Baltic Sea. For a second, a vision crossed his mind. A long green apron, sparkling optics and a crowd of beautiful people on the other side of the bar. That was a chapter of his own story and he dismissed it as shallow and dull. Plus he'd heard it before.

"Ursula is smart. I mean really smart. She understands how to make people sit up and listen. She and Risto had an idea. It's all about public perception, you see? Black and white, good and evil, aggressor and victim. The news painted us as aggressors, whiny millennials claiming entitlement, ungrateful for the benefits and ignorant of the sacrifices made by previous generations. Ursula said we had to change the narrative, making it more about our sacrifices, our loss, turning a cosy story of a nostalgic past into a dystopian future."

It wasn't clear exactly why Theo's knuckles had gone pale while clutching the steering wheel. He decided to be magnanimous and put it down to the uncertainty of the weather.

"We're going to have a lot of time to discuss this, and we should because I am interested in what you have to say. Right now, Aleksis, I need you to tell me where we're going and what I should expect. When I go into a situation like this, I need to have a picture in my mind. Can you tell me a little bit about this cave? How do you get to it, how do you deliver food, why can't Valpuri and Samu get out on their own? Paint me a picture, will you?"

Aleksis shot him a quick glance and turned to look out of the passenger seat window. "It's a place Risto knows. His father works at the golf club and Risto used to play there when he was a kid. There's a cave, pretty deep, which is open to the sea. He and his friends had a rope ladder. They used to climb down there, make a fire, drink beer, grill fish, you know the kind of thing. No one could find you down there."

"And that's where you decided to hide Valpuri and Samu? How could you be sure they wouldn't get out? How could you be sure ..." He hesitated, framing his words with care. "How could you be sure they would be safe?"

As the minibus drove across the bridge, Theo swallowed and clenched his jaw. Waves billowed across the motorway, battering vehicles and forcing all traffic to creep along at 30 kph. The road was reduced to one lane only; cars, lorries and buses crept in single file across the wild water.

Theo's concentration was 100% on the road ahead, but he sensed Aleksis leaning forward to observe the dramatic conditions.

"It's not far. On the other side of the bridge, we take a left at Sarvvik and go a little way towards the coast. We are about ten minutes away. We have to keep going." Aleksis was rocking, as if to propel the vehicle forward by his own force of movement.

"I don't plan to stop," said Theo. "Tell me, how could you be sure they were safe? You heard what Samu's mother said? He needs regular medication, no triggers such as cold and damp and his emergency inhaler in case of an attack. You took that into account, right?"

"It wasn't up to me! I didn't want to do this but they had it all planned. They didn't tell me, they didn't tell Tuula until the last minute. They said everything was organised and all we had to do was follow the plan. So we did." He sniffed but Theo could tell he was not crying. "We always do. Samu always has an inhaler on him and we didn't mean for this to go on so long."

"You said we take a left at Sarvvik. That means this exit, yes?"

"Yes. Left here."

For the next few minutes, they stayed silent and tense, the only communication being Aleksis's directions. The road soon became little more than a washed-out track and Theo struggled to keep the decrepit old bus moving forward.

"Could we dump the bus and walk from here?" he asked.

"We need the bus! That's the only way we can lower a ladder or a rope. We need the bus," panted Aleksis, his voice high-pitched and breathless. "It's only another hundred metres. Keep going, please, keep going!"

Even with his lights on full beam, Theo could barely see where he was going. The edge of the cliffs loomed closer and he had to make a judgement call. He stopped the bus and switched off the engine.

"No! Keep going!" shrieked Aleksis. "We have to help them!"

Theo inflated his ribcage and addressed the hyper individual in the passenger seat with a powerful, but modulated voice. "If we drive any further in these conditions, I am putting us both in danger. The bus stays here and we'll walk to locate this access point. I'm sorry, Aleksis, but I need to alert the emergency services. Anyone exposed to this weather, whether they are healthy or not, is at serious risk. No more messing about, lives are on the line. Theirs and ours. Come on."

The kid, to his credit, didn't protest, and scrambled into the back.

He tried 112 but his phone refused to cooperate. He switched on location services so hopefully he could be tracked. After two attempts at calling Beatrice failed, Theo sent her a message with their location and an alert to call police, ambulance and whatever version of coastguards existed in Finland. He just had to hope the message would get sent when the signal returned.

Over his shoulder, he saw Aleksis stuffing cans into his rucksack. "Forget the food! All we need is rope, the first aid kit, fluid and blankets. Give me that ..." he didn't know the Swedish word for tarpaulin. "... thing!" He saw the confusion in the guy's eyes. "The green canvas sheet with the holes! Come on, Aleksis, now's the time to forget the rest of this shit and do right by your friends. Mind the door as you get out, this wind is insane!"

The door slid back and exposed them to the full ferocious force of the storm. Instantly, Theo was blinded by rain and his hood blew off his head. He sheltered behind the bus, tied his hood under his chin and followed the beam of Aleksis's torch.

Chapter 33

The minute Beatrice arrived back at the hotel, she knew it was a bad idea. There was no way she could settle without knowing where Theo was and what he was doing. The view from the windows of her hotel room brought home the violence and fury of the storm. Boats rocked, bucked and crashed up against the sea wall, while the sea bubbled and frothed like a volcano. On top of that, she had no choice but to listen to all the voicemails she had thus far studiously ignored.

Before braving the furious voices of her loved ones, she needed sustenance. Conditions such as this called for comfort food. She ordered fish soup with crusty bread and a half bottle of white wine. She switched on the TV with the sound down and faced her punishment.

Her phone showed messages from Matthew, Catinca, Adrian and Gabriel. Gabriel but not Tanya? Maybe the bride-to-be was too angry to even speak.

She pressed Play.

`I'm used to you hiding behind electronic communication when you're being evasive and I was not fooled for an instant. But delaying your return by a day merited the common decency of a phone call. If not to me, then to Tanya. Passing the buck to Theo is beneath you, Old`

Thing.

With a wince, she acknowledged the truth in what Matthew said. This disappointment in his tone was painful to hear. The next message began to play.

What you playing at? We are all rolling up sleeves and mucking in to make Tanya's wedding a success. Where are you, mate? Shoulda sodding been here this morning. This is your responsibility as well as ours. Sort yourself out!

Beatrice muttered to herself. "That's the whole point. With all of you on hand, what difference does one more person make?" Then she pictured the scornful expression on Catinca's face and realised that line of argument would not wash.

Beatrice Stubbs, I cannot believe I have to make this call. Do you have any idea how awkward this is! When Will and I got married, you couldn't do enough. Now, two days before Tanya marries her dream man, you go AWOL. It's not good enough. Will is driving to the airport tomorrow and you had better be on that flight. The one that you should have been on this morning. Yes, I can read airline timetables and your flight took off and landed as scheduled. I mean it, Beatrice. This is not funny.

She took a swig of her wine and tallied up how many apologies she owed. Before the next message played, she'd already lost count.

Hello, Beatrice. This is Gabriel. I hear you're not coming back until tomorrow. Right now, Tanya is emotionally fragile. I know you think she's got enough support from family and friends. What you don't realise is how much you mean to her. You're probably busy and I understand that, but could you at least give her a `call? Oh, yeah, Luke is here and says he still loves you.`

Disappointment, anger, outrage, reproach and appeal to loyalty all had an effect, but nothing punched her in the solar plexus quite like that simple message from Luke. She swallowed the lump in her throat and blew her nose in the napkin. Her first instinct was to call Tanya. Her gaze ranged the room as she pondered what to say. Then a picture on the television caught her eye.

The twin images of Valpuri Peura and Samuel Pekkanen filled the screen. Beatrice scrabbled for the remote and turned up the volume. Her frustration reached screaming point when she couldn't recognise a single word in the newsreader's delivery. Then the image switched to a map, showing the southern coast of Finland and across the Baltic Sea, the northern coast of Estonia. The capital city of Tallinn was circled in red. Her jaw dropped open and snapped shut again as her phone rang.

"Beatrice Stubbs speaking."

"This is Sahlberg. We have new information, Ms Stubbs."

Beatrice jerked to attention. "Is this about the news? I've been watching. I couldn't understand it all but they definitely mentioned Tallinn."

"Yes, they mentioned Tallinn and repeated everything on the recording you gave me. We have a better quality audio version and a transcript in English if you would like to read. But my reason for calling is regarding the caves at Malmen. Do you have any information from your assistant?"

Beatrice took her handset from her ear and looked at the screen, although she already knew she had received nothing from Theo. "Not yet. The signal goes off and on. I'm sure he will let me know when he can."

"We interviewed another member of the Gaia Warriors this afternoon. A young woman called Tuula Sirkka. She confirms the information you have about the caves and has given us an approximate location. We are travelling there immediately."

"I want to come! I mean, sorry, please may I come with you? I'm worried about my assistant and I can do nothing to help sitting here."

Sahlberg hesitated for a second. "You can do nothing to help anyway. We are already on the road with two patrol cars and an ambulance. Stay in your hotel. This is a police matter now."

"Detective!" she squeaked, but he had already rung off. Somebody really should have a word with that man about phone etiquette.

She scrolled through recent calls and pressed a number.

An efficient voice answered instantly. "Hello, Beatrice. I saw the news."

"Me too. Astrid, the police have a rough idea of where the kids might be hidden. There are some caves in an area called Malmen. The police want me to stay in my hotel, but I'd ..."

"I'll collect you in twenty minutes. Have you got any waterproofs?"

"Thank you so much! No, not exactly. More tourist type of gear. Have you heard from Karoliina?"

"Yes. She knows. See you soon."

Twenty minutes. Long enough to make a well overdue phone call.

She was just about to press Tanya's number when somebody knocked on the door. Either Astrid had a broomstick or Beatrice had an unexpected visitor. She sidled up to the spyhole and peeked out. Nothing. Not even a view of an empty corridor. She froze. Whoever wanted access had blocked her view. Not a good sign.

Someone rapped again and her breath became shallow. She retreated to the balcony door. All she need do was hop over the little wall onto Theo's balcony and get into his room. If it was open. If he'd locked his balcony door, she was trapped, with who knows what waiting outside.

She twisted the lock and jumped as a voice came through the door. "Maintenance, Mrs Stubbs. Your air-conditioning is leaking onto the floor below. May we come in?"

She drew the curtains, eased open the door, grabbed her bag, slipped through the gap and closed the door behind her. The wind blew her hair wildly around her head as she kept her face pressed to the gap in the curtains. Inside, the room door opened and the bulk of the Nordic giant filled the doorway. With a squeak of fear, she hopped over the barrier and tried the handle of Theo's room, praying his distraction after the morning's phone call had made him careless. To her immense relief, it opened.

The man would work out where she'd gone and come after her, that much was clear. She locked the balcony door, closed the curtains and scuttled across the carpet. With great caution, she peeped out of the spyhole at the corridor.

No one there. She opened the room door silently and checked in both directions. The corridor was empty. But to get to the lifts, she had to walk past her own room. Astrid's voice echoed in her head. *Nobody uses the stairs.* She dodged out of Theo's room, round the corner and into the stairwell. Her instinct was to rush downwards, but the same would occur to any pursuer. She opted for up, taking the stairs two at a time.

Chapter 34

This was suicide. Climbing down into blackness on a metal ladder in high winds and torrential rain would be an act of wilful self-harm. Gusts of wind pushed and shoved Theo with all the force of aggressive commuters on the Central Line. He leaned against the pressure and bent his knees to keep his balance. When Aleksis uncovered the ladder, it was as if the kid had pulled a rabbit out of the hat, the solution to all their problems. Theo stared at him, incredulous, shaking his head. Sure, the metal foundation securing the thing to the rock looked sturdy enough to be trusted on a summer afternoon. Today, no way.

"No way!" he yelled at Aleksis. "I'm not going down there and you can't with a broken wrist. Give me that torch!" He crawled towards the aperture of the cave and shone the torch below, trying to make out any signs of life. The drop to the ground was around twelve metres and visibility close to zero. As far as the pathetically weak torch beam illuminated the cave, he could see nothing but dark shapes and patches of sand.

Theo beckoned Aleksis to join him and they each wrapped an arm around the metal ladder. Aleksis held the torch and Theo cupped his hands around his mouth, calling a 'hello' into the chamber below. The wind whipped his voice away as if it were a sparrow's fart. He tried again. Nothing. Then Aleksis pointed with his left hand, shining the torch with his right. Theo squinted into the gloom and spotted the glint of a plastic water bottle. It wasn't much, but it was a sign someone had recently occupied the space. Aleksis shone the torch in a semicircle around the area and they both spotted the encroaching waves at the same time. The cave was going to flood and anything down there would be swept out to sea.

Gathering all his strength, Theo focused his attention on the space below. He assessed the risks and considered the alternatives. The wind whipped his plaits so that the beads struck his face. There was no choice but to act.

"Roll down the ladder!" he shouted. "I'm going to get the bus and reverse it as close as I can. We'll attach the winch to the tow bar and I'll take the tarp down there. If I find them, you will need to drive the bus forward and winch them back up. Can you drive, Aleksis? Can you handle this bus with one arm?"

The kid's face looked like a Halloween mask. "I don't have a licence, but I think so. Yes, I think so. I'll do the ladder."

Theo left him the torch and used his tiny Maglite to illuminate the path ahead. It seemed to take twice as long to reach the minibus as it had to leave it. Once inside, he started the engine and wrenched the wheel to the right. The cliff top was rocky and rough, terrain which could be unpredictable, but less slippery and muddy than the track. Forcing the vehicle ahead until he was at a right angle to the original direction, Theo thrust it into reverse. He allowed the force of gravity to ease him closer to the cliffs, using the brake to slow his progress and twisting around to judge the distance by the reverse lights. The whole time, his hand hovered over the handbrake. Aleksis stood to one side, leaning into the wind.

Theo reversed as close as he dared. He left the bus in first gear, yanked at the handbrake and called Aleksis to take his place. The boom of the waves echoing through the caves below them tightened his nerves, but he spent precious minutes showing Aleksis exactly how he wanted him to move the vehicle.

"Avoid the track. Drive onto the rocks, the brush. If you go on the track, the wheels will get stuck and all you will do is spin mud. Keep the lights on and flash full beam on and off. We want to attract attention. Come on, first I need to get down there and judge the situation. We're going to need to communicate and there's no way you'll hear me. If I want you to drive, I'll flash my light twice. You flash back twice to show you've understood, OK?"

"I understand. The ladder is down and I packed the rucksack. Medicine, water, heat blankets, tarp, first-aid kit and Swiss Army knife." He shrugged at Theo's bewildered expression. "You never know. Please, take my gloves."

"Good thinking," agreed Theo. "Keep calling emergency services. Aleksis, listen. This is the most important thing you have ever done. Three lives depend on you."

It was time to go. Theo zipped up his rain jacket, shouldered the rucksack and stepped out into the brutal storm.

The worst part was getting onto the ladder. The rungs were slippery and Theo struggled to find his footing as the wind seemed determined to help him descend the quickest way. After the first few tentative steps, the descent got easier. He took conscious breaths and reassured himself after every move. Hand grip, foot grip, hand grip, foot grip, look down, check next rung, hand grip, foot grip. Only once did he look up and vowed not to do it again. The tiny speck of Aleksis's torchlight made him realise the depths to which he had descended. His heartbeat raced so hard he had to stop and breathe himself calmer.

His foot touched sand and he released a long shaky sigh. He pulled out his torch and scanned the immediate area, spotting the water bottle right away. What he had perceived as a lump of rock from above, he now saw was a sleeping bag. He hunched over the soggy fabric and found the opening. He pulled back the hood and saw the pale blue face of Samu Pekkanen. His breath caught and he took off his glove. Pressing his fingers on the boy's neck, he searched for signs of life. Even above the ozone and seawater, Theo could smell the kid was lying in his own waste. He closed his eyes and concentrated on calming his own breath. The pounding waves, the dervish wails of the wind and the impossibility of the task ahead of him faded into the background. He reached out a hand and laid it under Samu's ear. There, just under his index finger, a regular movement indicated a thready pulse and with a leap of optimism, he noticed long, dragging breaths as the kid's torso rose and fell.

He threw off the rucksack, wedging his torch under his armpit and located the inhaler. With one swift movement, he dragged down the zip and hauled out Samu's upper body. Like husking a corn on the cob, he drew back the waterproof, the fleece and the scarf to expose his head completely. The torch slipped and he swore. In order to administer this dose, he needed three hands. He took the Maglite in his teeth, directing the beam to Samu's face with its blue lips and closed eyes. With one decisive movement, he pressed the mouthpiece between his teeth and pumped. He waited thirty seconds and pumped again, repeating the process till he had counted ten times. Samu's condition remained the same and he slumped forward. Theo's instinct told him to leave him there, rather than lay him on his back.

For now, Samu was still alive. Theo covered him with one of the heat blankets and shone his torch at the other lumps on this spit of sand. Where was Valpuri? Surf roared in through the cave mouth, splashing as close as Samu's feet. Theo cupped his hands around his mouth once again.

"VALPURI! Where are you? Valpuri! VALPURI!"

His voice echoed around the chamber but long after it had died away, there was no reply. With a grim sigh, he got up to search. If she wasn't in the cave, there was only one other place she could have gone. He glanced out at the ocean, its power terrifying as it smashed against the cliffs, and tried not to imagine what it could do to a human body.

Chapter 35

Only one sense could be trusted. She ignored all the messages from her ears, her nose and her eyes. Her sense of taste had given up days ago. All she knew now was how to feel. She slipped in and out of consciousness and could not be sure where the rainbows came from. They started in the corner of her eyes, glittering like a kaleidoscope, like sunlight on a fjord, progressing across her vision and refracting light. Where the light came from, she had no idea. Down here, in the damp and the darkness, there were no rainbows.

Sometimes, she saw stained glass like the windows of Helsinki Cathedral. Once or twice, she saw an eye. Whose eye she couldn't be sure, but it looked like a dinosaur, or maybe a rabbit. While her eyes painted psychedelic pictures, her ears presented her with an orchestra. Carl Orff, Philip Glass, Max Richter and Markku Peltola synthesised into a composition in praise of the planet. All the instruments were forces of nature, imposing as glaziers, icebergs, volcanoes, leaving the listener feeling as insignificant as a grain of sand.

All in her mind. A fine mind, her teacher had said. A fine mind to find, no precious metals to mine, for they are not mine, these fine finds. Your daughter has a fine mind. You'll find a fine mind in Valpuri Peura. Valpuri. Valpuri. VALPURI!

Her eyes were closed yet filled with colours. The orchestra

reached yet another crescendo and there was a new note to the melody. A voice, calling her name. It wasn't Samu. He hadn't called anyone's name for hours. She curled backwards, reassuring herself of his warmth, his presence, his life. He was still there, still breathing, still warm. She relaxed and withdrew into herself, returning her attention to the rainbows.

VALPURI! The voice echoed around the cave as if Poseidon himself was standing in the cave mouth, emptying his mighty oceanic lungs to reverberate around the walls. VALPURI?

She tried to open her mouth, unsticking her lips and answered the call with all the volume of baby's cough. The effort exhausted her and she allowed her body to retract into the foetal position, willing the pretty pictures to return.

A light shone in her eyes, making her squint and recoil. Fingers pressed at her neck, parted her lips and squirted fluid into her mouth. At the same time, the ground shifted, lifting her and Samu, still curled together like sea-horses, a few centimetres higher. Poseidon had sent his waves to take them home.

Chapter 36

In the ladies' changing rooms in the hotel gym on the tenth floor, Beatrice sat in a shower cubicle, sending a message to Astrid. No one else was using the pool or the machines but her ears were alert to the sounds of anyone entering the facility. Astrid did not respond, probably because she was on her motorbike. Beatrice got to her feet, unable to sit still and paced around the pool, keeping an eye on the door.

The ring of her telephone made her jump. An incoming call from Karoliina and several other notifications.

"Hello, Karoliina?" She could offer no other conversation opener without giving herself away. She yanked out her headphones so she could talk and simultaneously check if anything had come through from Theo.

"Hello, Beatrice, I'm on my way back from Kolkko. I'm receiving contradictory reports on the latest developments. Do you know where the missing teenagers are and if they are OK?"

Beatrice acknowledged the fact that Karoliina's first concern was for Valpuri and Samu, a point in her favour. "We think we know where they are but have no information as to their state of health. I'm soon heading towards the suspected location."

There was silence at the end of the line until Karoliina stated, "Which is not in Estonia."

"No. I'm afraid the organised crime syndicate in Tallinn story was a smokescreen to flush out an informant." She hesitated, unsure what more to say.

Karoliina had no such qualms. "That is why my husband is currently being questioned by the Helsinki police, yes?"

A text message appeared from Theo. She opened it and scanned the contents. It contained a geographical location and exhorted her to call emergency services. It was essential Sahlberg have this information now.

"Karoliina, I'm afraid I have to go but I will keep you informed as to all developments regarding the young people. Everything else will have to wait. Goodbye."

She forwarded Theo's message to the detective and called him to ensure he'd received it.

"Thank you, Ms Stubbs. That is a big help. We are around ten minutes away. Everyone … is doing their best."

Beatrice recognised how Sahlberg had ducked a reassuring platitude, remembering who he was talking to. 'Everyone will be OK' was a phrase Beatrice was unlikely to swallow. But everyone doing their best was all she could hope for.

She ended the call without telling him her immediate intentions and saw a tall figure silhouetted in the doorway of the gym. Her breath caught for a second until she saw the figure was carrying motorcycle helmets.

Astrid strode towards her, dressed in leathers and carrying a bag. Beatrice wasn't wild about motorcycle riding at the best of times, leave alone in weather with ambitions to a hurricane.

"Come, put this on and let's go."

"Is it safe?"

Astrid's green eyes met hers. "The hotel or the bike? I don't know. We'll wear our helmets in the lift so no one will recognise you. As for the weather, these are not ideal driving conditions, but I've seen worse. Do you need a hand?"

Beatrice was struggling to put on the one-piece waterproof bodysuit. The width was sufficient but the length was ridiculous.

The crotch came to halfway up her legs and her feet reached as far as the knees. Astrid stood behind her and heaved the garment up, as if it were a toddler's nappy. By the time she found the elasticated ankle holes, the legs were concertinaed like an accordion. Her reflection in the gym mirrors looked like a small child in a dinosaur costume.

Zipping up the neck, Astrid gave an apologetic smile. "We're not exactly the same size, but at least you'll be dry."

"I understand the Malmen area is around half an hour's drive from Helsinki. At least, that's how long it would take in normal weather. As a local expert, what's our ETA?"

The young woman lifted her shoulders to her ears. "We don't know exactly where we're going. The weather conditions are unpredictable. The short answer is I have no idea."

"We do know where we're going, actually." She showed Astrid the text.

"OK. Everything depends on the state of the roads. Listen, the most important thing to keep us safe on the road is to relax. Counter-intuitive, I know, but you lean with me and don't tense up. Let's go."

Tensing, leaning or any other kind of normal movement was hard to imagine in her outfit, but she wedged on her helmet and waddled after Astrid to the lifts.

The idea of white nights had long since disappeared from the sky and relentless swirls of rain came in from the coast. Within seconds of leaving the lobby, her helmet fogged up and she could barely see the neon stripes on Astrid's biker gear as she led the way to the large motorcycle.

"Zip up your jacket to the top and put on your gloves," Astrid commanded.

Beatrice did as she was told and struggled to get astride the pillion. Astrid took her wrists and pulled them around her own waist. Beatrice shuffled closer, using Astrid's back as a windbreak. The engine powered up and they took off into the storm.

Just relax, lean with her, don't tense up, she reminded herself and made a determined effort to breathe deeply. The bike moved through the city streets at an unhurried pace, weaving slightly when a gust of wind hit them broadsides. Astrid leaned from side to side as they took the corners, almost part of the machine. With surprising speed, Beatrice learned to copy her. The danger from the rain and wind was their inconsistency. One minute it would die down to a showery breeze then assault them with a physical force. Water crept its way down her neck but the constant speed of the bike cleared her visor, so she could see where they were going.

She noticed Astrid tried to avoid stopping at traffic lights, slowing long before a stop signal and keeping momentum as soon as it changed. It made sense. A stationary bike would be harder and heavier to hold upright. Once out of the suburbs, they crossed a bridge, one of the most terrifying experiences of Beatrice's life. Relaxing was nigh on impossible. She almost screamed when Astrid overtook a truck and after they had passed the vehicle, a wall of water attacked from the sea. Astrid navigated with a diagonal lean, cutting through the wave at speed. They were both dripping wet and the seat was slippery.

She clung to her driver and echoed her every move apart from the knee thing. When the gale knocked them off course, Astrid would use her knee like a sail, catching the airstream to pull them upright. Beatrice judged it better to leave such manoeuvres to the expert.

Through the next stretch of urbanisation, apartment blocks shielded them from the wind and the tension in Beatrice's body reduced from all-out panic to manageable fear for her life. They faced the next challenge when crossing the bridge to Malmen. Beatrice was shivering with cold and anticipation. On seeing waves pounding the span, all energy and hope drained from her.

She closed her eyes and trusted her body to move with Astrid, to move with the bike and keep them going forward.

This bridge was much shorter and traffic was down to one lane in each direction. Cars and buses created a pattern of brake lights as they inched across, stopping and starting. To Beatrice's horror, she realised they would have to come to a halt and somehow try keeping 500lbs of machinery from falling over and crushing them. She glanced down at her wet legs and walking boots, convinced she would be unable to manage it.

Astrid spurred the bike forwards and to Beatrice's amazement, slid the beast past the waiting vehicles, maintaining momentum as she followed the white lines. The traffic offered them some protection against the pounding ocean and they reached the other side only marginally wetter than before. She indicated and pulled off the main road towards a place called Sarvvik. The landscape turned black and featureless with few signs of life.

After rumbling along a country lane for a few minutes, Beatrice spotted flashing lights. Astrid guided the bike down the turning to the golf course and parked up behind the building. Beatrice released her and got off, her legs wobbling as if she'd run a marathon.

She lifted her visor. "You are amazing!"

Astrid took off her helmet and tugged her scarf up to protect her ears. "You did pretty well yourself. What now?"

"Let's go and see what's going on."

Chapter 37

Any hope of the storm subsiding was long forgotten. The waves raced closer and wilder, making a mockery of Theo's feeble efforts to drag the sleeping bag containing Samu and Valpuri out of their reach. The tide was coming in at a pace he could never outrun. By his own calculations, he had fewer than ten minutes before the cave flooded completely. Once the raging sea entered the space, everything within it would be battered against the rocks. As he worked on dragging the tarpaulin from his rucksack, the waves rushed at his ankles, threatening, teasing, relentless.

The tarp was only strong enough to take one, even in perfect conditions. The odds against any one of them getting out of the cave looked grim. With an inexperienced driver at the wheel of the minibus, lethal winds and communication between him and Aleksis almost negligible, it was clear this could never work. He had to make a choice.

Option one was to risk someone's life by placing one of them in the tarpaulin and flashing his torch at the surface. In the unlikely event Aleksis could winch one body to the surface, by the time the winch returned, the other two would have drowned. Valpuri was delirious and incapable of taking instructions, yet occasionally violently active. She had lashed out at him when he tried to give her fluid. There was an alternative: leave them both here and try to scramble up the ladder before the waves took him down with them.

A voice echoed around his head. *Not your fight, mate. Get out and save yourself. You did what you could. No time for heroics.* In that instant, Theo retreated from it all, shutting out the terrifying booms of the encroaching surf, the tortured screams of the wind and his own panicky breath. He turned his attention inwards and pressed two fingers between his brows. *What do I do?* The answer came before he had even completed the thought. *Use your strength.*

He whipped around and caught hold of the sleeping bag before the waves made yet another attempt to snatch it. He unzipped it, rolled Samu out and onto the tarpaulin, clipped it onto the winch and lifted his head to the gap high above. He fumbled with his Maglite and pressed the light twice. Nothing happened. He tried again, suppressing his panic. No response. Where the hell was Aleksis? There was not enough time for Theo to climb to the surface and drive the minibus himself. He looked behind him to see the curled form of Valpuri washing out to sea. With a violent curse, he splashed after her and grabbed the hood of her fleece. He carried her in a fireman's lift back to the aperture and faced the fact he could not save both these people. He wasn't even sure he could save himself.

A bitter sob escaped him and he placed a hand on the first rung of the metal ladder. The extra weight of the girl across his shoulder made every step agonising and he constantly adjusted his balance. After four heaves upward, a grinding sound forced him to halt. With small jerky movements, the winch dragged the tarpaulin towards the surface. Its progress was painfully slow and its cargo swung in the air like a body of a hanged man. Aleksis had followed instructions and a comatose Samu was out of the sea's reach. Just. Theo released a long ragged breath and continued his progress. Hand up, foot up, change grasp on Valpuri's jeans, hand up, foot up.

They were on the final third of the ascent when Theo spotted the approaching disaster. As the winch dragged the tarpaulin higher, the wind and gravity began to swing Samu's cradle in a wider and wider arc. Each time it swung left, it came a few centimetres closer to the metal ladder. At its current trajectory, in another three steps it would hit them. If he stopped where he was, carrying the limp body of Valpuri Peura, the heavily laden tarpaulin would hit the metal ladder instead of them. Whether that would cause enough damage to knock them from their precarious perch into the roiling sea below, Theo could only guess. His only other option was to climb faster, at the risk of losing his grip on the ladder or on Valpuri. Even if he could escape a direct blow, the tarpaulin would smash into the ladder, potentially tearing it from its foundations.

He stopped, staring at the imminent threat as if it were the blade of a guillotine. His body screamed in protest; the tendons in his forearms burned, the pain in his shoulders and neck transformed his muscles into lumps of concrete and his exhausted thighs trembled like a weightlifter. All he could do was wrap one arm, knee and ankle around the ladder and hope he could hold on.

The tarp swung closer, black, malevolent and merciless. On this sweep, it reached an arm's breadth from the ladder, scraping against the cave wall. Theo cringed, only too aware that there was only one layer of canvas and heat blanket between unforgiving stone and a fragile human body. He clutched his arm tighter around Valpuri's legs, repeating the same words over and over again.

"I won't let you go. I won't let you go. I won't let you go."

The tarp reached its opposite peak and began its lethal return journey. Theo wanted to close his eyes but forced himself to stare at their nemesis, an unstoppable natural force.

And then it halted. The tarp dropped around two metres, no longer swinging from side to side but spinning in a slow rotation. The winch held solid but immobile, leaving Samu in mid-air. Fear and adrenalin pulsed through Theo's body and although he wanted to cry with relief, it wasn't over yet. He unwound himself from his defensive position and continued his slow, torturous climb.

Water shot up in a jet to his left and Theo saw the cave had now flooded, forcing surf into a spout beside them. The furious sea extended one last vengeful finger to try and claim them as its own. Six rungs left and he would be at the surface. He would carry Valpuri to the minivan, take over from Aleksis and winch Samu to the surface. This could still be OK. Six more rungs. His grip was slippery as every part of his body was soaked by sweat, rain, seawater and tears.

Sudden illumination shone into the blackness. Torches, voices and flashing blue lights told him the cavalry had arrived. Hand up, foot up, change grip, hand up, foot up, hands grasping his armpits, hands lifting the girl's weight from his shoulder, hands easing him onto solid ground, voices saying things he couldn't understand. His body began trembling to an extent he could not control. But it wasn't over. He had to get to the minibus. The cave was flooding and Samu was still dangling over the waves, fragile as a canary in a cage.

Chapter 38

If there was one thing Beatrice hated, it was being relegated to the role of bystander. She wasn't wild about being on the front line either, but at least she had a better view. She stood beside Astrid, holding her helmet and drawing her hood up against the rain, trying to make sense of what was happening around her. Huddles of people were sharing information and officers in wet weather clothing ran in various directions. Much as she wanted to stamp her metaphorical foot, she had no jurisdiction here and simply had to wait.

Detective Sahlberg spotted her and did a double take. He held up a hand as if to say he would be with her in a moment. Mollified, she waited until the man had done his job. He finished his conversation and marched towards her, his face thunderous. A series of shouts drew all heads towards a spot further down the coast. Faintly, but unmistakably, a vehicle was flashing its lights. Emergency staff scrambled to their respective vehicles and Sahlberg pointed towards a plain sedan, motioning for Beatrice and Astrid to get in. She didn't need asking twice, beyond relieved to escape the driving needles of constant rain.

The police vehicles crawled along the tracks towards the flashing lights at a pace Beatrice found intolerable yet understood. Screeching in there like the Dukes of Hazzard could potentially endanger whoever was calling for help. She checked her phone one more time with every expectation of no news from Theo. She was right.

Sahlberg's car pulled in behind the semicircle of vehicles surrounding a rundown-looking minibus, whose lights were no longer flashing. Two uniforms were speaking to a person in the driver seat. He or she was invisible to Beatrice as the bus's headlights remained on full beam. She reached for the door handle, impatient to know what was going on. Sahlberg looked over his shoulder and shook his head.

"No. You two can't go out here until we assess the situation. Too risky. Sorry, but I have to keep everyone safe. Stay in the car, please." He zipped up his waterproof jacket and heaved open his door. Beatrice squinted through the rain, trying to guess what was going on. Thankfully, Sahlberg's driver kept the wipers going at full speed, clearing a view of the scene.

Sahlberg and one of the uniformed officers helped a slight-framed person from the driver seat and the other uniform took his place. A flurry of activity erupted, paramedics and police personnel making their way cautiously but with purpose towards the cliff edge. Leaning as far as she could, Beatrice peered into the confusion, willing Theo to make an appearance. Eventually her frustration got the better of her and she opened the door. Instantly, the wind blew it shut. The driver raised his eyes to the mirror.

"Detective Sahlberg said you stay here. You must stay." With the touch of his finger he locked the doors.

She clenched her fists but would not, could not argue. Then into the police headlights strode Sahlberg. He and the driver exchanged a sharp conversation through the wind, Sahlberg indicating towards the bus behind them. The driver unlocked the doors and got out. Beatrice watched as he struggled against the wind and climbed into the driver's seat of the minibus.

"What were they saying?" she asked Astrid.

"The bus has a winch and someone's on the other end. They

need an experienced driver to pull it out of the cave."

Sahlberg gave the driver the thumbs-up, who dipped the headlights and moved the bus forward, just a short way, then paused as if awaiting feedback. Sahlberg spoke into his police radio and guided the driver forward with slow movements of his hand. Two medics ran past to the left of Beatrice, carrying a stretcher. Her curiosity would wait no longer. She exited the car, holding on to the door as if her life depended on it, then let Nature slam it shut with enough force to rattle teeth.

Never in her life had she experienced winds so forceful it felt she was being physically punched. Afraid of losing her balance, she squatted against the patrol car and reconsidered her plan of moving closer to the cliff edge. Until she saw Theo.

Paramedics were hunched over two people; one inert, one protesting and gesticulating towards the cliff edge. She scuttled across the brush and rocks, her footing unsteady, but her focus on her injured assistant. Was the other teenager on the end of the winch?

Before she could get close enough, a police officer blocked her path.

She protested, yelling. "I need to speak to Theo! I'm his boss!" but the man shook his head and directed her backwards. She retreated to stand beside Astrid, followed by the first group of paramedics carrying someone whose body, but thankfully not head, was covered in a silver sheet. Another pair of uniforms guided Theo in the opposite direction. Beatrice crouched behind the ambulance, protecting herself from the wind. Nothing made any sense until she saw half a dozen officers forming a human chain as the bus winched something the shape of a walrus out of the cave and onto the cliffs above.

Paramedics and police officers battled the weather, leaning against the wind and struggling towards the package at the end of the winch. The cluster of high-vis jackets blocked Beatrice's perspective entirely. She released an unladylike curse and stood up, coming face to face with Theo.

They stared at each other for a moment, both blinking against the wind and rain lashing their faces. A burly man in paramedic's gear tried to move him on but Beatrice ran into their path, throwing her arms around Theo's neck.

"Are you hurt? I was so worried! What happened? No one is telling me anything and it's driving me mad. Theo, are you all right?"

He reached up a hand to clasp her wrist. "I think so. It was pretty bloody dodgy but I managed to get Valpuri out. Beatrice, find out what's happening with Samu. I have to go in the ambulance, but I can't rest until I know Samu is OK. Will you let me know? Please?"

"Of course I will. Go, get treatment, get better and I'll join you as soon as I can. Go, Theo, you're an absolute hero."

He succumbed to the insistence of the officer, who guided him into the back of the ambulance. The paramedics slammed the doors. She watched the flashing lights creep in the direction of the main road, wiping away the water on her face, unsure if it was spray or tears.

It was one in the morning when one of the doctors came to find her. She couldn't cope with sitting in the relatives' room with Samu's mother and the Peura family, so found herself a cushioned bench in another corridor while she waited for news.

"Excuse me, are you with Mr Theo Wolfe?"

Beatrice's eyes opened like lighthouse shutters. She hadn't even realised she'd fallen asleep.

"Yes, he's my assistant. Can he fly?" She opened her mouth and shut it again, confused by her own question. "Sorry, I mean is he fine?"

The doctor gave her an uncertain smile. "Yes, he is fine. He needs rest and fluids for twenty-four hours but we can release him on Saturday morning."

"Saturday? That's too ..." Beatrice swallowed and closed her eyes. "Can I see him?"

"You can visit Mr Wolfe tomorrow. I mean, later today. Visitors' hours are from ten till twelve. I must go now."

"Doctor, just one more thing. Theo was involved in an incident with Valpuri Peura and Samu Pekkanen. I'm not a relative but can you give me any information as to their state of health? I promise you I'm not a journalist! And neither is Theo."

The doctor rubbed her nose, a weary gesture. "I understand, but this is a police investigation. I have instructions to update you on the situation regarding Mr Wolfe. That is all. The doctor treating those young people has already spoken to the family. If you want to know their state of health, it's better if you ask them."

"I can inform you on that topic." Sahlberg stepped out from behind a coffee machine.

The doctor took the opportunity to escape, a look of relief crossing her face.

Sahlberg's face was weary and his clothes crumpled after the evening's drama, but the haunted expression he'd worn since the first time they met was absent. He hitched up his trousers and sat beside her. "Samu Pekkanen is on a ventilator to assist his breathing. He is out of danger although further tests will be required to ascertain whether the attacks caused any permanent damage. Valpuri Peura is responding well to treatment for dehydration and minor injuries. She will stay under supervision for the next couple of days and go home at the weekend."

"Thank you. I'm so relieved you found them."

"Correction: we found them. Your advice was helpful and without Mr Wolfe, things would have been very different. You should get some rest. As I understand it, you plan to return to the UK at lunchtime. I will need to take a full statement from you and your colleague. Perhaps we could do that later this morning?" He looked at his watch. "Let's say eight o'clock and afterwards a driver will take you directly to the airport."

"That would be ideal, but I'm not sure the hospital will release Theo so early. They told me they need to keep him in for twenty-four hours."

Sahlberg yawned and stood up. "Come back here for eight am. We can complete the formalities and I will make sure you both catch your flight and get out of the country."

He made it sound like they were being deported. "That's very kind of you. But I'd rather not go back to the hotel. You see, I think someone is following me." She explained the sightings of the big blond and how he had entered her room.

Sahlberg's concentration snapped into focus. He found something on his phone and showed it to her. "Did he look like this?"

It was the same man, in a black and white still from a video camera. "That's him!"

"He's also the one we've been looking for in connection with the murder of Juppo Seppä. The fact he is following you does not make me happy. I will arrange a hotel room somewhere else and send an officer to collect your suitcases."

"Thank you, Detective Sahlberg. You are very kind."

"Efficient, that's all. Goodnight."

Chapter 39

Yet again, the ring tone on her phone kicked off a good hour before her alarm. After four hours' sleep, Beatrice's mind was mush. She scrabbled for her glasses so she could read the name on the screen.

"Hello, Astrid, is everything all right?"

"Yes, perfectly fine. I just arrived at the office and wanted to check on you and your friends."

Beatrice scrunched up her eyes in disbelief. Arriving at the office at seven am? She gave a précis of what Sahlberg had said and thanked her again for going above and beyond the call of duty.

"I can't say it was a pleasure," Astrid replied, "but you did offer me an opportunity to do some good. Thank you and I wish you a safe trip home."

"What about you? Can you collect your bike today?"

"Yes. Karoliina's driver is taking me out to Malmen this morning. Look at the weather. It's a lovely day for a ride."

When Astrid rang off, Beatrice padded across the carpet to look out of the window of the budget hotel window. Helsinki's innocent blue skies and glorious sunshine could fool a person into believing the previous day's weather tantrum had been nothing more than a dream. If the storm had passed, there should be no impediment to her and Theo flying back to

London. A fact which would please Detective Sahlberg just as much as them.

To Beatrice's great annoyance, there was an infestation of journalists outside the hospital. Bristling with microphones and cameras, they scuttled across the visitors' car park to accost her the moment she got out of her taxi. There was no question of making a graceful dash through the automatic doors, head bowed, muttering no comment, because she had to help the taxi driver lug two suitcases from the boot.

When she finally got inside the building, the first person she saw was Sahlberg, looking pointedly at his watch.

"You try battling your way through a forest of microphones and cameras while people yell questions at your face!" she snapped.

He gave her an incredulous look. "I did."

"While carrying two suitcases?"

He did not reply but signalled to a uniformed female officer who took charge of Beatrice's luggage. Then he strode away down the corridor in the direction of Accident and Emergency. Beatrice gave the back of his head an evil stare but fell into step behind him.

Theo was awake when they entered the room and greeted her with a huge smile. Forgetting her professional pose in front of Sahlberg, she ran across the room to clasp his hands and kiss his cheek.

"How are you? Where does it hurt? Is anything broken?"

"The X-rays show no broken bones, just severely strained muscles. I had my breakfast two hours ago and now I'm keen to get out of here. What's the news on the kids?"

Beatrice looked to Sahlberg.

"Samu is conscious and the medical team believe he will make a full recovery. Valpuri is still weak but will be released tomorrow. Your doctor tells me you are doing well enough to be discharged. Once we take your statements, I will escort you and Ms Stubbs to the airport to catch a flight to London."

Theo let out a deep sigh and closed his eyes. Then he opened them and fixed Sahlberg with a serious expression. "What about Aleksis? What happens to him?"

"This is why I need your statement. Risto Vanhanen and Ursula Saari have been charged with abduction and obstruction of justice. We believe Aleksis and Tuula were manipulated by the older couple and do not wish to place them under arrest. Your testimony will be essential in proving their true intentions. Are you willing to give a statement?"

"Of course. Let's do it."

A knock at the door preceded the entrance of the police woman who had taken charge of their luggage.

"This is my colleague, Officer Halme. Could we begin? I will need to speak to you individually. Ms Stubbs, would you wait outside when I speak to Mr Wolfe?"

"Yes of course. I'll go and get some breakfast." She kissed Theo's cheek and squeezed his hand. "I'm going to be the first to say this before you get tired of hearing it. You, Theo Wolfe, are a bloody hero."

Theo shook his head, his eyes staring at the bed sheet.

"And what's more," added Beatrice. "I have excellent taste in assistants. Back in a bit."

She left the room, casting a snotty look at Sahlberg, and went in search of the canteen.

It was an uncomfortable feeling being on the other side of the table, even though it wasn't a police interrogation room, but a corner of the nurses' station. While she answered all Sahlberg's questions as truthfully as she could, she knew exactly how the detective was watching her for nervous tics with all the intensity of a poker player. Just as she would have done if she were in his shoes. When he finished testing all aspects of her story, he escorted her to the waiting room and reunited her with Theo.

The patient was now showered and dressed but all semblance of normality fell away when he stood up, pain contorting his face. Beatrice offered him her hand. He took it and gave her a reassuring squeeze.

"I'm all right. Really. You should have seen the state of me after the London Marathon."

Officer Halme materialised at his side with their luggage and a wheelchair. She quelled Theo's resistance with a brisk shake of her head. "The doctor discharges you on the condition you use a chair. Please, Mr Wolfe. Think how much easier boarding your flight will be. This way, it's better for all of us."

The slight blush in the woman's cheeks did not escape Beatrice's notice. Women simply fell at Theo's feet. How was it possible he was still single?

He capitulated and allowed the officer to guide him into the chair. Halme took the suitcases, Sahlberg steered Theo's chair and Beatrice was left to trot alongside. They were waiting for the lift when a female voice called out.

"Theo! Wait!"

They turned to see another wheelchair speeding in their direction, propelled by a large blonde Goth. In the chair sat a skinny little wraith wrapped in blankets. The police officers tensed and both adopted an alert stance. The Goth skidded to a halt right in front of Theo, her eyes shining.

"Valpuri wants to say thank you," she said.

Beatrice's jaw dropped as she realised the scrawny creature in the wheelchair was one of the reasons that brought her to Finland. Valpuri Peura, if not exactly in the best of health, was alive and sitting right in front of them. Her appearance was wretched, gaunt and bruised, exacerbated by tears streaming down her cheeks as she stared at Theo. She blinked and swallowed but could not seem to express words. The Goth girl, who fitted Theo's description of Tuula, reversed and manoeuvred so the two chairs sat side by side. The lift doors opened and closed, but no one moved.

Valpuri swiped at her face with both hands and attempted to speak. She only managed one word.

"You ..."

Her face collapsed and her chest heaved. Tuula placed both hands on her shoulders.

To Beatrice's astonishment, Theo was crying too. He twisted sideways and reached out to hold the girl, who wrapped her arms around him in a fierce embrace. Moments passed while they hugged each other. In a subtle move, Beatrice withdrew a packet of tissues from her pocket and handed one to Tuula and another to Officer Halme. She even offered one to Sahlberg, who refused but with a gentle smile. Moments passed and the lift opened again, releasing nurses with an empty trolley bed.

Theo broke the embrace and gave Beatrice a red-eyed signal. She hit the button to hold the lift. They shuffled into the elevator and Tuula and Valpuri's gazes stayed on them until the doors closed.

No one spoke on the descent to the ground floor. Sahlberg and Theo were behind Officer Halme and Beatrice, who both faced the door. A ping announced their arrival and the doors peeled back. Standing outside was a huge man with a blond ponytail. They stared at each other for a frozen second, then Beatrice recovered herself.

She pointed at the man. "There he is!" she yelled, at the same time Officer Halme shouted something in Finnish.

The big man took off across the hospital foyer, covering the distance at considerable speed, Sahlberg and Halme hot on his heels. People stared at the pursuit, simply standing back out of the way. Sahlberg shouted something and withdrew his weapon. Just then, two orderlies ran into the fleeing man's path, tackling him around the legs and neck. He ejected the one from his back but the leg-tackler toppled him off balance, bringing him to the tiled floor with a painful crash.

By the time Beatrice had wheeled Theo close enough to see past the crowd, the police had got the man in cuffs and were heaving him to his feet. The captured giant didn't say a word but looked around the crowd until he spotted Beatrice. He stared at her until two more officers took him outside and eased him into a patrol car.

Sahlberg came over to join them. "That was the man who was following you?" he asked.

"Yes. The one who was in my room. I'm 100% sure."

"Officer Halme will escort him to the police station and later today, he and I are going to have a very interesting conversation."

"What was he doing here?" asked Theo.

Sahlberg collected the cases and led them outside. "I can't say for sure, but it seems he was following Ms Stubbs. It's a very good thing that I can make sure you get safely to the airport."

Beatrice had to agree.

Chapter 40

What better reception committee than DI William Quinn? Practical and understanding, he took control of the wheelchair at Heathrow Arrivals Hall and in under half an hour, bundled them both into Gabriel's Land Rover. The rear had been converted into a comfortable double bed with the use of yoga mats, a duvet, fresh pillows and a flask of tea. Theo allowed Will to pick him up and carry him inside without a single complaint. Will secured the cases onto the roof rack and they headed down the M4.

"The flight was right on time, I see," he observed. "Just like yesterday's."

She shot him a wary look.

"Don't worry, we haven't told anyone else it wasn't cancelled by the storm."

She waited until they had passed Heston Services and checked Theo was asleep before she asked the inevitable question. "How much trouble am I in?"

Will shot her a quick half-smile and returned his attention to the road. "You'll have to do a whole lot of penance for this one. Blame the storm for the delay and make a whole lot of effort with Tanya. She's hurt, Beatrice, and you have to take responsibility for that. The best way of pouring oil on troubled waters is to play up your success. You found those kids and saved two lives."

"I didn't. That was all Theo."

Will exhaled sharply. "Award the badges some other time. Concentrate on what's important to Tanya, Gabriel, Luke and Matthew. Seriously, Beatrice, you must pay attention to the family and notice the details. Nothing is more important."

Chastened, Beatrice said nothing for several miles.

"I'm sorry. I know you're not asking for an apology, but I apologise anyway. Catinca and Adrian will yell and shout and shame me, and I am prepared for that. The ones I really feel I've disappointed are Tanya and Gabriel. I'll do everything I can to make up for my absence."

Will gave her a strange look. "Don't compensate for your absence, Beatrice. Instead, be present. As coppers, we're trained to observe, read between the lines and work out what's going on. You can't do that when you're not there. Your family and your friends depend on you. I know this will hurt you and I'm sorry I have to say it. Frankly, you're letting them down. Stop being selective and self-indulgent. Let other people sort out their own problems. Direct your intelligence where it's most effective. Be present."

She had no answer to that.

"Do you mind if I listen to the news?" Will asked. "Just want to catch up on the football scores. You can have a nap if you like. I'll make sure we'll make it to the wedding rehearsal by six."

Beatrice turned her face to the window, wearied to her bones by yet another confrontation with reality. "Of course you can listen to the news or the football or whatever you like. I'm going to rest my eyes for a few minutes."

She closed her eyes and girded herself to commence battle with her most fearful opponent.

Voices woke her from a light doze. Or at least she thought it had been light, until she saw signs for Upton St Nicholas. Apparently she had been asleep for over three hours. She rubbed her hands over her face and straightened. Theo was sitting cross-legged behind their seats, a blanket over his shoulders and a cup of tea between his hands.

"And she's back in the room," said Theo. "Do you want some tea? I saved you a cup."

She stretched her arms to the roof of the Land Rover and yawned. "We're almost home now. I'll wait for a fresh brew with Matthew. How are you feeling?"

"Better. I was just saying to Will, I think I might skip the wedding rehearsal tonight so I'll be fit for the ceremony tomorrow."

"Good idea. I'm sure we have something wholesome and restorative in the fridge. Then while we are out, you can kick back and relax on the sofa."

Theo didn't respond for a second and Will's voice filled the gap. "No need for that. We booked Theo a room at The Angel. That way, he can join us if he feels like it, or stay in his room if he doesn't. You and Matthew should have some time alone. I'll drop you off and take Theo to the pub."

Beatrice looked at her watch. "If that suits you, Theo, it's fine with me. We only have an hour and a half before we are supposed to be at rehearsal. Will, you're incredibly good to come and fetch us and deal with all the fallout while I was gone. You're the calm before the storm. I fully expect to get a severe tongue lashing from Adrian and Catinca. Worst of all, I'm dreading what Tanya has to say."

Will pulled up onto the little forecourt in front of the cottage and got out to unstrap Beatrice's case. Before Beatrice could undo her seatbelt, Theo placed a hand on her shoulder.

"Can you not tell anyone what happened? Not yet. I need time to process this."

"Oh. If you want. But people really should know what a heroic thing you did."

To her surprise, Theo shook his head. "I'm no hero. Don't ask me why 'cos I can't talk about it. Just don't tell anyone. Make out we helped the police. OK?"

"If that's what you want. You take care and I'll see you later." She patted his hand.

Matthew opened the door and Huggy Bear hared out to meet them, bouncing on her back legs, tail wagging. Beatrice made a fuss of the dog and embraced Matthew. Will took her suitcase into the hallway, gave her a hug and got back in the vehicle. She blew a kiss at Theo as the vehicle crunched back into the lane.

She faced Matthew once again, relieved to see his smile. "We need to talk, but perhaps tomorrow. I'm cutting it fine, I know that. Are you all right? Are you prepared?"

"It's good to see you, Old Thing. We are all in fine form, thanks to William Quinn. He's been an absolute brick, you know. Shall we have a pot of tea before bedecking ourselves in all our finery?" He picked up her suitcase and took it up the stairs.

"Good plan. I'll put the kettle on. Do we have to do get all gussied up this evening? It's only a rehearsal and a pub dinner." Dumpling prowled into the hallway, wound himself around Beatrice's legs and led her into the kitchen. She followed, to find Huggy Bear sitting in her basket next to the Aga, gnawing on a chew. She boiled the kettle, made the tea and sat sifting through her post while she waited for Matthew to return. After a while, she stood up and cocked her head to listen. What earth was he doing up there?

She checked his office and the living room, then trudged up the stairs to see if he had answered a call of nature. When she got to the landing, Matthew was standing there, her suitcase at his feet.

"Matthew? What is it?"

His head rotated slowly to face her. "Which room?" he asked. "Where should put this bag?" He indicated the suitcase with an expression of complete bewilderment.

She looked into his eyes, wondering if this was some sort of passive aggressive rebuke. But Matthew didn't do passive aggressive and not much in the way of rebukes. "It's my bag so it belongs in our room. Where else?" She pointed at the door of their bedroom, took the case and shoved it just inside the door. "Come downstairs now, your tea is getting cold."

"Righty ho. Nothing worse than cold tea."

The car park of The Angel was crowded so Matthew parked the Volkswagen on the other side of the village green. As Beatrice got out of the car, she could already see the marquee was filled with people, most of whom would be absolutely furious with her. She hesitated, fighting the urge to get back in the car and run away. Matthew scooped up her hand and pulled her towards him, placing a kiss on her cheek.

"I'm jolly glad you made it," he said. "Will and Adrian have been absolutely marvellous but I really don't think I could do this on my own."

Beatrice squeezed his hand and pressed her head against his shoulder. "Come on, Prof, let's face the music." They made their way over a wooden walkway towards the marquee, hand in hand, admiring the solar powered lights guiding their path. The entrance was framed by an archway of greenery and they paused, ostensibly to admire the florist's skill, but more realistically to gather their strength. She looked up at Matthew and was about to quote Julius Caesar when a small boy hurtled across the parquet floor and launched himself at Beatrice.

Luke's arms encircled her waist and administered a crushing hug. "Beatrice! Where have you been? Hello, Granddad. Didn't you bring Huggy Bear? They said you were trapped in a storm in Finland and it was really dangerous. Where is Theo? You know Will's been helping me and Granddad with our speech. I can't tell you what it's about, because it has to be a surprise, but I promise you it's gonna be really, really good. Not even Mum knows what we going to say, do you, Mum?"

Beatrice looked up to see Tanya approaching, her face unreadable. It seemed all activity in the marquee ceased and every head turned in their direction.

She held out her arms and Beatrice enfolded her into a hug. Neither spoke for a moment until Tanya whispered, "I'm so glad you're home." Then she released her and placed her hands on her hips. "About bloody time!"

"Mum!" Luke gasped. "You swore!"

"Sorry about that but she deserves it. Right, woman, get into position. Dad, you're over here with me. Luke, what are you doing? You can't sit with Beatrice. You *know* why, the best man has to be at the front. Go stand by Gabe, like a good boy. Marianne, round up the bridesmaids, will you? Mum, leave those decorations alone or I swear I'll set Catinca on you."

When the rehearsal party entered the function room at The Angel, it was filled with the scent of flowers, all prepared for tomorrow's reception. Beatrice found herself taking huge inhalations as she took her seat at the table. She made sure to greet all those she had so far missed and wedged herself between Adrian and Catinca. She pacified Luke with a place directly opposite her. Adrian announced their plans to holiday in Devon for the following week and Beatrice promptly invited them to dinner on Tuesday.

The party ate mushroom risotto with olive ciabatta and drank a light Pinot Noir. Tanya was taking no chances with stomach upsets before the big day. Catinca and Adrian satisfied themselves with her apologies and did not subject her to a lecture. Just as dessert – ginger and pear sorbet – was served, the door opened and Theo limped in. Reactions to his arrival were positive, but not the standing ovation of a returning hero. Questions as to his physical state were easily deflected by Beatrice's vague statement that he'd been 'overdoing' it. He gave her a grateful smile. Catinca found him a chair next to her. He joined in the dessert, refused the wine and ingratiated himself with Adrian by admiring his shirt.

Beatrice left her place to mingle with the other guests. She shared a joke with Pam about escaping the hen night, chatted to Gabriel and his mother, complimented Marianne on the results of her diet and eavesdropped on Matthew's conversation with Gordon, the landlord. At ten o'clock, people started making moves to leave. She said her goodbyes, passed Theo talking to Marianne and gave him an extra squeeze on his shoulder on the way out. Tanya stayed behind to say one last farewell to Gabriel and then joined her, Matthew and Luke to walk back to the cottage.

Tanya sniffed. "Next time I see him will be when I walk up the aisle. I can't believe this is finally happening. Me, getting married!" She linked arms with Beatrice. "I'm so happy I could float off like a balloon," she said, looking up at the night sky glittering with stars.

"Very traditional of you to spend the night before apart, but I'm glad because you'll be with us," said Matthew, trudging ahead, holding Luke's hand.

"You say that now, but wait till the chaos descends in the morning, Dad. You'll wish you were well out of it."

"Me and Granddad will be well out of it. We're going to get ready at our house."

Matthew chuckled. "Quite right, Small Fry."

Chapter 41

Dear Beatrice

Thank you for sending your invoice. I have now made payment in full and added a little extra as a personal thank you.

Firstly, to your assistant. To put himself at risk like that was an extraordinary act of courage and those two young people owe him their lives. I visited them both today and am happy to say they are recovering well. What a gift it is to be young!

Secondly, to you. My gratitude may sound strange since your actions precipitated the end of my marriage. However, what you and Astrid proved, I had long suspected. Confronted with the evidence, my primary emotion is relief at no longer having to pretend.

The Neljä plant at Kolkko opens tomorrow and everything will go as planned. On Monday, I will begin two separate divorce proceedings. The first from my faithless, alcoholic husband. The second is to divest myself of another partnership gone sour - my working relationship with Ville Ikonen.

I cannot imagine you keep up with Finnish news, so let me summarise. The false news report resulted in the termination of Päivi Aho's employment. Aggrieved, she made allegations about the influence of the paper's owner. Channel 6 is owned by a media company which after a legal demand for information, transpired to be a subsidiary of Scanski Solutions. Nothing has been proven but I believe Ville Ikonen has been using the TV news as his own personal mouthpiece to manipulate public opinion.

On that note, there is overwhelming sympathy for the two rescued teenagers, but a great deal of anger at their culpable colleagues. When Valpuri and Samu are fully recovered, I intend to invite them and their families to the plant. Along with any other environmentalists who will bring an open mind. If they still believe what we are doing is wrong in face of scientific facts, we will politely agree to disagree. There is an irony in that the cave where they were found contains radon gas in the bedrock. The anti-nuclear protestors hid two of their members in a place which exposed them to high levels of radiation.

I am sorry to say the other four leaders of the Gaia Warriors will face trial. On speaking with Detective Sahlberg, I have decided to finance the defence team for the younger two.

Sahlberg also informed me that he intends to charge the man arrested at the hospital with Juppo Seppä's murder. His name is Karl Marin, well-known to German police as muscle-for-hire, happy to provoke violence at football matches, protest marches and so on. Sahlberg suspects him of vigilante justice and has a witness ready to testify against him. The Helsinki police force want to know who paid him to dispose of Seppä. The aim of charging him with murder is less to achieve a guilty verdict, but to flush out his employer. I have my own suspicions - see above. Let's hope it works.

Thank you once again for all you have done and I wish you every success in your future career.

With best wishes
Karoliina Nurmi

Saturday's weather was perfect for a midsummer wedding. A party of twenty attended the registry office to witness Gabriel and Tanya exchange their vows. Luke discharged his duties without a fault, bringing a lump to Beatrice's throat. She would not allow herself to cry, though. That was Pam's prerogative. Everyone exclaimed over the beauty of Tanya's dress. The designer herself wore a buttermilk-coloured dirndl sprigged with wildflowers. Catinca's hair was plaited around her head and her Converse trainers were meadow green, a contemporary take on a Swiss milkmaid.

On entering the marquee on the village green for the reception, Beatrice was charmed to see the remainder of the guests had taken the natural theme to heart. Anyone looking into the tent, and there were plenty of curious glances as villagers crossed from one side to another, would see the whole spectrum of rainbow colours with an emphasis on the verdant. The wedding 'breakfast' was a variation on ploughman's lunch with fruit, salad, pickles and cheese. The simplicity was refreshing and made for some excellent photographs. Matthew made a short but touching speech, only prompted twice by Will when he forgot his lines. Luke's speech was not much longer but it was funny, moving and delivered with feeling. Adrian nudged Beatrice, both blinking away tears as they applauded wildly.

The cake was a surprise. That was the one item where Tanya had given her mother free rein, so Beatrice was expecting something classic, ornate and rococo. So she joined in the oohs and aahs when Susie from The Angel carried it into the marquee. The plate bore a woodland scene, with a 'tree stump' at the centre. Around it were ferns, leaves and flowers and on the top, ladybirds, butterflies and bees. As Susie passed, she spotted a heart 'carved' into the tree's bark, with the letters T & G inside. It was charming, thoughtful and so pretty it seemed a pity to cut it up. Everyone wanted photographs of the happy couple posing by their bespoke confection before they began dismantling it to share between their guests.

Another toast meant more Prosecco, in which Beatrice happily partook. Guests began to move around the marquee, so she got up from her place and went in search of Theo. She'd hardly seen him all day. She found him trying to explain why he wasn't going to dance to three of the bridesmaids.

"Leave the man in peace. He's had a tough week. Look, see Adrian over there? Go and ask him. He's a terrific dancer, as is his husband. I need a word with Theo on important professional business." She sat in one of the recently vacated seats and watched as the young women persuaded Adrian onto the dance floor in seconds.

"You're not wrong. He's quite a mover," Theo observed. "Never seen him dance before."

"I don't suppose there was much opportunity when you were working at his wine bar. Have you had a good day?"

Theo gazed around the marquee with a contented smile. "I love weddings. This was one of the best. What about that cake?"

"Wasn't it brilliant? I must compliment Pam on such a fitting concept. Are you completely exhausted or do you fancy wandering over to the pub for a quiet chat? I really do want to talk business for five minutes and I have something for you."

They slunk away from the dancers and across the green to The Angel. Theo was still limping from the damage to his hamstring, so Beatrice parked him at a table outside and went in to get the drinks.

"Here you are. G&T with ice and lemon. This is a lovely time of day. Warm and dozy without the heat of midday. I heard from Karoliina last night."

"Oh yeah? Any news?"

Beatrice relayed the content of the email, keeping her voice low enough so other tables could not overhear. Then she opened her bag and withdrew an envelope.

"She also paid us extra. Me for exposing her husband and you for that heroic rescue."

Theo didn't take the envelope. Beatrice peered into his face.

"Theo?"

He looked down at his glass, stirring the twizzle stick, his plaits screening his face from view. "I can't take it. Not the cash, not the praise, none of it. I don't deserve any gratitude. This is not 'oh anyone would have done the same' modesty shtick. I mean it. I don't deserve it."

Confused by his apparent embarrassment, Beatrice asked, "Why not?"

He took a long time to answer. Beatrice sipped her gin, and soaked in the idyllic setting of late afternoon sun bathing the village in golden light.

"You ever feel like there are two of you?" asked Theo, his voice quiet. He met her eyes. "There's you-on-a-good-day, who wants to do the right thing. That you who ran into the traffic to save an old geezer from being flattened by a bus. Who said no to a relationship because you don't want to hurt someone. Who climbed into a cave during a storm to stop some kids from drowning. That you is the person you really want to be."

He removed the twizzle stick and took a long draught of his

drink. "Then there's another you. The lazy, selfish cynic who says 'what's the point?' That voice inside telling you the old geezer will be dead soon anyway, to take your kicks where you can and bollocks to her broken heart. That voice told me to leave them down there and get out."

Beatrice placed her hand on his. "The point is, you didn't listen. You ignored the voice and rescued them. You picked the right fork in the road."

He shook his head with such vehemence his beads clicked against one another. "I made a choice. Aleksis didn't respond to my torch signal. I thought he'd gone or given up or something. So I left Samu there and took Valpuri. I chose her, not him. When the winch started to work, I was well up the ladder. I abandoned him, Beatrice. I left him to drown." He pulled his hand away and placed it over his eyes.

She gave him a moment. "I'm not going to argue with you. You made a horrible choice under impossible conditions. The thing is, they both survived and that is thanks to you. It is!" she insisted as his head shook again, this time more slowly. "You put him in that sling thingy, you carried her up the ladder, you showed Aleksis what to do. You didn't listen to the voice. And to answer your question, yes, I do feel like there are two of me."

He removed his hand from his eyes and cradled his chin between finger and thumb to listen, his brown eyes illuminated by the sinking sun.

"Some time back, when I was still a detective with the Met, I did a job in Germany. That's where I encountered the expression '*Innerer Schweinehund*'. It means inner pigdog, the negative part of you that focuses on the worst case scenario, that whispers poisonous thoughts of jealousy, fans flames of anger, convinces you that it's all hopeless. Those vile beasts are awfully fond of the phrase: *what's the point?* It takes a lot of effort to fight them. Some of us find ourselves unequal to the task, requiring reinforcements."

His gaze searched her face and she did not flinch. "Yeah, that makes some sense. I used to see it as the black side of me."

"It may be late in the day to bring this up but ..."

Theo snorted but the sound was devoid of humour. "Good point. Poor use of language. What I want to say is that I have a selfish part, seeking reasons to disengage, take no responsibility. *Keep out of it, mate, not your problem*. Know what I mean? My conscience goes over and over that moment. What if Aleksis hadn't managed to get the minibus moving? Samu would ..."

"But Aleksis did and Samu didn't. Listen to me, Theo, you cannot put yourself through the guilt and self-recrimination you *might* have felt had things been different. That's a common feature of PTSD. Which is why you are taking next week off to recuperate. Don't interrupt me! Look at the facts. Neither Samu nor Valpuri would be here now if it weren't for you. Now I appreciate you don't want to wear the hero's mantle, but I insist you take the cash. Otherwise I will keep it and blow the lot on having my hair done."

A reluctant smile lifted his cheeks. "Catinca thinks you should."

"I know. The wretched creature wants me to have another of those blond shiny dos and I flatly refuse. The natural look works for me. Do you fancy another or should we head back to the party? I promise to protect you from those predatory bridesmaids."

They got up from the pub bench and Theo tucked the envelope into his jacket. "Thank you. For this and for letting me bend your ear. As bosses go, you're solid gold."

"Don't tell Adrian that, he's fiercely competitive. Ooh, it sounds like the ceilidh's starting. I love a Scottish reel."

They linked arms and wandered back across the village green to join the party.

Chapter 42

The beach glittered and shone after last night's rain. Helvi always took her walk when it grew light and in summer, that was anytime she wanted. She trod carefully across the stones, watching for flotsam and jetsam of interest, saving her appreciation of the horizon till she reached the shore. Otso was still sniffing and scratching at a rock pool, tail wagging and ears alert. She hoped he had learned his lesson from the last time he bothered a crab.

The sea rolled in, a deep blue tinged with pink from the reflection of the sky. Foam bubbled and fizzled out as each ripple reached the beach. Helvi paused, raising her face to the horizon and filling her lungs. A bark made her look over her shoulder. Two seagulls soared gracefully into the air, leaving Otso far behind. The silly young Spitz continued to bark, his curly tail in constant motion.

"Otso!" called Helvi, trying to preserve the peace of the morning. The dog scrambled across the pebbles, his tongue lolling and white teeth visible.

"Come here and shh. This is our quiet time." The dog stared up at her with such eagerness, she could not resist. A piece of driftwood lay a few paces away. She reached for it, stroking the sea-softened contours with her fingertips. Otso barked and barked and reversed along the beach. Helvi hurled the log as far as her muscles could manage and the excitable Spitz took off in pursuit.

Helvi laughed at his triumphant return, log between his jaws. Her peaceful morning rituals were considerably less calm since adopting this noisy bundle of gingery fur. She stared out at the horizon, setting her mood for the day. Sea air penetrated her whole being and she said her thank yous to the planet as she absorbed its bounty.

Three throws later, she called Otso to heel so they could return to her beach house. They were almost at her garden path when Helvi looked down and saw Otso had discarded the driftwood in preference for a plastic bottle. She took it from his mouth and carried it inside. A water bottle, cap still on with some rubbish stuffed inside. A sound of disgust escaped her as she poured some kibble for Otso.

Throwing plastic into the sea? Finns were supposed to have the highest environmental awareness in the whole of Europe. She placed the bottle in the recycling bin and washed her hands while shaking her head.

Kids these days.

Dear Reader

I hope you enjoyed WHITE NIGHT, Beatrice and Theo's Finnish case. To let you into a secret, the story didn't stop there. Another adventure was banging at the door impatient to come out. So immediately after I'd finished this book, I began on the next, which starts two days after WHITE NIGHT ends. Tanya and Gabriel are on honeymoon in Mallorca when events take a strange turn. The first chapter is included at the end of this book. THE WOMAN IN THE FRAME will be published in July 2020.

Acknowledgements

For her expertise on Finland, Finnish culture and nuclear power, I would like to thank Iida Ruishalme for her time and patience with my questions and also for her intriguing blog, https://thoughtscapism.com/. As always, I am indebted to Florian Bielmann, Jane Dixon Smith and Julia Gibbs. Any errors are entirely my own.

Message from JJ Marsh

I hope you enjoyed *White Night*. I have also written The Beatrice Stubbs Series, European crime fiction:

BEHIND CLOSED DOORS
RAW MATERIAL
TREAD SOFTLY
COLD PRESSED
HUMAN RITES
BAD APPLES
SNOW ANGEL
HONEY TRAP
BLACK WIDOW

I have also written standalone novels:

AN EMPTY VESSEL
ODD NUMBERS

And a short-story collection:

APPEARANCES GREETING A POINT OF VIEW

For more information, visit jjmarshauthor.com

For occasional updates, news, deals and a FREE exclusive prequel: *Black Dogs, Yellow Butterflies*, subscribe to my newsletter on jjmarshauthor.com

If you would recommend this book to a friend, please do so by writing a review. Your tip helps other readers discover their next favourite read. It can be short and only takes a minute.

Thank you.

The Woman in the Frame

By JJ Marsh

Chapter 1

It was a strange sensation to put on shoes after two days of going barefoot. She decided against applying make-up because it reminded her of the usual dreary routine at home. Instead, she slicked Vaseline over her eyebrows and on her lips. Her husband was a big fan of the natural look. Facing herself in the mirror, she could see why. Her skin glowed, her eyes shone and her hair seemed grateful for a rest from daily blow dries.

Tanya put on a petrol-coloured cotton maxi dress and added the silver earrings Gabriel had bought her that morning in Port de Sóller. She was ready to meet their hosts and prepared to be on her best behaviour. With a last spray of scent, she wandered out onto the veranda where the man of her dreams was waiting, one ankle crossed over his knee, gazing out at the extraordinary view of sandstone buildings descending in circles down the hill. On the table sat two glasses of Aperol spritz, the orangey liquid the colour of a Caribbean sunset.

On hearing her footsteps, he looked over his shoulder with a smile. Her heart swelled and she wondered if she would ever get used to living with a man overjoyed by her mere existence.

"You look lovely," he said. "Then again, you always do."

"Thanks. I didn't want to overdo it, you know. I packed a proper evening dress and high heels, but it feels inappropriate for a casual dinner with bohemian artists. The thing is, I'm a tiny bit nervous. Maybe a drink would help. When do we have to leave?"

He passed her aperitif across the table and reached out to take her hand. "When we're ready. It's around a twenty-minute walk to their place, I reckon. They said to turn up any time after eight. Relax, it'll be just like having dinner with my mum. They're a pair of arty old hippies, so absolutely no reason to be nervous."

She sank into the chair and picked up a glass, asking herself what she had done to deserve such luck. "Your mum is not a celebrated artist who can flog her latest creation for a seven-figure sum. Which is one of the many reasons I adore her."

They drank in comfortable silence, listening to the cicadas' natural accompaniment to the evening symphony of birdsong. At ten to eight, Gabriel took the empty glasses into the kitchen, picked up the bottle of wine they had bought as a gift and took Tanya's hand.

The walk took under twenty minutes, despite Tanya dragging her heels to gaze into gardens, cafés, restaurants and other people's homes. A little over a quarter of an hour after they left their tiny cottage, they wandered up a slightly posher road towards the white walls of a villa. Nothing about the entrance identified the owner as one of Europe's most revered artists. Large metal gates were closed but nothing else suggested that this particular compound contained anyone special. Gabriel pressed the buzzer and the gates swung open.

Dogs barked as they drew closer to the building and Gabriel dropped to his haunches, greeting the two tatty-looking Irish wolfhounds on their own level. A woman appeared at the kitchen door, glass in hand, calling the animals.

"Harris, get down! Heel, Balfour!" she called. "Fear not, they look dangerous but they're nothing more than noisy and daft. Welcome, Gabriel and his lovely bride! Come over here and let me see you both. It's too romantic for words."

The dogs herded them towards the main house and the smell of grilling fish. Ophelia Moffatt came down the path to greet them, her kaftan wafting around her body like an Indian dancer's veils. She kissed Gabriel on both cheeks and rested her hands on Tanya's shoulders.

"I'm Ophelia, but you can call me Philly. Everyone does, the disrespectful bastards. Tanya, I am delighted to meet you. May I offer my most sincere congratulations? I'm brimming with joy at you darling people and this young man is radiating love like a Ready Brek kid. How are you finding the cottage? It's on the rustic side, that much I know, but we did our best to make it worthy of a honeymoon suite. Let's go in and have a snifter. My Long Island Iced Tea is getting warm." She slugged the remainder of her drink and Tanya managed to get a word in.

"Pleased to meet you too! The cottage is just perfect. We're really grateful. It's incredibly kind of you to lend us your cottage as a wedding present. I hardly ever get to travel, so this is more of treat than you can imagine."

Philly clutched Tanya's arm and peered past her to look at Gabriel. "I adore her already. I may cry before the night is done. Harris, put that down, you filthy beast! Come along, my dears, before that useless man buggers up the fish."

On the patio stood a portly grey-haired man wearing an apron and brandishing a pair of barbecue tongs at the wolfhounds. "Here you are!" He dropped the tongs onto the table and opened his arms. "Gabriel Shaw, let me look at you. Heavens above, my godson, a married man! I feel ancient. First things first, introduce me to your beautiful bride." He embraced Gabriel with real affection and Tanya found she was smiling.

"You don't look ancient," said Gabriel. "You look better than ever. Hoagy, this is Tanya, my wonderful wife. Tanya, meet my godfather, Alexander Moffatt, known to his friends as Hoagy."

Tanya held out a hand which he took and lifted to his lips. "Charmed, Tanya, quite charmed to meet you, dear girl. I'm so sorry I couldn't attend your wedding, but I don't travel, you see. I'm doing my best to become a hermit. Tonight we'll celebrate the occasion all over again with cava and plenty of it! Philly, bring these people an aperitif and you may as well top mine up whilst you're there. Have a seat, Tanya, I need to keep an eye on the fish."

"It's lovely to meet you, Mr Moffatt. Thank you so much for the use of your cottage."

"Hoagy, please. It's only solicitors who call me Mr Moffatt. Gabriel, tell me all about your mother. Is she well? Is she happy you married such a delightful woman?"

As the two men conversed beside the barbeque, Philly placed a tray of glasses on the table and sat opposite Tanya. "Chin, chin, my dear" she said, raising her Long Island Iced Tea. "We're family now. I hear you have a little boy. How old is he?"

"Seven. His name is Luke. Along with my dad, he was sort of best man at the wedding. He made a speech and everything." To her astonishment, her eyes prickled with tears. She had seen Luke only yesterday morning and spoken to him that afternoon, but still.

"You miss him," said Philly, her eyes soft. "I understand. When my husband left me and my daughter, we became each other's entire worlds. Never spending a day apart until the custody agreement. He took her every other weekend and those forty-eight hours were absolute torture."

Tanya pinched the bridge of her nose. "That's it. Most of the time I worry about how much he needs me, but sometimes I think it's the other way around."

Philly took a long draught of her cocktail. "All the times you pick up their toys, their shoes and dream of having some time to yourself. Then when it happens?"

"I know! Don't get me wrong, I'm deliriously happy to be alone with Gabe. I love the freedom, the lack of responsibility and I know Luke's being spoilt rotten by the rest of the family.

It's just, you know, not being able to kiss him good night, smell his hair, I ..."

Philly passed her a tissue and Tanya patted the corner of her eyes, sniffing.

"Hellfire and damnation, woman, you've already made her cry?" Hoagy boomed. "What the devil did you put in her drink?"

In a second, Gabriel was by her side. "Tanya? Are you OK?"

"She's fine! Tanya and I are bonding over shared experiences, that is all. Unlike the testicularly challenged, women find it perfectly acceptable to express emotion. Gabriel, here's your aperitif. As for you, you interfering old windbag, just concentrate on not burning the bloody fish."

"The fish is nearing perfection, light of my life, star in my firmament. Fetch the salad and the bread, give Romy a call and let's eat! Pass my glass before you go, would you?"

Tanya gave Gabriel a reassuring smile and squeezed his hand. "I was telling her about Luke, that's all," she murmured. "It just hit me how much I miss him."

"Me too." Gabriel bent to kiss her lightly on the lips.

Philly shooed the dogs out of the way and placed a wooden bowl the size of a coracle in the centre of the table. The salad, fresh and colourful, was enough to feed ten people. She pulled a baguette from the crook of her arm and a bottle of salad dressing from her pocket.

"We thought cava to start unless you prefer wine? Harris? Harris! Where's Romy? Where's Romy? Go fetch! Fetch Romy!" The wolfhound paced away into the garden. "Good dog! So? Fizz all round? Gabriel, would you open these for me, darling boy?" She produced two bottles of unlabelled wine.

Tanya was watching Gabriel uncork the cava so didn't see the new arrival until she was halfway across the lawn. Like a dancer, she moved with feather-light grace, brushing past shrubs and beneath overhanging branches, the dog following in her footsteps. Her white dress was as thin and floaty as tissue paper and her feet were bare. Blonde hair fell in waves around her face as she picked her way up the patio steps.

Hoagy stopped in the midst of placing a platter piled high with fish on the table to stare at the girl with open admiration.

Philly tipped her head at the new arrival. "Romy, come say hello to our guests. This is Gabriel, Hoagy's godson and this is Tanya, his brand new wife. Tanya, Gabriel, this is Romy."

Her large blue eyes glossed over them both. She waggled a pale hand, like a child being told to wave goodbye. "Hello, Gabriel. Hello, Tanya."

Tanya waved back. "Hello. Nice to meet you." She was the most startlingly beautiful girl, with a heart-shaped face and golden skin, and such fabulous hair she could have walked out of a shampoo commercial.

"Hello, Ronnie," said Gabriel, half out of his chair, hand extended.

The girl didn't look at him, picking at her fingernails. "Romy. Short for Rosemary." Her voice lifted at the end of each phrase, as if she was asking a question.

Philly looked up from the glass she was pouring. "Dig in, one and all. Romy, are you going to sit down or stand there making the place look untidy? Out of the way, Balfour."

Romy slid into a chair, stroking the dog's head. "He says he's hungry."

"He's always bloody hungry. Tanya, help yourself to salad. Now then, a toast. To Gabriel and Tanya, may their lives together be filled with love and happiness!"

Everyone raised their glasses and repeated Philly's words, clinking their flutes together in the centre. Hoagy drained his glass in one and smacked his lips together.

"Thirsty work, grilling fish. Philly, I'll take a refill when you're ready. *Buen provecho*!"

"*Buen provecho*," they replied and began to eat.

The fish was perfect, charred and crispy on the outside, but flaky and sweet on the inside. The salad was a delicious, crunchy balance with warm bread as a crusty accompaniment. Fresh, simple food, beautifully cooked, Tanya's favourite kind. She complimented Hoagy on his cookery skills.

"Most kind of you to say so. Yet even as I snatch the compliment with both hands, it's hard to go wrong with ingredients as divine as sea bass caught this morning. Ha! Gabriel, do you remember that time I took you mackerel fishing off the coast at Dawlish?" He grinned at Tanya. "He was only ten years old or so. Poor lad got sick as a dog, while I was up at the bow, throwing myself into the adventure as if I was Hemingway." He roared with laughter, one hand on his stomach, the other holding his fork.

Less Hemingway and more Henry VIII, thought Tanya. His face, so familiar from Sunday supplement profiles, had a photogenic quality. The deep-set eyes radiated light, which switched from sparkle to laser as the conversation switched from fishing trips to forestry work, rival artists, politics and the merits of Spanish cava versus French champagne. It wasn't hard to see why so many women had fallen for his charms. At least a decade younger than her husband, Philly joined in the debate, offering unvarnished opinions and much dry wit. Tanya liked them both enormously.

Reluctant to exclude anyone, Tanya tried to draw Romy into the conversation. The girl ate nothing Philly had put onto her plate, just tearing off bits of bread to feed the dogs.

"Not hungry?" she asked, while Gabriel was trying to get Hoagy to tell a particular story from his youth. The girl looked up at her, blinking in surprise.

"I am hungry, actually. I've had nothing but two bowls of Coco Pops all day. But I don't eat fish. It disgusts me."

It seems bizarre that Philly would serve her daughter fish if she had made the choice not to eat it. "Oh, I see. Are you a vegan? Gabriel and I are trying to eat more plant-based food. It just seems a shame not to eat fish when you're on Mallorca. It's so fresh."

Romy reached out a hand and touched Tanya's earring. "These are pretty. How much did they cost?"

Tanya was taken aback. "I don't know. They were a present."

Something attracted the dog's attention and he bounded down the drive, barking and cavorting with his canine companion. Romy grabbed hold of the cava bottle and topped up her glass until the bubbles flowed over the rim. She bent her head and sucked up the overspill from the tablecloth.

"Romy! Not in front of our guests, please!" Philly said, handing her a napkin.

"I'm hungry," whined Romy, dropping the napkin onto her plate of uneaten food. "When are we having dessert?"

Hoagy tore off a lump of baguette and pushed the salad bowl towards the girl. "Eat some greens and have some bread. But don't feed any more to those damned curs. Why don't you try a piece of this fish? I promise you it's a trigeminal delight." He stabbed a piece of fish with his fork and lifted it towards her plate.

She recoiled and pushed his hand away, her bottom lip sticking out like a sulky child. It was difficult to assess the girl's age, but she had to be in her mid-twenties. Tanya could not understand why they treated her like a truculent teenager. Romy arched back in her chair, clasping her hands behind her head and tilted her face towards the emerging stars. It was impossible not to notice her breasts, pushing at the flimsy material of her dress, nipples pointing skyward. For a moment, no one spoke until Philly broke the moment.

"That reminds me, for dessert we have Rum Babas. Unless anyone prefers cheese?"

Gabriel and Tanya stifled embarrassed laughter while Hoagy clapped cupped palms together in applause, summoning both dogs. Apparently unaware of Philly's wisecrack, Romy dropped her elbows on the table and lifted a beseeching face as if she were Oliver Twist.

"Rum baba for me, please. Is there any ice cream?" She gave Philly a winsome smile and then seemed to see Gabriel for the first time. "Did Hoagy say you are his godson? He's never mentioned you before. Keeping you a secret, I see."

As Philly gathered plates, Tanya stood up to give her a hand. The gesture was driven mostly by good manners, wishing to be a well-behaved guest and partly to escape from the embarrassingly obvious flirtation aimed at her husband.

In the kitchen, she helped load the dishwasher and put the remaining salad in the fridge. She opted for cheese rather than a Rum Baba. She had never been one for a pudding.

"In that case, you dear sweet thing, I'll join you and we will have a glass of port. We'll leave the sticky sweet stuff to the men. I wouldn't mind betting Romy will eat at least three desserts, so they won't go to waste." She rummaged around in the fridge. "I have Reblochon, Danish Blue and unless that greedy swine has filched it, a slab of Manchego somewhere. Grab a couple of figs and a pear from the fruit bowl, and we shall dine like queens."

Tanya obeyed, placing the fruit on the tray. "You and your daughter don't look alike. Same with me and my son. It's as if my genes aren't represented at all, at least in the physical sense."

"My daughter? Oh, you mean Romy! Didn't Gabriel explain? No, probably not, things have changed since he was last here. My daughter lives in Houston these days and I rarely see her. No, don't sympathise, that's a good thing. She grew up to be a thoroughly unpleasant human being whose sole motivation is judging other people. As you say, one's genes aren't represented at all. Don't tell me that old sot has drunk all the port!" She swanned through a brickwork arch into another room.

Tanya didn't press the point, concerned she had touched on a sensitive area, but when Philly breezed back from living room with a bottle of port in each hand, she continued her explanation.

"Moral is, only reproduce with the bland. Seeing as Gabriel is extraordinarily handsome, I'd say my advice won't wash with you, dearest girl. No, Romy is not related. Either to myself or Hoagy, which is a damn good thing. Her role is rather different. She's his muse." She placed five desserts on the tray and crossed her eyes at Tanya. "I know. Could we be any more eighteenth century? But he only paints when he's inspired by an individual. They tend to be females in their twenties, nubile, acquiescent and easily impressed. Romy is the latest in a long line. Shall we go rescue your husband? It's far too late for mine."

On the walk back to the cottage, Gabriel's arm around her shoulders, hers around his waist, they said little, digesting the evening and enjoying the warm breeze blowing in from the sea. At one corner, the vista opened up towards the valley and they stopped to soak in the landscape.

Gabriel's voice rumbled into her ear. "There's something special about this place. I don't how to describe it but it feels good for the soul. Am I being too esoteric?" His arms wrapped around her waist and his stubbled chin rested on her shoulder.

She inhaled the scent of honeysuckle and bougainvillea and basil, wafting on the night air. "It is special. Nothing like I expected. My image was sun, sea, sand and some other stuff beginning with S. This is different, but in a really good way. Tonight was so much fun."

"They loved you. Who wouldn't? You were so natural and friendly and fitted right in. I could see he was impressed with your comments on his work. So much more than a pretty face."

Tanya's mind flipped back to the studio visit. While Romy was eating her third dessert and pleading with Philly for a glass of port, Hoagy had taken his guests to the inner sanctum, allowing them a preview of his work in progress. Accompanied by the two hairy hounds, they wandered to the end of the garden to the studio, a two-storey stone outbuilding. Inside, canvases leaned against every wall.

Hoagy shut the dogs outside and dialled up the lights to display his work. The focus on his model's body was hard to overlook. Hoagy painted Romy as she performed her yoga routines, naked. The poses themselves were elegant, graceful and artistic, but exposed the young woman in a way that made Tanya uncomfortable. Not just the personal areas of her body, but the sense of being a voyeur at a private ritual. She hid her awkwardness by asking questions about sketches and motion, how to transfer the fluidity of movement onto a canvas.

He answered in detail, his voice growing more voluble and passionate as he described his method. Upstairs, he showed them Romy's room, a futon in the centre and windows on each side where she practised each morning. Hoagy captured the magic and took it downstairs to convey it to canvas.

"Yeah, his paintings are striking. I can see why he's such a big deal in the art world." She paused, hesitant to express any criticism. Then she reminded herself this was Gabriel, her husband and there should be no secrets. "The whole muse thing, though. Don't you find that a bit weird?"

He kissed her neck and they began walking down the hill. "Weird, freaky, and if I can get all millennial for a second, TMI."

A delighted laugh escaped her. "TMI? Too right. I just met the girl so I'd prefer a longer acquaintance before being exposed to her undercarriage." She intertwined her fingers in his. "The paintings themselves were pretty kinky, but the set-up is what really messes with my head. She lives above his studio, he paints her naked, she has dinner with them both and he toddles off to bed with his wife? Sorry, but WTF?"

"WTAF." Gabriel unlocked the door to their tiny cottage and kicked off his shoes.

In the kitchen, Tanya stashed the Tupperware full of leftover fish in the fridge. Philly had insisted they take it as they left. "Do you want a nightcap?" she called.

"Herbal tea for me. My stomach is swilling with alcohol. You know, Hoagy's always been this way. Philly is his third wife and I reckon she might last the distance. She can handle the whole 'muse' narrative. Heather always says Hoagy found a way to make infidelity not only acceptable but lucrative."

"Was your mum ever one of his lovers?" Tanya asked, filling a pan to boil water. "Oh my God, you're not his illegitimate son, are you?"

Gabriel stretched out on the sofa, yawning like an overfed lion. "Nope. Heather was going through her lesbian phase when she and Hoagy were at Slade. He and my mother were close but in that you-really-get-on-my-tits-but-I'm-looking-out-for-you kind of way. Hoagy had already hit the big time when Heather got pregnant with me. He sent her a five-figure cheque, with a note saying 'This is your freedom to decide'. So she decided. She chose to go through with the pregnancy and made him my godfather. That's it."

"A very decent man. Even if he does paint his lovers' bits and sell them for obscene amounts of cash. Here's your tea. Gabe?"

He opened his eyes. "What?"

"Did you fancy her? I mean, I'd understand if you did. Romy is one of those catwalk creatures you cannot believe exist. Luminous, glowing and all the other words they put on the packaging of face creams. She's got the body of a teenager and thanks to Hoagy's pictures, you've seen what's under the hood. If I was a bloke, I think I'd fancy the arse off her. I could tell she wanted to jump your bones."

He sat up to sip his tea. "I've seen what's 'under the hood'? 'Jump my bones'? Where do you come up with these expressions? Tanya, I made myself clear when we tied the knot. In my eyes, there's only ever been one woman I wanted. Cobweb or Mustardseed or whatever she calls herself holds no interest for me. Does that answer your question? Come here."

Tanya forgot all about her tea.

Printed in Great Britain
by Amazon